Chosen
People

By Karen Grigsby Bates
Chosen People
Plain Brown Wrapper

Chosen People

An Alex Powell Novel

KAREN GRIGSBY BATES

AVON
TRADE

An Imprint of HarperCollinsPublishers

HarperCollins books may be purchased for educational, business, or sales promotional use. For information please write: Special Markets Department, HarperCollins Publishers, 10 East 53rd Street, New York, NY 10022.

FIRST EDITION

Designed by Ellen Cipriano

Library of Congress Cataloging-in-Publication Data

Bates, Karen Grigsby.
    Chosen people: an Alex Powell novel / by Karen Grigsby
Bates.—1st ed.
      p. cm.
ISBN-13: 978-0-06-055972-4
ISBN-10: 0-06-055972-1
1. African American women journalists—Fiction.
2. Murder—Investigation—California—Los Angeles—Fiction.
3. Los Angeles (Calif.)—Fiction. I. Title.

PS3602.A86C47 2006
813'.54—dc22   2005057201

06 07 08 09 10 10 9 8 7 6 5 4 3 2 1

In memoriam:

Anita W. Addison

beloved friend,
gone far too soon

I would hope that our congregations would feel responsible toward inviting people of all kinds into their membership and not feel that certain people are our kind. Our kind must be all people.

The Right Reverend John Melville Burgess,
1909–2003

Acknowledgments

Heartfelt thanks to:

Faith Hampton Childs, who got Alex the first time around and who has battled on her behalf ever since.

The good folks at HarperCollins: Carrie Feron and Selina McLemore. May Chen, who jumped on this horse in midstream and rode it to the finish line. Samantha Hagerbaumer who labored to make Alex visible to the larger world.

My *Basic Black* partner, Karen Hudson Freeman, for several years' worth of conversations about black folk and class stratification.

Callie Crossley and Lauren Adams DeLeon, whose droll Southern wit continues to replenish Signe's well. And Kelly Carter, whose lifestyle most of us can only dream of.

Vivian Davidson Hewitt, for allowing me to hijack wholesale her essence on Aunt Edith's behalf.

Babes on Books, for more than a decade of friendship and support.

The Norton Thanksgiving Group, for more than two decades of friendship and support.

Les Femmes Anciennes du Déjeuner: *encore, et encore, et encore!*

Writer friends too numerous to mention who have passed on words of support and encouragement.

Jill Goodman and Margo Haward, devoted e-pals.

Marcy DeVeaux, a one-woman tornado of energy and good ideas.

Gwendolyn Osborne, for her no-nonsense critiques of just about everything.

James Fugate, Tom Hamilton, and Kate Mattes for being so kind so early in the game.

My mother, Miriam Grigsby Bates, and sister, Patricia M. Bates, and my bajillion relatives, for always having my back.

Bruce W. Talamon and Jordan A.B. Talamon, who have had to live with both me *and* Alex for a long, long time. Love you both, this much.

And finally, to the book clubs, libraries, and ad hoc reading groups across the country who have given Alex and her crew a home: many, many thanks.

Chosen
People

Chapter One

James Simpson Lee Hastings Jr. was a chunk of the nineteenth century that had been vomited into the lap of the twenty-first. Simp Hastings, as he'd been known since his days at an East Coast boarding school, had been a moderately competent Boston accountant who had put himself on the mainstream media's map by becoming the social arbiter of modern Negro society. His gossipy history of same, *Chosen People,* had briefly been on the *New York Times* bestseller list. Since then, Hastings had all but quit his day job to make the circuit, describing to innocent and unknowing white people who counts—and who doesn't—in black communities across the country. Apparently, they found him fascinating, because he kept a full lecture calendar: the Junior League, the Kiwanis, the alumni associations of various colleges and universities that were underrepresented in the diversity department were all avid customers.

His West Coast part of a speaking tour had landed him

here in Los Angeles, at Eso Won, one of the country's biggest and best black bookstores. I'd dropped by to see, firsthand, what all the fuss was about, and perhaps to get a column out of it.

My name is Alex Powell, and I am a journalist. I write a column for the *Los Angeles Standard* that runs in the metro section on Thursdays and Sundays, and I'm always looking for good ideas.

This, however, might not have been one of them. Simp Hastings's book had been the cause of considerable ire in several black communities across the country. He'd been able to write it despite the fact that many of the upper-crust black folks about whom Simp had chosen to write had resolutely refused to talk to him. "If we keep quiet," one Philadelphia doyenne had sniffed, "perhaps he'll just go away."

A few had cooperated, though, and, augmented by a raft of eager wannabes, given him interviews. As a result, *Chosen People* spent several hundred pages chronicling the "I-gots" of a certain kind of black person, and listing the Right Clubs and Organizations to which strivers would strive to belong.

Some of the Negro Old Guard thought Simp suspect as well as traitorous. "Really," grumbled one Chicago doctor, "who is he, anyway? I've never heard of him. My children have never heard of him." A Charleston socialite from a family that had been living in that city for over one hundred and fifty years simply sighed. "The bad part is, they get it wrong and we—myself included, I'm sorry to say—don't speak up and correct them when they *do*."

Black activists who'd struggled for decades to minimize class differences among us in the interest of developing a more progressive social agenda that would benefit us all were furious. They felt that Simp was ripping the scab off old hurts covering touchy issues such as skin color, hair texture, and the keenness of one's features. They bitterly mocked his now-trademark inquiry to every new acquaintance: *"Do I know your people?"*

So here I was, at seven P.M. on a rainy April evening, crowded into a standing-room-only group of people who'd come to be given The Word from J.S.L. Hastings Jr., as he was listed on the book's cover.

The room seemed to be about equally divided between business-suited professionals and Afrocentrically dressed people in cowrie-tipped dreadlocks and clothes from (or inspired by) the Motherland. The room quieted as Hastings stepped to the podium.

"Good evening," he began.

His voice was high-pitched and boyish, like Mike Tyson's. But unlike Tyson's Bronx accent, Simpson's was a carefully aped Locust Valley lockjaw, a nasal, almost whiny voice, kind of like Thurston Howell III's had been on *Gilligan's Island*.

And unlike the onetime heavyweight champ's massive body, James Simpson Lee Hastings Jr.'s was tiny, almost elfin. His skin was a deep, unattractive yellow—almost orange, as if he'd just recovered from a severe case of jaundice. His dark hair was crunched in poorly suppressed waves all about his head. There was less of his chin than there should have been, proportionately speaking, and his nose stuck out of his flat-cheeked face like Pinocchio's.

Hastings did possess two saving graces, however: he had a magnificent set of teeth—white, even, and natural—and beautiful eyes that seemed to change color from bright green to gold to light brown, depending on the light.

At the moment, they were greenish, and fairly snapping with excitement—and maybe just a little malice. Hastings shot his cuffs, straightened his tie, took a drink from the glass of flat mineral water that had been placed at his elbow, and smiled out at the assembled.

"Good evening," he cooed to the audience, again.

"Good evening," the audience dutifully responded.

"*Wassup?*" yelled some wag from the back.

When the laughter subsided, Simp Hastings continued.

"What's up, indeed? That's why we're here tonight, isn't it, to discuss what is up with the depiction of black people in this country. For too long, the only images of us have been of happy slaves, buffoons, or gangbangers. Today, when the media writes about 'real black life,' it's always welfare mothers with eight children—Baby Daddy ladies—gangbangers, and crack addicts."

There were murmurs of assent from some in the audience.

"Well, I'm sure those people exist—I know they do—but those people are not my people. *My* people get up and go to work every day, and they are successful at what they do . . ."

"Um-hum." A fiftyish lady in a burgundy tweed suit nodded.

"*My* people live in lovely homes, with original art on the walls and inherited silver in their sideboard drawers . . ."

Two women my mother's age nudged each other as if to say "finally," while a young woman with expensively mono-grammed everythings—purse, tote bag, shoes, and earrings—waved her hand as if she were in church, not Eso Won, and shouted, "Tell it!"

"*My* people have been summering with other people like them, in the same places, for decades . . ."

"Hincty muthafucka," snorted a man near me, shaking his head in disgust.

"*My* people are not ashamed to have servants, and they know what to do with them . . ."

Less certain looks all around.

"In short," Simp Hastings concluded, "my people have not been discussed by mainstream America, which has no idea we exist. Which is why I wrote *Chosen People*. I want America to know that we are here. I want us to take our rightful place in American society. I want people with money and taste and breeding to stop hiding these assets and to be proud of them. We *should* be proud: we are *special*. We are *different*. We are *chosen*. And now is our time to shine."

Vigorous applause broke out from the people who felt as Simp did. Others kept their hands in their pockets, frowning. Some people shook their heads, as if they couldn't believe what they were hearing. And about four folks simply got up and left.

During all this, a white magazine journalist for the local

monthly was scribbling furiously in his notebook. Clearly he'd never met or heard anyone like J.S.L. Hastings Jr. and he was fascinated, as white people usually are.

"Now, I could go on for hours," Hastings said. "My fiancée—whom some of you may know: she has an M.D. and a J.D. from Yale and she's a medical correspondent for *The Today Show,* Dr. Sheila Howe?—says I go on all the time. But I'll stop, because I'm sure you have questions, and I'd love to hear them. And answer them."

So saying, he drank some more water, and looked over the rim of his glass at the audience. You could hear chairs squeaking as people shifted.

"Come on, don't be shy! What's on your mind? Tell me!"

A tall, thin woman rose slowly. She was elegantly dressed, all in beige, with a cream-colored cashmere shawl draped gracefully about her shoulders.

"What I'd like to know, Mr. Hastings, is this: *why?*"

He blinked.

"I beg your pardon?"

"Why bring all this up now? We've gone through so much as a people; this is such a hurtful subject for many in our community. Why do you insist on raising it?"

Her voice was well modulated and confident. She was probably in her early seventies. Her gold bangles jingled softly as she sat again.

"Well, Mrs . . . ?"

"Elton," she called out. "Grace Elton."

"Oh, my God—I cannot believe I'm talking to you,

finally!" Simp squeaked. He looked out at his audience. "Does anybody here not know who this is?"

Many people looked at him like "duh—of course we do." A few people shrugged, confused. They didn't remain unenlightened for long.

"This is the wife of Dr. Howard Elton, one of the premier civil rights activists in this city," Simp trilled. "Dr. Elton's father established the first black hospital in Los Angeles. You may be too young to remember any of this—I am, too, actually, but I did my homework: the hospital Dr. Elton senior started is now Los Angeles Municipal Children's Hospital!"

Gasps of recognition, interspersed with a few "I didn't know that's."

"You're *exactly* who I wanted in this book," Simp chided the woman old enough to be his mother. "You should have let me interview you."

Mrs. Elton rose again, and looked squarely at him.

"I had no interest in being in your book, Mr. Simpson. Like my late husband, I feel strongly that if we are to move forward as a people, we have to concentrate on what binds us together, not focus on those things that could tear us apart. This book never should have been written. Or perhaps it should have—but by someone else. I have no quarrel with a book that outlines the achievements of successful blacks, whatever their backgrounds. But this is not that book. This is merely a . . . a *shopping list* of things to have and to get, and a wretched catalog of the worst snobberies and sillinesses some of our people insist on displaying. So I *have* become a Chosen Person: I have chosen to remove myself from any association with this book or what it stands for. I wish some of the people who had decided otherwise had had second thoughts. And I pity you, Mr. Hastings. You have completely missed the boat on what being black means in this day and age."

It was a good speech, delivered at some cost, apparently, because toward the end, Mrs. Elton's voice had begun to quaver.

"I'm sorry." Grace Elton turned and apologized to those around her. "I'm becoming a little emotional. I wish you all a good evening."

And wrapping her shawl more closely around her, the chic Mrs. Elton picked up her purse and left to thundering applause.

Simp Hastings wasn't fazed in the least.

"*Well,*" he huffed, "*some* people are still in denial about their station in life. Such a pity. She would have been fabulous to include. Other questions?"

It went on for about a half hour, with varying degrees of civility: Why had he included So and So but not Thus and Such? Why hadn't he thought to include more cities in the Midwest? Would he consider, ever, doing a history of "the best sororities and fraternities? White folks need to understand we've had these organizations for years . . ." Was it true that he'd signed on as a consultant to a Movie of the Week about life on one of the East Coast's now-vanished black summer resorts?

After the questions, Simp Hastings signed books for another half hour. Some people bought loads—one for themselves, several as presents. Many people bought them for their children "because they need to know this about us."

Toward the end, a thirtyish man with long dreadlocks and a Malcolm X T-shirt came up to the signing table, leaned forward, and said softly:

"We should be beyond this shit by now. It's niggers like you that are holding us back. You need to rethink your utility to the community, *brother*."

The menace in his voice was unmistakable.

"I'll be sure to do that," Simp said blandly, as the angry man stalked out of the store.

"What's with him?" wondered Logo Lady, who was having three books signed.

"E-N-V-Y," Simp said, looking at her knowingly. She nodded, and slipped the books into a stylish tote with a big metal G on the front.

Hastings had promised a brief interview after all this was over to both me and the white guy from the city magazine, so we hung around waiting for the last person to receive a signed book.

Unfortunately for the remaining few, Eso Won had run out of books. Simp had sold seventy-five in under thirty minutes.

"Oh, no!" one disappointed customer moaned. "I wanted to give one to my mother for her birthday."

"We're getting another shipment in two days," the store owner assured her.

"My mother's birthday is *tomorrow*," the woman said stonily.

The owner retreated to the cash register, muttering something about "last-minute Negroes who think they can just throw a present together when their mama's birthday is the same day, *every year* . . ."

Disappointed Customer rolled her eyes at him.

"Know what? I think I have a few extra in the back of my car," Simp said. "Let me go out and look, and if I do, they're yours."

"Oh, would you? Thank you! Do I make the check out to you?"

"Yes," he called, as he walked out into the misty night air. "I'll be right back."

Either he had a huge trunk, he was a smoker, or he was having trouble finding the books, because after ten minutes, Simp Hastings hadn't returned.

"Maybe he's out having a smoke," someone suggested.

"Or he's making a call on his cell phone."

"Or," said the bookstore owner, "he can't see. Those rental cars are notorious for leaving off as many of the essentials as possible. I'll bring him a flashlight."

He was back in forty-five seconds, looking ashen.

"Call the police—now!" he snapped to his cashier.

The few of us left in the store looked up.

"Something bad has happened," the store owner said testily. "Nobody go outside."

Which, of course, is what everyone did, immediately.

Logo Lady started screaming at once. I pushed her aside to look, and wished I hadn't. The white guy from the city magazine leaned over into the bushes and quietly threw up.

There, lying on the ground, promised books in his out-stretched hand, was James Simpson Lee Hastings Jr., wearing an ear-to-ear grin.

On his neck.

Chapter Two

The police came almost immediately. A couple of uniforms on the 3–11 shift happened to have been eating "lunch" at a fast-food burger joint right up the street, so when the bookstore clerk dialed 911, she got results. Practically before Logo Lady had stopped screaming they arrived, lights flashing, motor roaring, siren blaring. We were all bathed in the surreal glow of red, then blue strobes.

The driver was Japanese-American and identified himself as Lieutenant Hirata. His partner, Officer Lisette Nelson, was a lanky sister with long, wavy hair that had been carefully French braided and pushed up under her cap. They looked at Simp's body, then each other.

"We'd appreciate it, folks, if you'd all go back into the store now," Lieutenant Hirata said blandly.

"This has been very traumatic," Logo Lady wailed. "Can't we just go home?"

"Afraid not, ma'am," the lieutenant said politely. "We'll

need to take statements from you all. We'll try to be quick about it."

Some people were anxious to have their fifteen minutes with the officers, others were resentful that their movement had been curtailed.

"Look," one older woman protested. "I got groceries in the car. My frozen food is gonna melt. I just stopped in here for a minute to get a book signed for my grandbaby. I don't know who killed that man." Her wig, gray and poufy, shook in indignation.

"Yes, ma'am," Officer Nelson soothed, taking her by the elbow and moving her toward the store's doors. "I'll personally see that they question you first so you can be on your way."

"Well, okay . . ." The elderly woman peered at Nelson closely. "One of the po-leece gonna walk me to my car, too? It's dark out here."

"Yes, ma'am, I'll see that you have an escort . . ." Nelson's voice, low and respectful, trailed off as they walked farther away. I joined the rest of the crowd and walked inside.

Norman Wilkens, Eso Won's tart-tongued co-owner, had persuaded the Christian lady who ran the Manna from Heaven Bakery next door to reopen her shop and send over cookies and brownies. His more amiable partner, Lester Robinson, had gone in back and dragged out the coffee urn, and soon the smell of Sumatra was wafting through the store.

"Folks," Lieutenant Hirata began, "we're going to try to

13

get you out of here and home as quickly as possible. Detectives are on their way to take your statements, so we'd appreciate it if you wouldn't speak about what's happened outside until they get here. That's so you'll remember as much as possible."

And, of course, so anybody with a mind to coordinating stories would have a harder time doing it.

"Just have some coffee and browse," Norman suggested. Lester looked at him, amazed. It was well-known to Eso Won regulars that if the uninformed came in with food or drink, Norman would loudly tell them: "I'm sorry, my brother, but you got to park that pork up here at the register. Food and unpaid-for books don't mix." Or, "Miss, I'll take your drink and hold it here until you're ready to ring up."

People who protested the policy would be told they'd probably be more comfortable shopping elsewhere. "You see the sign," Norman would point out for disbelieving would-have-been customers. "We reserve the right to refuse service to *anyone.*" Hint, hint.

Norman's standards, stringent as they were, had earned Eso Won a devoted following of readers, browsers, and, most important, buyers, who willingly came from all over the city to surf the well-stocked shelves for black literature, nonfiction, art books, and greeting cards. My girlfriend Signe insists that I bring her every time she comes from New York to visit, and she never fails to buy so much it has to be shipped back in a big old box.

She loved that Norman wouldn't sell to just anyone.

"He's like Idi Amin would be if he owned a bookstore," she said, admiringly, the first time she met him. "My way or the highway."

"Yeah, except Amin would probably have *eaten* some of his customers, which would tend to discourage repeat business," I pointed out.

"Oh, please." Signe had waved her hand in a get-outta-here gesture. "Don't nobody know for sure he ever did that. He just boasted about having done it."

Close enough for jazz. If I had run into the former Ugandan dictator—when he was still living, rumor had him everywhere from being happily installed in a Gstaad *Schloss* with gold bathroom fixtures to foaming-at-the-mouth in the end stages of syphilis, being tenderly cared for by a group of Belgian nuns in a convent somewhere—I'd have given him a wide berth. Either fate, considering the havoc he'd wreaked on his poor subjects, was way too good for him.

Anyway, I'd have to call Signe when I got home to tell her that Idi was feeding the masses tonight, not feeding *off* them, and *letting them eat while they read!* This, definitely, was an occasion of note.

The doors opened and two guys from Robbery-Homicide came in. Apparently they'd been outside for a few moments, scoping the body. One went straight to Norman and Lester. He talked briefly with them for a moment, nodded, then motioned to the second guy. They divided up and walked quietly to the first two people—one, as promised, was the gray-wigged lady—and began writing in their notebooks.

I was trying to read lips without much success when I felt a hand on my shoulder.

"If I was even mildly acquainted with you, I'd keep clear of you, because every time I see you there's a dead body in the room. How do you account for that coincidence?"

I looked at him and sighed.

"You know that isn't true—I saw you a couple of months ago and the only thing dead in the room was that hunk of cow you polished off at dinner. And to be perfectly accurate, you and I have only been in a room *once* with a dead body."

He grinned. "For normal people, that would be one time too many."

"Hasn't anyone told you? Normal is boring."

James V. Marron and I had met last summer at the National Association of Black Journalists conference, which had been held here in Los Angeles. The publisher of one of the country's biggest and best magazines, *Diaspora*, had been killed during the conference, and I had helped Marron a bit in locating the one what done it. We'd maintained a casual friendship since then, wary of the traditional love-hate relationship between cops and reporters. He was way out of his neighborhood—he usually worked out of the West Hollywood bureau—but they move cops around all the time, so I shouldn't have been surprised.

"Know anything about all this?" Marron asked, jerking his chin toward the outside door and Simp Hastings's now-draped body. The coroner's people had taken what photos they needed and all the standard stuff—body temperature, testing for rigor mortis and lividity, nail parings, blood typing—and were now prepared to remove the body.

"Not really. I'd just barely met him. He was going to sit for an interview after the signing was over. Now I guess I'll have to start from scratch—and my column is due in about a minute and a half."

He gave me a disgusted, "you reporters are slime" look. "I'm so *very* sorry, Mr.—what's his name?"

"Simpson, like O.J."

He rolled his eyes. "We'da all been better off if the *other* Mr. Simpson was being loaded into the meat wagon out there."

L.A. cops hated O.J. Simpson because, after the most highly publicized trial since the Lindbergh baby kidnapping, the former pro athlete walked after being accused of killing his wife and a visitor to her home. Since then, cop shops around the city (and beyond) abounded with bitter O.J. jokes. Not that the jokee in question was doing much to defuse things. Seemed like every week, the tabs had photos of him with the latest bimbette, accompanied by breathless headlines: OJ CALLS COPS AS NICOLE LOOKALIKE OD'S! OJ: TALK TO ME LIKE THAT AND I'LL KILL YOU! And so forth. All helped by his witless proclivity to give impromptu interviews in which he managed, metaphorically speaking, to shoot himself in the foot using his weapon of choice: horribly mangled syntax.

In working to find the answer to who killed Everett

Carson last summer, Marron and I had developed a wary respect for each other. With the exception of the *Miami Trib*'s über-crime-reporter, Edna Buchanan, female reporters dealing with cops—especially the macho divisions like homicide, robbery, and vice—have a hard way to go. My way was harder because I often criticized police procedure in the city's colored neighborhoods, which tended to be much heavier-handed when administering justice than in the more gilded parts of the city where colored people aren't as much in evidence without lawn mowers or strollers, anyway.

So Marron and I saw each other from time to time, sometimes over lunch, sometimes in a foursome with his woman of the moment and my man of the past year, with whom I had a commuting relationship. The last time I'd seen him, we four had been out to dinner because Paul had been in town and the guys, who'd gotten along famously during the only other time I'd been in a room with a dead body, wanted to see each other. So we'd enjoyed the evening over a couple of bottles of wine.

This wasn't nearly as much fun.

The two plainclothes were finishing up with the remainder of the half-dozen or so people left. Lester was rolling the now-depleted coffeepot to the store's tiny kitchen. Norman was opening the door for each departing guest, wishing him or her a polite good night.

"You see anything?" Marron asked me, more as a formality than anything else.

"Nope. Mixed crowd of Old Guard types, professionals,

and scientific socialists. All here for different reasons, but none of them raving, or armed."

"Too bad." Marron sighed. "No confrontations, anything like that?"

"Well, now that you mention it . . ."

Marron looked up expectantly and drew a small notebook and an even smaller pencil out of his jacket pocket.

"Speak."

"This won't get anyone in trouble, will it?"

"This is a *homicide* investigation, Bo Peep. We would *love* it if somebody got in trouble."

"As long as he or she is the right person, I don't have a problem with that. I just have a problem with you all going willy-nilly after everybody—"

"Powell, would you stop—this is *me* you're talking to. Now what happened?"

I took a deep breath. I'm not a seize-the-time-off-the-swine type anyway, and I'd grown to respect some aspects of the LAPD's job since meeting Marron, but the department has a bad reputation among the city's darker residents, and I'd been cautioned about them almost as soon as I'd moved to L.A. So fingering someone on a "maybe" didn't seem like such a bright idea. On the other hand, if it would help find whoever sliced Simp Hastings . . .

"Here's the thing: he came, he sat, he dispensed wisdom—or his equivalent of it—for the first fifteen minutes. Then a lady in the audience rose and told him he shouldn't have written the book because it was just a shopping list that wannabes could use to social-climb, and it would only further fracture us as a community—"

"Whoa. I can only write but so fast. Who was this lady?"

"Grace Elton. Her husband started the children's hospital here. They're considered one of the first families of Old Guard L.A."

"Black L.A., you mean?" Marron looked up from his notebook.

"If I'd meant black L.A., I'd have *said* black L.A."

"No need to be testy, Miss Daisy. Did they fight?"

"No—she just said her piece, gathered up her things, and left."

He looked at me expectantly.

"Oh, please—she drives a Volvo. How many violent perps have you run into who drive Volvos?"

He thought for a minute, then nodded.

"Point taken. Who was the other person?"

"I don't know him, but I've seen him in the black papers here. He's a longtime community activist. You always see him in the same bunch as Sharif Muhammed and Jefferson Sparks, that crowd."

"The White Man Is the Root of All Evil crowd?" Marron smiled.

"Those fools." Lester snorted. He'd come up behind me and I hadn't heard.

"They just *love* the sound of their own voices. Drop a pop can out the window on Crenshaw and they gotta call a press conference to announce the start of a new committee for urban restoration, maintenance, and beautification."

I grinned. "They do tend to lecture a little much for my taste."

Norman groaned. "And ever since 1992, y'all white media come out with your notebooks and tape recorders and video-cams ready whenever they announce they have something to say." He shook his head.

"Well, talk to my white folks. This colored child tries to tell them wassup, but they think they know better than me, y'know?"

He nodded. Marron frowned, impatient.

"I'd love to hang around and listen to this diatribe, but is there a *point* to all this, regarding the mystery man in question?"

"His name is Kwaku Halstead," Lester offered, coming to join us. "I see him over at the Y, when we play pickup. Community-minded brother."

Marron nodded. "And why might his presence have been considered worrisome?" He looked pointedly at me, as did the other two.

"Only because I heard what he said to Simp about ten minutes before Simp was . . . you know."

"Slashed? Murdered? Should I use another word?" The two plainclothes and the two officers were walking toward us.

"Either of those will do. It's just that he told Simp he needed to rethink his utility to the community. He seemed angry when he said it—he sort of hissed it. Then he left. But he could've been angry and not had anything to do with this. Other than having been here in the first place."

Marron looked at me, then at the posse advancing on us.

"I may need to talk to you more about this, but for now, Ms. Powell, you're free to go."

I looked at him askance and started to ask when he'd begun addressing me so formally, but Norman's raised eyebrows indicated I might want to think about that. Maybe Marron didn't want his colleagues to know how well he knew me; given how pissed off my police accountability columns made some LAPD employees, that would make sense.

"Uh, thanks. You have my card, and can reach me at that number, or via my pager, if you need to. I'm in town for the foreseeable future."

And saying my good-nights, I walked to the door.

"I'll see you out," Norman volunteered.

"Thanks."

As we left, Lester had begun to herd the remainder of the Eso Won crowd to the door. A nice-looking guy in a suit was offering to walk Logo Lady to her car—"can't be too careful," he warned—and she gratefully accepted.

"You think Kwaku did it?" Norman asked casually.

"Nah. The obvious person never does it. Not in books, anyway." The strip mall in which Eso Won was located was closed tight. The bakery lady, having sold most of her wares to Lester earlier that evening, had prudently locked herself in her minivan and gone home to her family. The fast-food joint run by a Korean couple was locked and dark, as was the nail salon they'd bought adjacent to the Seoul Food Palace. If you'd told me three years ago that you could get Negroes to eat kimchee, I'd have laughed in your face. But the Kims were doing land-office business, selling fried chicken, potato salad, greens, and a spicy side of the Korean national condiment. Live and learn.

The only people left, besides Eso Won patrons and the cops, were a family of Latinos struggling out of the about-to-close Laundromat with an enormous load of neatly folded laundry. Everyone carried something: Mami and Papi lugged the flat pieces between them, junior and his sister had a bag apiece. Even the baby's stroller was supporting a small duffel of carefully folded clothes. They passed us, nodding pleasantly, and, chattering to each other softly in Spanish, loaded up an old Ford wagon with their clean clothes and linens.

Norman watched silently, then said quietly: "Was a time when you could be black and look forward to a future in this city. No more. Between the Koreans and the Mexicans . . ." He stopped and shook himself. I waited.

"It's not the same city anymore, Alex."

"Nobody's city is, Norman. That's what change is all about."

We'd arrived at my car, which he regarded with frank disgust.

"Well, here's one thing that never changes—and needs to. Don't them white people pay you enough for a decent ride?"

Norman drove a Lincoln Navigator. The back was always filled with books and book-related junk.

"Now, see how inconsistent you are? You're always raging against black folks who do not have, in your words—"

"Pot nor window," Norman finished, unabashed.

"But baby, this is *L.A.*" He pointed to my beat-up ancient orange BMW." "If you were white, I'd say you had a trust fund and just didn't give a damn, but that ain't the case."

"Not this evening, anyway. Thanks for walking me out. And don't worry—I won't help the cops finger the wrong brother. I'm not in this at all."

Norman nodded, shut the door after I got in, and waved me off into the misty spring evening. As I drove north on La Brea, the tires rolling over the gleaming, empty street kept up a steady mantra: *I'm not in this, I'm not in this, I'm not in this . . .*

Too bad saying so didn't make it so.

Chapter Three

Through a serendipitous set of circumstances, I'd lucked out and found a guesthouse on the grounds of a large home in Hancock Park when I first moved to L.A. My landlord, Sally Fergueson, is an opinionated little dynamo of a lady, and a prima facie example of why you shouldn't judge a book by its cover.

On the outside, Sally looks like all those other carefully coiffed ladies who run the Music Center and the various museum boards and the Charities That Count. The Old Money has wrinkles it wouldn't deign to have retouched ("I've earned every one," Sally likes to say), clothes that are fashionably timeless, and jewelry just big enough that it would be pointless for it to be fake—and vulgar for it to be any larger. They are slowly being replaced by taut-faced, bleached-blond, helmet-headed women of a certain age who revel in their outsized possessions—everything from cars to houses to jewels—and who engage personal publicists to make sure their names and tightened faces appear in the papers and glossy lifestyle mags several times a year.

Sally and I had a great relationship: we kept each other company when we had a mind to, and spoke our minds freely about whatever we discussed, be it politics or race or art. At least once a week I'd receive an invitation up to the Big House, and we'd have drinks and dinner. She wasn't too crazy about my nickname for her huge Mediterranean-style home, though.

"Would you please stop calling it that, Alexa," she'd chastise. "I am *not* Scarlett O'Hara. And you, certainly, are not Mammy."

"Yassum," I'd inevitably reply, pissing her off further.

"Oh, you are the *most* aggravating girl when you've a mind to be."

True enough. When Signe was in town, Sally would come down to the Little House; Signe and I would cook for her, and we'd have a "Girls' Night In," with rented videos, Cosmopolitans, the whole nine. Sally loves it; she's seventy-two and totally cool.

And an outrageous flirt, to boot. Which was why the man I was seeing, Paul Butler, adored coming to visit. I'd like to say it was my not-inconsiderable charm alone that drew him from Washington, D.C., about once a month, but I know better. But more on that later.

My house was quiet when I pulled up. Just the whisper of the floating pool cleaner at the side of the house, and the sigh of leaves in the many trees planted on the grounds. Sally had added some security lights after I was attacked last year. I told her it was unnecessary—I'd known my attacker and he'd come for me in broad daylight—but Sally insisted. "It will make *me* feel better, even if you don't care, so I'm exercising my landlord's prerogative: they're going in."

She flexed her muscle like that so infrequently I didn't have the heart to fight her about it, so we let it be. Now, after what had happened this evening, I was kind of glad the extra lighting clearly indicated nobody was lurking about my doorway.

Inside, it was quiet, too. I could see my message machine light blinking across the room on the pass-through counter that divided the kitchen from the dining area. Dropping my tote on the dining room table, I walked across the rug and hit the button.

"Hey, girl, how'd the L.A. Negroes react to Simp Hastings's lecture? I told you they went *wild* up here when he did that cocktail thing at the Century Club. Call me with the 911 tomorrow. I'm in the office all day. Bye."

As usual, Signe's thick Memphis accent made "bye" sound like "bah." She'd written a profile of Simp for the *New York Times Magazine* ("Who Is This Man, And Why Is He Driving Black America Crazy?") and was curious as to what I thought. She was going to be *plenty* surprised when I called her with the 411, which one of my New York aunts had mistakenly referred to as the 911 in a misplaced effort to be down with the peeps. We thought it was hilarious, and it had turned into a sort of shorthand for us, an inside joke, which quickly became a newsroom standard because we couldn't keep it to ourselves. On to message two:

"So what did you think?" Paul Butler's voice. "Were you charming, or snippy? Was there a full house, like there was when he spoke at Metropolitan Baptist when he was here? They're *still* arguing about him up on the Gold Coast. Call me with the 911."

See what I mean? Everybody uses Aunt Edith's phrase. They probably don't even remember the original digits.

I did want to gossip with Signe, but since she was usually in bed by midnight, it was probably too late. And Paul was probably in bed, too, although he often called in what had to be the middle of the night for him, which meant he was up working on something. But even if it had been early enough to call Signe or Paul, there was something else I had to do first. I picked up the phone on the pass-through and dialed.

"Fine."

"Do you do that when you're at home, too? Don't most people assume it *would* be a Fine who answered the phone?"

There was a long-suffering sigh at the other end. "It can't be a nightmare, because I haven't gone to bed yet. Although it's late enough that I should have been there by now . . ." (*Translation: what underling would be cheeky enough to disturb me in my hard-earned free time?*)

"A.S., have I ever called you at home when it wasn't an emergency?"

"No," my editor conceded. "So what is it this time? Your

end of town have an earthquake? We didn't feel it up here and nobody else called . . ."

"No, this is a different kind of seismic activity, but you'll be feeling the ripples soon enough. Remember I told you I was going to do an interview with Simp Hastings?"

"Who?"

"Sorry. James Simpson Lee Hastings Jr."

"Oh, that silver-spoon black guy?"

I grinned to myself. Not bad for a man who is, in Signe's immortal description, "critically Caucasian."

"Yeah, that guy. Well I went to Eso Won Books to hear him lecture, but a funny thing happened before I could interview him."

"Don't tell me the *News* got him first."

"Worse—for him, anyway: somebody killed him."

Silence.

I paced the kitchen in my bare feet, enjoying the coolness of the big Mexican pavers on my stockinged soles.

"You're serious? He's *dead*?"

"Quite. Neck slit. In the parking lot. Nobody knows who did it yet."

"Jesus. I'd better call Hanrahan."

Charlie Hanrahan was the night editor on Metro. He probably already knew, since someone in his shop is almost always listening to the police scanner.

Then another thought struck him: "I guess your piece on Hastings is as dead as he is, huh?"

I shrugged. "I thought it was at first, but maybe not. The

issues he raised are still very much alive in the community, and they're worth discussing."

"Even outside the community? And by community, I presume you mean—"

"Yes, A.S., mah peoples—but *your* people are fascinated with this kind of stuff, too, so I imagine it will be read."

"Fine. I suppose the police want you to omit certain details?"

"Believe it or not, Jim Marron was one of the people who answered the 911. He was in the neighborhood for something. He said he trusts my discretion."

"Really?"

Well, not in so many words. What Marron had really said was "write what you gotta, but don't fuck me, Powell. I take enough shit just for knowing you." But A.S. didn't need to hear language like that at this time of night, right?

Big yawn came through the phone. "Powell, it's almost time for the news. I'm going to call Hanrahan first and see if he can squeeze anything into the late edition. Otherwise, we'll run your column a day early; Sasha Leibowitz is still out with whatever goddamn bug has half the newsroom out sick. Maybe she'll be up to writing her column on Wednesday."

Thanks to the aberrant patterns of El Niño, it had been an unusually rainy and bleak winter, and the newsroom had been hit pretty hard by a series of flus. The latest gave you a sore throat, an insanely high temperature, and left you so weak you had to take a nap even after you got up to go to the bathroom. Sasha was a plucky babe, and I'd seen her write through all kinds of crises, but if she was down with this sore-throat thing, they'd better plan on running a repeat column. Or leaving a big white space where she would have been featured.

"Gotta go. Gotta write. I'll see you in the morning."

"Yep." And he hung up. A.S. never says good-bye. I pointed this out to him once and he looked puzzled. "What for? Doesn't my hanging up signify we're finished?" From his standpoint, I guess it does.

It was almost two A.M. on the East Coast. I was really sorry it was too late to call Signe, who usually hits the hay right after Ted Koppel touches his chin at her, just before *Nightline* runs its credits. I'd actually met Koppel at a conference on race and the media in (when else?) February, and told him my best friend had an unbreakable "date" with him every night. He thought that was funny, and I thought I'd give her a thrill, so I called her on my cell phone while we were standing there and the two of them carried on like long-lost buddies. (He looks stern, but he's a huge flirt, as is Signe.) Ted told Signe she had "a marvelous name—your mother must be an extraordinary woman," and promised that, from then on, he'd send her a special sign when he was on air: "I'll tap my chin. It'll be our little secret."

Uh-huh. Signe told everybody who cared and everybody who didn't, so there wasn't hardly anybody who didn't know that when Koppel stroked his cleft at the show's end, he was really saying, "Magnolia Mouth, wassup?" Since then we three have gotten together for dinner a couple of times, and almost gotten kicked out of each restaurant we were in, those two were so loud. Even if nobody recognized Ted Koppel's face, they got the voice right away. An autograph and a big tip, courtesy of his ABC expense account, kept us from being bounced every time.

I decided it was too late to call Washington, too. Then the phone rang. A.S. wanting to micromanage something, I thought.

"Forget something?" I teased.

"No, *you* did. Forgot to call and give me the 911." The warm baritone oozed through the phone, and I smiled.

"I thought you'd have been in bed ages ago. I was going to call you tomorrow at work."

"I had dinner with a bunch of folks from the Black Caucus. The *Times* was paying, and it wasn't a voting night, so we were there forever. I've only been home for about forty-five minutes."

"Well, you had more fun than I did." And I recounted the highlights of the evening for him.

"Do you have an internal magnet for corpses or something? This is twice in one year."

"Yeah, that's what Marron said. But actually, it's not twice in one *calendar* year." The last corpse I'd seen had been six months earlier, in August. He ignored my technicality.

"Are you okay?"

"I guess. Mostly weirded out."

"They don't know who did it?"

"Too early to say. There was this ticked-off brother in

dreads there, and an older woman who was really upset with him. But being upset, or even seriously mad at someone, doesn't mean you want to kill them." Lucky for me that's the case, since many of my readers get seriously upset with what I write from time to time.

"I worry about you, Powell."

"I'm fine. I think whoever did this was completely interested in doing it to a specific person, and did. Marron says all his personal effects were with him. He was wearing a three-thousand-dollar watch, and had a wallet full of cash and credit cards. None of that was touched. Although they haven't released that information to the general public yet."

"You writing about it?"

"A.S. and I were just discussing that. Yes, about the issues, not necessarily the murder. Beyond the fact that there was one, I mean."

He sighed. I could picture him propped up in his big bed, several pillows behind his back and books and papers spread over the part I slept on when I was there. His laptop could be up and running on the nightstand. His watch would be carefully placed on the base of the reading lamp, face up. His wallet would be on the dresser. The room would be quiet, dim, and just warm enough. On weekends, he often put a fire in the fireplace he was lucky enough to have in his bedroom. I wished I was there.

"I wish you were here—I miss you."

"Well, if you can hold on for two days, I will be. I'm off to San Jose tomorrow to meet with some Silicon Valley brothers.

Then up to San Francisco to talk to our Internet folks about an all-politics page. Then, if you're not busy accumulating more dead people, I'll stop down and spend the weekend with you. Sound good?"

"Sounds better than good. When are you coming in?"

"Not sure yet. I'll probably just catch a commuter flight when I'm done. If I have any warning, I'll let you know. Otherwise, I'll just find something to do till you get home."

Woo-hoo. By Thursday he'd be here. Which meant I had to get cracking.

"Guess I'd better go write, then, so I'll be free for more important things on Thursday."

"Guess you'd better, because the way I'm feeling, you'll probably go to work late on Friday."

I grinned. The bad thing about cross-country relationships is the distance; the good thing is the sex: when you don't get to have it that often, you make sure it's da bomb.

"You're good, boy, but I can type with one hand if I have to. I *never* blow a deadline."

"Why would you, when there are much more interesting things to blow than deadlines?" he purred.

"Good-bye, pervert. Gotta write."

"Bye, Einstein. See you Thursday. Be ready."

Actually, I was ready right *now*, but it would have to wait till Thursday.

I peeled out of my work clothes, put on a warm pair of sweats, because L.A. in early April is still pretty chilly in the evenings, turned on my laptop, and got down to business.

WHOSE KIND OF PEOPLE?
By Alex Powell
Standard columnist

Even people who'd never met him had strong opinions about James Simpson Lee Hastings, Jr.

For some he was, at long last, a person who celebrated out loud what they could only say among themselves behind closed doors: there are blacks and there are blacks, "and we'd not like to be confused with the Other Kind, thank you," a woman at Eso Won Books informed me last night, where Hastings was reading from his new book, *Chosen People*. "*Our* kind is a different breed entirely, and it's time for mainstream [read white, well-educated] America to take notice of that," she said firmly. "Simp Hastings has brought us out of the closet."

For others, Hastings was a finely honed wedge for social division, a throwback to a less kind and decidedly less gentle day when our community discriminated against itself, even as the larger white world continued to insist that we remain in our assigned, second-class places. So though we were not welcome in the ballrooms of the large downtown hotels, a way was made within the community to provide a venue for wedding receptions, cotillions, and ladies' luncheons. An entire social structure was built in black Los Angeles; it paralleled, but never intersected, its equals in the city's white social environs.

Admirable that, but looking at photos from the time, one can see why Simp Hastings's insistence on recognizing the Negro upper classes has riled some people so much: the teas, the dances, the cotillions, frolics, and luncheons were uniformly populated by a certain kind of black person: the women usually ran the gamut, as Dorothy Parker once said of an actress, "from A to B"— from porcelain to pale praline. Their mates might have been a bit darker (but not much) but they made up for that "deficit" by being wealthy, powerful, or both. There was an invisible Do Not Cross barrier that many of the Other Kind of black folks felt spoke pointedly to them.

Simp Hastings, with his exaltation of black achievement, has also managed to raise the hurtful specter of black-on-black exclusion. Which is why Eso Won was packed last night with two kinds of black folks: those who were proud to have been in the book (or who wished they had been, and were angling for an introduction so they'd be included in the sequel) and those who, for myriad and often radically different reasons, wished he'd never written it.

At the end of the evening, some people left highly satisfied that the invisible black America they live in but never see reflected in the mainstream had finally been made visible. Others left thinking that the turn of this century is going to look depressingly like the turn of the last one, when fair skin and naturally straight hair were considered a premium and social circles could be entered only at the say-so of arbitrarily selected gatekeepers.

Our ongoing fascination with history, hierarchy, and

hue all combine to make Simp Hastings a very controversial speaker and writer. Controversial enough that at some point on Monday evening, someone sought to silence him permanently, and did, by killing him in Eso Won's parking lot. But killing the messenger doesn't automatically stifle the message. Or does it?

I had done all I could do for one evening. It was almost one-thirty my time by the time I filed the story and shut off my machine. I knew I'd need some sleep to face whatever wildness tomorrow was going to bring—and there would be some.

I'd bet on it, except I've never been a betting kind of girl.

Chapter Four

People on the East Coast talk bad about those of us who live out on the Left Coast, and are particularly vicious about those of us who, for one reason or another, find ourselves living in Los Angeles. To compensate for the nice weather we enjoy most of the year, some East Coast types feel they need to punish us. Some do it by claiming there is no cultural or intellectual life out here. Smart West Coast people don't even argue that; it only sounds defensive, like you've been recruited by the chamber of commerce to tick off all the cultural/intellectual stuff: libraries, museums, jazz joints, and so forth. Some do it by taunting us with the fact that, sooner or later, we're going to slide into the Pacific, and Western Nevada will become oceanfront property. So what? Sooner or later, something's gonna get us all.

And some, like my friend Signe, do it by calling at the crack of dawn because, hey, the day's already started back East "and y'all slugs should be up and at it, right?" Which is why

I was almost certain that the ringing phone as I exited the shower was going to be Magnolia Mouth. And when the machine picked up with the generic message Paul and Marron had insisted I install on the phone after I was attacked last summer, I *knew* it was Signe. She called the male mechanical voice that asks callers to *"please . . . leave . . . a . . . message . . . at . . . the . . . sound . . . of . . . the . . . tone"* White Boy, and talked to him like he was my personal servant:

"White Boy, tell that lazy girl you work for to pick up the phone—I cannot *believe* I had to hear this news from Patsy Yoo this morning."

Dripping a little and shivering a lot—the furnace, on a timer, hadn't kicked in yet—I grabbed the cordless and padded back into the bathroom, which was warm and misty and redolent of bulgarian rose, courtesy of the shower gel in my favorite scent Signe had given me for my birthday last fall.

"You *do* realize it's six-thirty, don't you?" I began.

"Uh-huh—and you *do* realize it's your sworn duty as my best friend to call me with the 911 before you tell anybody else. Whyn't you tell me somebody killed Simp Hastings?"

"Who told you?" I asked, stalling for a good excuse.

"Like I said . . ." Signe drawled, her thick Memphis accent, even after years of living in the benighted North, still making the words come out *"lak ah say-ed."*

"Oh, yeah, Yoo. How'd *she* know?" Patsy was the assistant Living editor at the *Times,* and she and Signe often worked together.

"Hel-*lo*: who's one of Yoo's best friends? Ashley Chang, a producer at *The Today Show*."

The light clicked on.

"Where the future Mrs. J.S.L. Hastings Junior is medical correspondent Dr. Sheila Howe."

It was getting to be a small colored world with a small *c*. Interesting.

I finished drying off and shrugged into my bathrobe, cradling the phone on my shoulder while firing up the kettle and taking the coffee bean sack out of the metal canister in which it's usually stored. Signe had put me on hold for a second ("my WP AME—back in a sec, don't hang up.") so I had time to fill the chamber of the coffee grinder, hit the button, and grind away for half a minute, and dump the whole lot into the French press before Signe came back. I was just putting the sack back into the can, a souvenir I got at a Paris flea market, when she came back on the line.

"Still there?"

"Yup. So what'd Patsy say?"

"Girl, the doctor just about had to be *medicated*. The police called her and she called her parents, then Patsy. She was hysterical. Kept screaming about how she knew 'they' were going to get him sooner or later, how jealous 'they' were of him, stuff like that."

I poured almost-boiling water over the heap of ground coffee in the glass pot, and immediately the comforting scent of mocha java filled my little kitchen. I got the milk out and poured some into the yellow ceramic pitcher I use just for this, stuck it into the microwave, and listened to Signe over the microwave's drone.

"So other than these hordes of nonelite, horrendously jealous, homicidally inclined black people, she just can't imagine who'd off her man?"

"Is the coffee ready yet? You know how mean you are before you've had a first cup . . ."

"I'm fixin' to rectify that terectly," I told her, amused.

The microwave timer chirped, and I poured the steaming milk into a cup and splashed coffee on top till it was just the right café au lait color. I took a deep, appreciative sniff, then a loud slurp, specifically for Signe's benefit.

"Oh, golly. I feel ever so much better now. Gee, you're right, I can be an awfully grumpy girl in the morning if I don't get my coffee . . ." I used the whitest, singsongiest voice I could, and was rewarded with Signe's chuckle.

"You sound like a cross between Alvin the Chipmunk and Shirley Temple."

"Whatever. So you know so much—are they talking arrangements for Simp yet?"

I took my coffee into my now-warmer bedroom (I'd turned the heat up as I was going into the kitchen) and looked into my closet. It looked like a black hole in there, since my favorite winter color was black—with the occasional splash of red. (Summer was mostly taupe, white, and pale blue.) What would I wear to work?

"Too early, but I did learn this: Dr. Sheila will probably be coming your way sometime soon, to, as she told Patsy 'get some answers from these people.' So you might want to be prepared."

"For what?" I wondered, rooting around for shoes that weren't suede and would therefore not be ruined by the still-rainy weather.

"I hear she can be . . . difficult." Signe giggled.

"And this is funny why?"

"Well, that's what they say about *you,* and you know it. So I'm thinking about asking her if she wants some company for the ride out there. I'm thinking I might be able to talk my WPs into a story on this whole business."

"*What* whole business?" I dragged out a pair of black gab trousers and a turtleneck of fine scarlet wool; they'd do.

"You know: grieving fiancée seeks justice for slain lover. They do 'em on white people all the time. Now it's our turn."

"Hmmm . . ."

"And if they don't let me do the story, I'm getting a cheap ticket and coming anyway—I want to be there when you two difficult babes meet."

"You're a sick person, know that? Gotta go. I'm going to punch in late at the plantation if I sit here talking to you much longer."

"Stay black, sisterwoman—or in your case, beige."

She hung up laughing and didn't hear my obscene, but salient, rejoinder.

Chapter Five

I could see as I finished dressing that news of Simp's death had been prominently featured on all the local television channels, and at least one national one. A sympathetic Katie Couric had mentioned it, too, on *The Today Show* when she noted that another doctor would be taking Sheila Howe's place, and why.

Looking like an alumna from an especially tony sorority house, Couric, freshly blonded with a string of pearls, gravely informed viewers that J.S.L. Hastings, "noted author and social commentator was the fiancé of our own Dr. Sheila Howe, medical correspondent for *Today*. Sheila will be back in a few weeks, but meanwhile, Sheila, if you're watching, you know our hearts and prayers are with you at this terrible, terrible time . . ." Couric's carefully lined and shadowed baby blues blinked back the empathy for which she'd become famous.

Simp's murder was mentioned on A.M. talk radio on the

way to work, and NPR did a little piece on *Morning Edition,* promising an in-depth piece on *All Things Considered* later today.

"Nice piece, Powell," called Karyn Palmer, a Metro reporter, as I walked to my desk.

"Thanks, K.P. You doing the news story?"

Karyn nodded her head in the affirmative and her head full of crazy corkscrew waves bounced and jiggled. "Yup— but just the who-what-when stuff. I hear they plan to make *you* go out and talk to people." She grinned. "I know how y'all columnists hate that."

I rolled my eyes and stuck out my tongue as I threw my stuff in the assigned cubby near my desk. Everyone assumes we columnists just sit at our desks and think Deep Thoughts, with no reporting involved. I spend at least as much time out in the street as the average beat reporter and they know it, but they also like to tease me about the fact that how and when I spend that time is up to me.

The anonymous mechanical lady who announces the number of messages you have waiting in the system blithely informed me that my voice mailbox was full, *"and is no longer available to receive messages. To listen to messages, press five . . ."*

And that's what I did for the next ten minutes. There were several. Many were from reporters at local television stations, wanting to know if I had any suggestions about whom to interview in what Norman sometimes called "the Nigwhazee" for stories they were working on about Simp. Norman himself called just to check in.

"I didn't see anything on the news about you this morning, Alex, so I assume you got home all right. People have been coming in here since the store opened. I must say, the brother's misfortune has been our good fortune." He didn't sound way broken up about that. Norman is serious about his money.

"Powell: lunch, one o'clock, the Gauguin Room. Guste wants to make sure we're on top of this thing and that *The Community*"—big pause for the sarcasm Fine always used to mock street activists and politicians—"is aware we're taking this seriously. Already Father Holier-Than-Thou wants to come in and lecture the editorial board." Father Holier-Than-Thou is actually Father August Holywell, a black Episcopal priest and community activist whose plummy baritone and impeccable vocabulary sometimes rubbed white folks in power the wrong way. Holywell's Harvard degrees (undergrad, the Episcopal Theological Seminary, *and* a doctorate in divinity) and a pedigree stretching back to the Revolutionary War made him harder to dismiss than some of the "street preachers" the paper's management politely ignored. And his status as a close friend of the president and first lady made him dangerous to antagonize. The fact that he would probably be the first black Suffern Bishop of the Los Angeles Episcopal Diocese, and hence the city's first black Episcopal archbishop eventually, didn't hurt, either. Hence the summons to lunch.

Finally, an even more interesting message:

"Ms. Powell, this is Sheila Howe. I read your column online a few months ago. I am leaving for Los Angeles later this afternoon and would appreciate it if you could take the time to see me tomorrow. I'm staying with my parents in Los Feliz, and I'll call after I've settled in." Her throaty voice broke, then sounded as if she'd been able to recover herself. "This is very hard, but I need to know more about what happened the night James . . . the night my fiancé was . . . was murdered. I look forward to speaking with you tomorrow." Her voice, clipped and precise, did not sound as if she would take no for an answer.

"End of messages." Hmmm . . . I flipped through my Rolodex and called my friend Ben Porter.

"Coroner's office."

"Hey, Ben, Alex Powell . . ."

"Hey, Alex. Should I thank you for keeping us in business? First that magazine editor and now this guy? Can I tell you how much media's been down here this morning?"

He didn't sound displeased. Ben was the perfect person for this job: he spoke well on his feet, didn't seem overly eager for attention (which made our starstruck chief coroner happy and secure), and was completely straight with reporters. If he knew something and could tell, he did. If he knew something and couldn't, he didn't bullshit you—he'd tell you, "I'm not allowed to release that information just yet." I liked him enough that I regularly took him to lunch every couple of months, partly because I genuinely enjoyed his company, and partly because when he *was* at liberty to release information, I was one of the reporters to whom he released it.

"I have a Simp Hastings question for you, Ben."

"Surprise, surprise." He laughed. "Shoot."

"Did he have family here? Has someone come down and ID'd the body yet?"

"Interesting you should ask. About fifteen minutes ago, his fiancée's mother came in, with an older woman. An aunt, I think."

"How'd she take it?"

"Which?"

"The aunt. Oh, hell, both of them."

"They did okay. Lots of silent tears, but they were all right. I think it unhinged them more that Channel Nine shoved a camera in their faces as they were leaving."

Ugh. Another reason I'll never work for TV. Not that they were beating down the door asking.

"Those poor women; having to battle their way through cameras *and* drive themselves home after all that trauma," I mused aloud, scanning my e-mail. I had twenty-five since last night; I'd cleared the in box when I left for home.

"Not that I can imagine you'd lose any sleep over this, Alex," Ben said, chuckling, "but 'those poor women' didn't drive themselves. Someone in a dark green Mercedes was at the wheel. And before you ask—no, I couldn't tell you who. Not my biz. And the windows were dark glass."

"Oh, well. Thanks, Ben. How about lunch next week, the Water Grill?"

"Love to, but I'll be in Dallas at a forensics conference. Push it back a week and you got a deal. My turn to pay, though." (We take turns paying, to keep our ethics people happy.)

"Twist my arm. Call me when you get back and we're on."

We said bye and hung up.

It was almost ten. At ten, a five-minute news highlight was broadcast on Channel 9. Which meant I'd need access to a television. I walked back to the Living and Style section and knocked on a closed door.

"Enter."

"It's almost ten; I hear some of Simp's relatives are on TV. Can I turn yours on for a moment?"

A long brown arm swathed in pink cashmere flipped in the direction of an old pie safe.

"You know where the remote is. Help yourself. I gotta make one more correction . . ."

Georgina Marks was squinting at her monitor as she absently mutilated a number 2 pencil with her white, white teeth. Georgie was about my best friend in the newsroom, six foot two of well-dressed Negro princesshood. Her office, with its Oriental carpets, antique furniture, and original art, was decorated better than most people's homes.

"Why shouldn't it be? I spend too many hours in this place for it to be dreary," she once pointed out, which placed her at distinct variance with most reporters and editors I know, who are not bothered by working in paper-strewn pigsties.

I moved a stack of style magazines and plopped down in her melon chintz slipper chair, remote in hand. A small

TV/VCR was on one shelf of the pie safe; beneath it was the center of a mini stereo system. The tiny speakers were hidden somewhere behind a couple of out-of-control ficus trees.

The dark screen brightened just in time for me to see Nancie Nguyen, the midday newsbite anchor, float into view.

"And in a startling development late last night, author and social commentator James Simpson Lee Hastings Junior was found dead in the parking lot of Eso Won Books in Baldwin Hills. Hastings, whose controversial new book, *Chosen People,* has generated heated discussion within the black community, was in town for a scheduled book signing . . ." The videotape showed the outside of Eso Won, with its big calendar in the front window that always advertised coming attractions so people driving up La Brea could see who'd be in the store during the next few weeks.

"Eso Won owner Norman Wilkens noted that Hastings's appearance had run true to form . . ."

Cut to a clip of Norman standing in the store, ringing up books, as he spoke to the reporter: "It's a book that a lot of people feel strongly about, and a lot of folks came out last night to express their opinions," he said, peering down at a charge card before sliding it through the credit card machine. "But nobody was violent in here; they never are. We won't stand for it, will we?" Nearby, Lester shook his head silently, bagging books, as the camera's lights glinted off his wire-framed glasses.

"Early this morning," the anchor droned, "Hastings's

soon-to-be in-laws, who live here in L.A., arrived at the morgue to identify his body . . ."

That's what I wanted to see. The camera showed two women, one in a trench coat, the other in what looked to be a silk raincoat with an expensive scarf tied, babushka-style, over her head. Despite the gloom, both women wore dark glasses. The two walked erectly, arm in arm, and seemed to be supporting each other. They batted away the microphones that were shoved in their faces, and quickly got into a dark green four-door Mercedes. The driver didn't get out and open the doors for them; he—or she—simply sped away after the women were safely inside.

The camera returned to Nguyen. "In other news . . ." I pressed the remote's button.

Markie looked up over her half-moon tortoiseshells.

"Your story?" she drawled.

"Seems to be. I heard that in addition to the column I was going to be doing another story on it for Metro. Or maybe contributing to one."

She laughed, and the little diamond studs in her brown lobes twinkled. "God forbid they should make a columnist do a little work." She teased.

I gave her the Universal Digit, and she just laughed harder.

"Fine says I have to have lunch with him to discuss how to handle Da Commoonity."

Georgie stretched her long pink arms, and the gold bangles up and down her right arm clinked softly.

"Oooh, yes—don't want to have restless natives, do we?" She grinned.

"Know anything about the players?"

"I've seen the doctor's mama around, at Links things, but I don't think she's in Mother's chapter. Or maybe she is and I just didn't notice." Georgie's mother had been in the premier L.A. chapter years ago, when they'd lived here for a while.

"I'm betting that if she *was* a Los Angeles Link, you'd have noticed. Your mother's chapter is the one where they hand the slots down from mother to daughter to grand-daughter," I reminded her unnecessarily, "and where out-siders have to wait for somebody without an heir to die before they're even *considered* for a place, remember?"

Georgie unfolded herself from behind her desk and stretched, showing yards of slim brown thigh and a coffee suede mini with knee-high boots to match. I had to give it to the girl—she wasn't the style editor for nothing.

"You know *your* spot was being held for a whole year, Contrary Short Person."

"Don't I? I thought they were going to have to carry Aunt Edith off after I declined . . ."

To my great-aunt's dismay, I was sociable enough, but not "social." *Sociable* meant going out for drinks, buying a ticket to the Links-sponsored Midsummer's Night Ball, and attending the cotillions when a friend's daughter came out. *Social* meant actually belonging to the organizations that put on such things, something Edith damn well knew I wouldn't do without being chloroformed. It's one of the few things my mother and I have in common.

"Anyway, whatever you might be able to pump your mom for—anything that doesn't involve me going to a cotillion, I mean—would be greatly appreciated."

I got up to go. Georgie's office, with its warm, indirect lighting ("flourescent lights probably give you cancer, you know . . ."), family photos, and vases of fresh flowers was so inviting it was hard to go back into the newsroom, with its modular pasteboard furniture, tweed cubicle dividers, and industrial carpeting. But it was time to get.

Georgie swiped a pink rose in full bloom out of a squat vase stuffed with them and walked me to the door.

"Here." She handed me the rose.

"That's so nice . . . thank you."

"It's not for you, it's for me." She smirked, leaning on the doorjamb.

"Whatchu talkin bout, Willis?"

"It's for me: every time I think of you working in that dumpy space it depresses me. The *least* you can do is put a flower in that mess. And I told you: whenever you're ready, my girlfriend Virginia will come by and straighten you out."

"One day soon, I promise," I lied. Virginia was one of those professional organizers who come in and throw out half your good junk, then rearrange the rest so you've got no idea where to find it. I still had the gift certificate from her services unused—courtesy of guess who?—somewhere at the bottom of my desk's center drawer. Who knows? I might actually call the woman before I die.

Temporarily conceding defeat, Georgie sighed, waved limply, and shut the door.

I walked back down the hall and returned to my desk. A green bottle half-filled with flat mineral water stood, forgotten, in one corner. I plunked the rose down in it. If Pellegrino was good for *my* insides, I figured it wouldn't hurt the rose none. The rose, gently unfolding already, seemed to agree.

Who said my work space didn't have atmosphere?

Chapter Six

The alarm on my PDA started chirping, telling me I had about five minutes to go to the bathroom, brush my hair, and get up to the Gauguin Room if I was going to be on time to meet with Fine and Father Holywell. Good thing I'd come dressed this morning—over the past couple of years, the newsroom had become so casual that the good reverend might be seeing me in jeans, something even I, fond as I am of casual dressing, would have been mortified about had it come to that. Episcopal, Baptist, or New Age, most black ministers expect a certain amount of decorum, even if you're not one of their parishioners. And as well as the Drum worked, it would only have been a minute or two before Aunt Edith was on the line, telling me what her former reverend had to say about her upstart niece. My mother would have been the call after that (after she and Edith had commiserated on my incorrigible ways), and the specter of the two of them beating up on me—concurrently or sequentially—was enough to make me give silent thanks that my all-black getup would earn me a dispensation from the Lecture Ladies. This time.

Fine and Holywell were sitting at a small table in the corner, discreetly away from the more occupied center of the room. The dark burlwood walls gleamed richly, the pale Berber carpets absorbed every footfall, and beautiful watercolors showing Tahitian women in various states of undress shone under the pinpoint spot lamps designed to highlight them.

The Gauguin Room was the jewel in the *Standard*'s corporate diadem. Eating there was a privilege jealously guarded by the senior editors whose prerogative it was to dine on the corporate tab. The Gauguin Room had been an institution since the early sixties, but there was a period when the room looked naked without the Gauguins on the wall. A little over two years ago, we'd inherited a new publisher who was very religious and who was distressed about the happy presence of the topless Tahitian ladies. "Not seemly," he'd snapped to his executive assistant. "Heads of state come in here. And what on earth would the archbishop say if he came to lunch and saw these?"

In fact, the French ambassador had come to lunch, and was delighted to see the collection of nubile Tahitians. "So intimate! It makes me homesick for when they were in the Jeu de Paume," he confessed. And the archbishop, who had been to lunch a lot over the years, had never been known to complain. But the new publisher was adamant: the nekkid islanders offended somebody. Some *specific* body with the power to order them down.

So they'd come down, and we'd endured much joking about the *"No 'gain Room"* from colleagues at other newspapers. Then about six months ago, the publisher decided to go back to Utah—he'd found Los Angeles a bad influence on his children—and the Gauguins, which had been languishing in a fireproof vault, had been rehung, amid much rejoicing. The archbishop had come for lunch the week after their re-installment and had declared to the *New York Times*, which ran a little article on the pictures' return, "it's like seeing old friends again." My guess was that the archbishop didn't have a lot of naked brown ladies for friends, but who knows?

Despite his collar, Father Holywell didn't seem to be uncomfortable with the ambiance, either. He was leaning back, gesturing expansively, when I approached the table. When he saw me he immediately stood. Fine rather reluctantly followed suit.

"Please don't get up for me," I murmured, as the priest pulled out a mahogany chair.

"Honey, do you know what Martha Wormley Holywell would do to me—even at this age—if I didn't stand for a lady?" He laughed. His smooth, walnut skin creased pleasantly at the corners of his smiling eyes, and his bald head shone.

"I can only imagine," I said, grinning. I turned to a rather puzzled-looking A.S. Fine.

"Home training is a very big thing, A.S., in our community.

About the worst insult someone could give you is to tell you you didn't have any."

"It's like saying your mama didn't raise you right," Father Holywell continued, picking up where I left off.

"Ah," Fine said, which could have meant "I get it" or "I don't get it, but I don't want to waste any more time on it, either."

After a waiter materialized at our sides to take orders (roast salmon and wild rice for Father H., the London broil with mushroom gravy for Fine, and roast chicken with mashed potatoes for me), Holywell looked at us both and began.

"The reason I asked to see Mr. Fine today is to impress upon him—upon you both—how potentially volatile this situation could become in the wake of Mr. Hastings's murder."

"You'll pardon me for saying so"—A.S. took a cautious sip of his iced tea—"but this doesn't strike me as the same thing as Latasha Harlins or Rodney King. It's not a matter of someone who's living at the margins of the economy being trod upon, yet again, by an unfeeling system, or being abused by authority. It seems to be a crime of passion."

"Just so," the reverend said smoothly. "And you are correct, Mr. Fine, in pointing out that Mr. Hastings did not come from the wretched among us. Quite the opposite, as a matter of fact."

Big salads arrived, and there was a moment of silence as our waiter gently ladled spoonfuls of vinaigrette over the crunchy green leaves. The priest took a small bite, swallowed, and continued.

"But here's the thing: there have been so many killings these past few years—by bad cops, most of them white, racial vigilantes, *all* of them white, and gang warriors—"

"*None* of them white," Fine pointed out.

"Touché," Father H. conceded.

"At any rate, so many of these remain unsolved by the police, or unaddressed by the courts, that the flashpoint in the community is getting very low. It doesn't matter that James Hastings was financially quite well off. It doesn't matter that the amount of education he possesses is far and above that of the average citizen in my community—"

"It doesn't matter that, from what I've heard of the guy, his only contact with the 'average citizen' in your community is to use them as a foil for his own elite fabulousness?" Fine pressed. "Why would anyone who'd met him feel obliged to protest on his behalf?"

"Because, Mr. Fine, Simp, um, James Hastings is the last link in a long chain of recently slain black men in this city about whom no one seems to care. The buck happened to have stopped with him. It could have been anyone—it *happened* to have been him."

There was momentary silence as Fine and the cleric chewed with manful concentration on their rather overcooked entrées. I took the opportunity to jump in for a second.

"And so what, exactly, would you like the paper to do for you, Father?"

He put down his fork and took a long swallow of his tea before speaking.

"I would like, Ms. Powell, for the *Standard* to pay close attention to what happens to Mr. Hastings from here on in."

"Um, isn't what happens next pretty conventional? He's autopsied, if he hasn't been yet, then they ship his body home, and his people bury him?"

Our waiter was silently placing glass bowls of gelato before us. He positioned a plate of cookies equidistant from each of us and retreated. I took a spoonful of the frosted scoop closest to me: hazelnut. Incredible.

"To answer your question, Ms. Powell, of course those steps will occur, and probably in that order. His parents, by the way, are both deceased. And he was an only child. But trust me, the community will soon feel it needs a closer examination of what happened last night and why. And what you want—what I *hope* you want—is for the *Standard* to be seen as *proactive*, rather than *reactive*, to this situation."

A.S. had been squirming, waiting to have his say, and the father's last remark was the catalyst for him to put his two cents in.

"Begging your pardon, Father, but I just don't see this as something that's any of our worry. Yes, we do occasionally do the 'tourist gets slain while visiting the City of Angels' story, but not very many of them—"

"Heavens, no," the priest said dryly, sipping decaf. "The hoteliers who advertise with you wouldn't like it very much if you did, would they?"

"Oh, please." Fine snorted. "That wall between edit and business is still there." Except when it isn't, and under the previous publisher there'd been some famous examples of cracks big enough to drive a delivery truck through the invisible wall that allegedly existed between the business side and its interests and the edit side and its precious integrity.

"Then if it's not ticking off the advertisers, pray tell, what *could* it be?" Father Holywell pressed.

"It's the fact that there's nothing *special* about this: he was a black guy, killed in a black neighborhood, on a weeknight, with no celebrities present and poor prospect for solving his murder. Where is the *story?*"

Whoa—that was blunt even for A.S., never a master of tact. The fact that he'd been so unvarnished with Holywell probably meant the priest had gotten to him.

Holywell put down his napkin and pushed back his chair.

"I believe the seeds I'd hoped to plant today are falling on infertile ground," he announced. "Thank you so much, Mr. Fine, for your time. And for lunch. I must be getting back to my parish."

Fine, after scanning the bill, signed it and pushed back his own chair. The priest had already placed himself behind mine and pulled it back to allow me to stand. I turned to thank him, and he winked. *Some of us,* the wink seemed to say, *still believe in manners.* He reached into an inner pocket, pulled out two business cards, and gave one to each of us.

"If events, as they evolve, indicate that the *Standard* might want to reconsider its approach to this unfortunate incident, I'd be happy to speak with either—or both—of you again," he said, as we walked to the elevator.

Fine nodded, and shook Father Holywell's outstretched hand. "I'll have to leave you here, Father, as I'm almost late for the afternoon story conference."

The cleric nodded graciously. "Of course." Fine disappeared first into the downward carriage, and we followed.

When it got to the third floor, he looked at me in surprise.

"I'm going to walk Father Holywell to the lobby," I explained. "I'll see you in a few."

The doors closed silently behind Fine. Holywell turned to me and grinned.

"Is this that home training you people are so famous for, or did you want to have a word with me without your White Person present?"

I grinned back. "How about 'all of the above'?"

He chuckled.

"I just wanted you to know this: Fine is a decent enough guy, but he reacts badly when he thinks he's being pushed. So all this talk of potential community reaction sounds to his ear—"

"Like I'm getting ready to do a Full Sharpton on him, eh?" Holywell smiled.

"Something like that."

"Well," he allowed, walking slowly to the door, "fear is sometimes a useful motivator, Alexa. Let's hope your WPs see the light soon—and that the light is not the Mason building going up. Again." The city's black insurance company had been engulfed by flames the night of the King verdict. Now, a decade later, it had arisen, Phoenix-like, from the ashes in the same spot, but we both doubted the old Los Angeles family that had established it would rebuild a second time if it came to that.

Father Holywell pulled a pair of dark glasses from his inner jacket and placed them carefully on his handsome face. "Let's keep in touch as this situation develops. Perhaps we can help each other out." He patted me on the shoulder like a fond uncle, then went through the brass-edged revolving doors.

I watched through the heavy plate glass as he walked purposefully down the street to the paper's guest parking lot. The afternoon rays of the early spring sun had glossed the granite buildings and cement sidewalks with a golden-orange glow, and walking into the waning light made him look like a man consumed by flame.

I hoped *metaphorical* flame was all we'd be seeing around here anytime soon, and slowly walked back to the elevators.

Chapter Seven

When I got back upstairs, A.S., who was talking to another section editor, saw me out of the corner of his eye. He quickly excused himself and came over to my cubby.

"You know, you're going to have to choose," he cautioned, slipping his glasses farther up his nose.

"Between what?" I asked, truly mystified.

"Between being a member in good standing of your community and being a good reporter."

I stared at him, stunned. *How dare he?*

"Number one, who says being black and being a good reporter are mutually exclusive? And number *two*—" My voice got a couple of notches louder, a no-no in this particular newsroom, which prided itself on its calm and civility. (*"Dead calm,"* as a media critic had once described it.) "What makes you think that just because I'm black, I'd give Holywell or anyone else a pass if they're pertinent to the story that I've been charged to report? And number *last . . .*"

It had gotten quieter around me, making my voice sound even louder than it was. Reporters love it when you fight with an editor right in front of them. Most often we get called into their glass-walled offices and the blinds are lowered before the metaphorical ass-kicking commences, and we have to rely on the "he-said, she-said" version afterward. Not nearly as satisfying as seeing the real deal unfold right before your very own beady eyes.

"How could you fix your mouth to ask that question? You don't question the objectivity of Sid Kramer, who covers the school board—and he has dinner with the superintendent once a month. At his *club*. Which has not a single black or Latino member and to which Sid also belongs. And do you question Muffie Chatsworth? She socializes with all the people she covers for Out and About—even when she's *not* doing a story. *Now* all of a sudden the rules are different? What, 'those Negroes are so emotional, they can't achieve the same journalistic remove' that the white folks, who possess plenty of conflicts of interest, do?"

Dead silence. A.S., now deeply crimson, squirmed.

"I have a meeting in five minutes. We can continue this later—in my office."

Uh-huh. Let's see if we ever finish *that* conversation.

"Whoo-wee." chortled Bob Knight, a sports reporter, as he passed by. "Boy thought he was a big dog, but he shoulda stayed up on the porch with the other puppies, huh? Wasn't ready for the tall grass he wandered into."

I grinned. "Today it might have been a good idea. There'll probably be payback but . . ." I shrugged.

"Sometimes a woman's gotta do what a woman's gotta do." Bob laughed. "Call me if you need some backup." Since Bob was always on the road with one team or another, I knew he probably didn't mean it, but it was nice of him to offer anyway.

"*Very* intelligent," a voice drawled behind me. I jumped.

"Could you maybe announce your presence before you sneak up on a person?" I asked Georgie. "What are you wearing, anyway, nun's shoes?"

"Sorta." Georgie had changed since this morning. Not an unusual occurence. She stuck out one narrow foot to display the patent-leather driving shoe that winked from beneath her gray wool trousers. The rubber-nubbed soles would have allowed her to move silently about the newsroom even if it hadn't been carpeted.

"Next time I'll bring the bearers and flower boys with me, since you need warning," she said. "But speaking of warnings, *I'm* warning *you:* fighting with one's editor in front of one's peers is *not* a smart career move."

"Well, I don't intend to be working for him for all of my career."

"Yeah." Georgie sniffed. "But your career here might end before you plan for it to, if you keep that up."

I hated to admit it, but she had a point.

"Okay, Voice of Reason," I purred. "Let's see what *you* would have said in a similar situation."

"In my office, please," Georgie instructed, "since I'm the only one of us who *has* an office. With a *door*," she emphasized, looking over the tops of her tortoiseshell reading glasses at the suddenly busy colleagues around us who, in traditional newsroom fashion, had indeed been listening to our conversation.

"And that door will be *closed*," Georgie intoned. Heads remained down, but I could see the beginning of smiles hovering around several mouths.

After we were settled and Georgie had poured me a cup of jasmine tea (and glared at me as I feebly made a motion toward the sugar bowl), I told her about Fine's assertion that black reporters can be good blacks or good reporters—but not both. She rolled her eyes in disgust.

"That's one of the most ignorant things I've heard in a long, long time. Which is saying something, considering the ignorant stuff I hear—including in this place—all day long."

"So now don't you feel badly about hollering at me?"

"I did not holler, I never *holler*," Georgie protested. "But I would have had that discussion with Fine in his office. And maybe even on paper. That kind of stupidity deserves to be documented. 'Cause who knows?" she continued, thoughtfully. "You might get a tidy settlement from it if you choose to go the court route."

Now *that* was an intelligent idea. Georgie Marks wasn't management material for nothing.

"Good point. I'm going to follow up with an e-mail."

"And don't let me tell you how to handle your trauma, but since I know you're going to send a copy to your higher-ups, maybe you should consider doing it subtly."

"You mean let my hand slip and just *happen* to blind-carbon the editor in chief?"

We beamed at each other. The current editor in chief was a true gentleman, a silver-haired, Southern-raised, second-generation civil rights activist from a borderline Southern state, and he would be appalled to, uh, *accidentally* learn of Fine's latest observation. Heh, heh.

"Far be it from me to tell you what to do," Georgie murmured. "Your call."

Mighty white of her, since we both knew what that call was going to be.

I decided I'd write my memo at home, from my own computer. If the paper's Stazi could tap into my AOL lines, so be it. But I wasn't going to contribute to my possible professional immolation by doing it on the intraoffice system. Even *I* am not *that* stupid.

That evening, when I arrived home, the little message light on my answering machine was blinking furiously. Wondering how many people had called in my absence, I got a pen and piece of paper and sat down to hear who wanted what.

"Hey, girl—I *am* coming out, no fooling, this weekend. Convinced the WP editor that this could be a big deal. I let them know the cheapo airline had round-trips for under four hundred dollars, and I have a ton of hotel miles, so I'll be at the Mondrian from Friday night on. I know you're going to be up under Paul on Friday, so I've made arrangements to have dinner with another friend, but I want to see y'all on Saturday, hear?" Signe left her cell number—as if I didn't know it by heart—and hung up.

Beep. "Hi, darling, it's your Aunt Edith. Wasn't that awful about poor Simp Hastings? I hope *you're* not involved in any of that . . . Anyway, turns out I will be in Los Angeles on Saturday and Sunday of this week. I've been asked to fill in for a lecturer at the Getty who got sick at the last moment, so they're flying me out and putting me up in the W, in Westwood. I guess that's not too far from the museum? Anyway, I have a dinner on Friday night with some docents, but I'm free for the rest of the weekend, so if you're in town, we should make plans to see each other. Saturday night would be good—nobody's taken that yet. Call me from the office tomorrow, okay? Ciao."

Boy, nobody comes to L.A. for a zillion years, then in *one* weekend, every damn body comes. And of course it's the weekend when I actually have a date. For the whole weekend. Oh, well, at least they all have their own rooms.

The last message was also from someone who did not live in Los Angeles:

"Ms. Powell, this is Dr. Sheila Howe. I have arrived in

Los Angeles, and I would like to see you at your earliest con-
venience. I'm staying with my parents, in Los Feliz. Here's
the number—and feel free to call early. We're very early ris-
ers, and I'll be on East Coast time." She left her parents' number. I turned on my laptop and typed it into one of the many
Internet search machines that can tell you who lives where, if
you provide the telephone number.

Whoa. According to the reverse directory, the Howes lived
very large on top of a big hill in Los Feliz, not too far from
Griffith Observatory. Judging from the lines on MapQuest,
the houses on the Howes' street, Barbary Lane, were old and
on very generous lots. The higher up the hill, the bigger the
lots and houses. And the Howes lived all the way at the top.
Any higher, they'd be going downhill into Glendale—
territory until recently reserved for cops, rednecks, and
newly rich Armenians. Guess she sounded snotty and rich
because she *was* rich. I made a mental note to ask Aunt Edith
about the Howes tomorrow when I dutifully called her back.

And since it was practically Wednesday, I'd have to start
thinking about what I was going to do with all these people.
It made sense, in a mental health way, to take them all to dinner somewhere. But who knew who Signe might be bringing
with her (there's always an intern or mentee of the moment). Or whether Aunt Edith might spontaneously invite a
couple of her seminar-mates to meet her favorite niece?

Or whether Paul might, as he has been known to do, run
into a friend at the airport and, on a whim, invite him to join
us for dinner? He would plan to pay, but he wouldn't know

there were about eight people besides me joining us. And if that were the case, I wouldn't let him, although we'd have to have a whispered fight about it and would probably end up splitting the bill because we're both so stubborn . . .

The whole thing was starting to give me a headache. Which is why I never entertain anyway. B. Smith has a job, Martha Stewart has a job, and I have a job. They are not the *same* job.

Until now, maybe. Because while going out to eat might be great for my mental health, it wouldn't be so hot for my frequently strained finances. I had money I could pull out of my savings account, but that was for emergencies. Which is what this was starting to feel like.

Two sessions with a good clinical psychologist, or a fine, homemade dinner for eight, with good wine?

Please. There's only one right answer. I would have to ask Sally for a caterer—an inexpensive ("never say cheap," Sally insists) caterer. And I'd invite Sally, too. Well, it would be made at *somebody's* home, so that's homemade, isn't it?

In for a penny, in for a pound.

Chapter Eight

With the morning light, sanity returned. I realized, in the shower, that what Sally and I considered inexpensive were worlds, maybe even galaxies, apart. I was going to have to bite the bullet and cook. It's not as if I *can't* do this, but it's not like I *want* to, either.

Since I'm almost as good a procrastinator as I am a writer, I managed to shove the whole issue of what I was going to feed my intended victims to the bottom of my list. I needed to get to work early if, as I suspected, I was going to have to spend a couple of hours out of the office with Dr. Sheila Howe.

She'd indicated in her message that she was an early riser, but I was hesitant to call her parents' home at seven-thirty. They weren't on East Coast time, and it wasn't, after all, three hours later for them. But then my phone started ringing, which meant I couldn't call anyone until I got whoever it was off the line.

I thought it might be Signe, or even Paul, but it was a *Standard* operator. Usually when they call you at home, it means someone from outside the paper is trying to reach you. The paper won't give them your number directly, but they will connect the person to you.

"Alex?" a smooth baritone asked. It was Bryan. There are six full-time operators on the general switchboard, and four of them are men—but Bryan is the only one who sounds like James Bond.

"Good morning, Bryan. What's up?"

"Dr. Sheila Howe wishes to be connected; will you accept?"

"Sure . . . I guess."

"Hold, please."

The next voice I heard was that of a very awake Sheila Howe. Apparently, waiting until I was in the office to call wasn't acceptable.

"Miss Powell?"

"Dr. Howe."

"I thought I'd take a chance and try you before you got to the office so we could set a time to meet today. Sorry about the operator, but I lost power on my Blackberry and all the recent numbers got erased. Anyway, as I said when we first talked, I'm an early riser. Would four this afternoon be convenient?"

Well, it would get me out of the office for a couple of hours, so that was cool. "Sure, four is fine. Where would you like to meet?"

"Actually, I was hoping you could come here. My mother

and great-aunt would like to meet you. We thought tea might work."

So we agreed on tea at four in Los Feliz. I hoped appearing in black pants and a black sweater would work for them. I added pearl earrings and pinned a gold dragonfly to one shoulder. It had tiny "diamonds" for eyes and "gold" filigree wings. Signe and I had spied it at a street fair in New York a few years ago. It was costume jewelry, but good costume jewelry. That would have to do to meet the Family Howe. I put on my raincoat and left for work.

I worked through lunch so I could leave a little early. I left a message with Fine's assistant, Francyne, and made sure my cell phone was on as I left the building. My white people like to know where I am at all times during the workday.

I could see that traffic was going to be fierce as soon as I got out of the garage. There used to be rush hour and non-rush-hour in Los Angeles, but in the years I'd been living here, both had merged into a seamless, eternal clog of traffic. Too many people in too many cars, said urban planners. But they didn't provide a viable alternative, so people who could afford cars kept driving them. And the freeways remained choked all day. Even when it wasn't rush hour.

Leaving at three from downtown to get to Los Feliz would take forever if I took the Hollywood Freeway, so I opted for surface streets. I wound my way west from City Hall by traveling down Temple, which turned into Beverly.

I went through downtown, past the shopping district, thronging with Hispanic immigrants from Mexico and Central America, buying fake designer T-shirts, luggage for trips home, and Spanish-language versions of popular movies. Past the soaring glass towers that allegedly would still be standing after the Big One because their foundations were on rollers. (As if that would matter when a 7.2 hits!) Past the lawyers in dark suits and administrative assistants wearing low heels and carrying small umbrellas. (It had stopped raining in mid-morning, but looked as if it would start again any minute). Past Koreatown, with its sleek strip malls advertising karaoke, boba drinks, and grilled short ribs, and storefront boutiques with beautiful silk clothes, both Western and traditional, all in tiny sizes. (Do Korean size 10 women exist, I wonder?)

I got to Western and hung a right, going north. After it climbed a hill, Western curved right, and blended into Los Feliz Boulevard. Los Feliz was lined with trees and large apartment buildings, some of which probably had beautiful nighttime views. The huge picture windows in many of the fancier buildings seemed to hint that might be the case. Just south of Los Feliz Boulevard was Laughlin Park, a private, gated community of mansions built during the days of silent film. Affluent actors still lived there, but they were greatly outnumbered by film industry executives, plastic surgeons, designers, and technology titans.

Past Vermont, the streets that ran uphill held single-story residences, not as large or as luxe as the ones in Laughlin

Park, but still nothing to sneer at. Following Sheila Howe's directions, I passed a number of streets with names related to pirates or the high seas: Galleon Drive, Dubloon Court, Lafitte Way. Barbary Lane was at the very top of the hill. Slipknot Road made a turn, right next to a four-level concrete house that Frank Lloyd Wright was supposed to have built (probably true—it looked uncomfortable enough to have been designed by him). And after that curve, Barbary Lane began. It ran along the spine of the hill. I couldn't see much from the road, but the views had to be splendid. Even on an overcast day like today.

On the Howes' street, I passed several hulking Tudors, a sort-of chateau that was probably built in the 1940s, and a homage to the Bauhaus school (concrete and chrome railings, and lots of glass with no shutters or curtains). Forty-four-oh-four Barbary Lane was a Georgian colonial set well back from the street. A chest-high brick wall surrounded the front lawn and its formal gardens, and a locked black wooden gate kept unwanted visitors at the street. I looked to the right; there was a small box imbedded in the brick, with a button. I pushed.

"Yes?" a voice asked quietly.

"I'm Alex Powell," I told the box. "I have a four o' clock appointment with Dr. Howe."

"Please come in, Miss Powell."

The gate buzzed, I pushed, and in a moment I was on Howe property. I walked on the serpentine brick pathway toward the house. The lawn was as green as something you'd see on a movie set. It was punctuated with several graceful weeping willows, and a few Japanese scarlet maples. Rose trees in square black planters flanked the wide wooden door. It opened just as I reached for the knob.

"Miss Powell? May I take your coat, please?" A stunning Latina smiled shyly and stretched out her arms, waiting for me to comply. She took the coat and opened a panel in the front hall that contained a closet. Once the door was closed, you'd never have known a door was there.

"Please follow me."

She led the way across the parquet-floored foyer, past a burlwood bombé topped with a large vase of lilacs. I walked past and breathed in their heady perfume. The young woman entered a doorway to the left and announced, "Miss Powell, Mrs. Howe." Then she gestured for me to go in.

Even though it was heavily overcast, the room was flooded with silvery light. The entire back of the Howe living room was glass, and overlooked the Los Angeles basin. The damp backyard, with its English herb garden and large swimming pool, was at least twenty feet below, so I guessed the public rooms—living room, dining room, den, and probably a library—were on the street level, but perhaps the bedrooms and guest rooms were on the ground floor.

"It *is* startling, isn't it? You'd never know this was here if you only saw the front of the house. Which is why we bought it. People don't need to know everything." The woman who addressed me walked across the room and extended her hand.

"Phyllis Howe, Miss Powell. Thank you for coming to see us. I'm sure you had a very busy day."

"I was happy to come. And please call me Alex." We shook.

"Sheila should be with us in a moment. I insisted she lie down for a bit. She's exhausted with all that's happened."

Phyllis Howe was probably in her late sixties, and still a handsome woman. My guess was that she had been striking but not cute when she was younger, and she had now grown into her face. It was oblong, with full, arched brows and pecan skin. She had high cheekbones and a nice mouth. No double chin. She was wearing the same thing I was—slacks and a sweater—only hers probably cost more than I make in a week. A silk scarf was wound around her neck, almost like a turtleneck. And she wore big mabe pearls rimmed in gold. If money could, indeed, talk, hers was saying "old money—recognize."

"How is Dr. Howe doing?"

"Of course she's devastated. She and Jamie were to be married next month. In addition to the trauma of his death, there are a thousand details to attend to." She paused and looked at me. "It's almost as much work to *undo* a wedding as it is to do one."

I thought of the caterers who would have to be called, the venue that would be canceled. Too late for the gown and the bridesmaids' dresses, I guess. But if there was a honeymoon, the airfare might be refundable . . .

"I would imagine that *would* be a lot of work," I murmured.

"*What* would be a lot of work?"

I knew that voice. I turned and saw Dr. Sheila Howe, dressed much as I was, black trousers and a black turtleneck. She was arm in arm with a woman older than her mother. Like the rest of us, the elderly lady wore slacks and a sweater, too. But she was all in white, which matched her white hair.

"Ms. Powell was just telling me about her day so far," the doctor's mother lied smoothly. She probably didn't want to further traumatize her daughter with talk about canceling weddings.

Like her mother, the doctor offered me her hand.

"Sheila Howe. And this is my great-aunt Mrs. Martha Dexter." Mrs. Dexter nodded, but did not extend her hand. Instead she sat wearily on one of the room's sofas.

"I asked Ms. Powell to come today because I think we need to find out as much as possible about Jamie's . . . about what happened to Jamie. She may have questions we can answer that would help find the person who did it."

The older women nodded.

The stunning Latina reappeared with a heavy silver tray. It had a teapot, and little silver vessels for cream, sugar, and hot water. White cups were stacked on the tray, as was a bowl of lemon slices. The maid—who apparently had no name, because no one ever used it when speaking to her—left and immediately returned with a large pottery plate that was laden with an assortment of cookies and tiny sandwiches.

Mrs. Howe passed plates and filled cups, all the while chatting about inconsequential stuff—a fashion show to benefit Young Black Scholars, who was and wasn't going back to the Vineyard from Los Angeles this summer, and whether we were having an especially late rainy season this year.

When we had all had a sip of our tea and a nibble at one of the cookies, Sheila Howe began.

"We already know this was not an accident. What we don't know, and what the police probably won't be able to find out, is why someone would hate Jamie enough to kill him."

"Jamie—is that his family nickname?"

Martha Dexter finally spoke. "Yes, it is—was. Apparently, Jamie's father was already called James, and the family didn't like Jim. His mother called him Jamie almost as soon as he was born."

"Then where did—"

Sheila Howe shrugged. "Probably boarding school or college. Seems to me boys always have to nickname each other, and somehow Simp stuck." She made a face, indicating her distaste. "I never liked it, so I never called him that."

"What have the police said so far?" I asked.

"Nothing of use," Phyllis Howe snapped. "We pushed them—after all those years of watching *Law and Order,* even *I* know that the longer it takes them to find something out, the slimmer the possibility of the crime ever being solved. We're approaching the forty-eight-hour mark; it's quite possible we'll never know anything . . ."

Sheila Howe's eyes began to fill, but her voice was firm.

"That's why we called you, Ms Powell."

"Alex, please."

"Alex, then. You work in a newsroom, you get out and

about. You wrote the piece in today's paper. You hear things."

"Yours is a very social family, Dr. Howe. I imagine you'd hear even more than I would on any given day."

She didn't urge me to call her Sheila.

"We are that, but people hardly know what to say to us, they feel so horrible that this has happened. I think they would be more forthcoming with someone . . ." She paused. I could see her trying to quickly figure out how to say it delicately.

"Someone not of their milieu?" I smiled. "You might be right."

I could hear breaths being released in the room. The Howes were indeed pillars of what many wags often refer to as the Nigwhazee. They probably would call themselves part of the Old Families of Los Angeles. They chose not to recognize that calling their family old would make their East Coast counterparts roll their eyes: to places like Boston, Philadelphia, St. Louis, Savannah, and Charleston, "old" means something completely different. For those places, "old" starts somewhere around the early 1800s, or earlier.

But the Howes were one of the oldest *black* families in L.A.—they went back to the late 1800s. I'd done my homework before I came: the first Howe to emigrate to the city came in 1898, with the railroad. Elijah Howe was a butler in a private Pullman owned by an Eastern banking family that spent its winters with others of their ilk in Pasadena. Old Elijah became a pillar of the region's colored community, and his descendants had done very well. And they were very clear about their place in the city: they were colored royalty and, when not doing good works, moved exclusively among their royal peers.

Sheila Howe was right—people might not be entirely forthcoming with her. If anyone had anything critical to say, they certainly wouldn't want to further hurt her with any ugly details. And people who wouldn't mind hurting her probably wouldn't want to alienate the Howes—they owned several Los Angeles businesses outright, many others as silent partners, and were scattered throughout the city's government elite. They could make life inconvenient, if not downright uncomfortable, for anyone who crossed or embarrassed them—something a critic would surely remember.

"So what, exactly, would you like to find out?"

Sheila Howe turned to her mother, who turned to the elderly aunt.

"We'd like to know who, if anyone, might have a problem with this family," the dowager said bluntly. "And anything else you might discover that could explain why this happened. Why we have been placed in this position."

"This position?" I repeated blankly.

"Now, Aunt Marty," Phyllis Howe began, "we don't really need to—"

"We do!" the elderly lady exploded. "We most certainly *do* need to know why everyone in town is talking about us, speculating about this death!"

Sheila Howe looked positively stricken. "It's not as if he

did this to *himself,* Aunt Marty," she began, but she, too, was cut off.

"*Nice* people do not find themselves in this position," Mrs. Dexter sniffed, "unless they associate with people who are *not* nice. I *told* you this would happen when that boy began to write that book. All the people who came out of the walls, insisting on being included. All the people who chose not to participate and who found themselves in that book anyway."

Mrs. Dexter was working herself into a lather. She shook her head so hard pins were flying out of her topknot. Her hand quivered as she shook it in my direction.

"This kind of preening, ostentatious display did not come from the *true* families," she warned. "This came from upstarts who want those who know no better to think they're more than they are! I *knew* this book was going to be trouble—and look what's happened. Our poor Sheila's name throughout the paper. People all across the city speculating about this family. It's *disgraceful!* Grandfather Elijah must be spinning in his grave!"

Sheila Howe was weeping silently. Her mother swiftly crossed the room and took her daughter in her arms. "Martha, that's *enough,*" she hissed. Aunt Martha merely sniffed and looked out onto the soggy garden.

"I should go, I'm sure Dr. Howe might want to rest for a while," I told them, as I rose. "I don't know that there's very much I can do, but I'll speak with you in a couple of days." I looked at Sheila, who had her head resting on her mother's shoulder; Phyllis Howe was stroking her daughter's hair and murmuring softly to her. She looked up and nodded.

"I'll see myself out," I told her.

I walked back through the lilac-scented hall and into the foyer. The Jennifer Lopez lookalike had disappeared to wherever it is servants go to wait until they're called. Left on my own, I spent about ten minutes pressing various parts of the paneled wall, until I finally found the door with my coat in it.

On the way down the hill, I switched on NPR. The local affiliate was doing the five-minute city wrap-up.

". . . and late this afternoon, Myron Bournewell, chair of the Los Angeles Community Foundation's board of trustees, apparently fell to his death from the twentieth-floor offices of his real estate firm, BroadBranch Development. Mr. Bournewell was alone when he died. Police have not ruled out foul play, but say a decision on the death will have to wait until an investigation is complete."

At the stoplight, I looked to my right and the woman in the VW next to me was listening to the radio, mouth agape. Clearly, we were both listening to the same thing. Myron Bournewell! He was as close to a Medici as this city would ever get. He funded museums, theaters, and libraries. The arts in Los Angeles flourished because of him. He had, single-handedly, shamed other affluent Angelenos into completing the funding for the city's new Arts Center, a building that had already been likened to the Eiffel Tower and the Sydney Opera House—the architectural symbol of a world-class destination.

I'd once interviewed him for a cover story for the *Standard*'s Sunday magazine, and found him delightful. Tall, perpetually tanned, with sapphire eyes and a shock of prematurely white hair, Myron Bournewell was one of the most pleasant, least affected billionaires ever born. He and his wife, Lydia, had been married for forty years and, by all accounts, were still a happy couple. On pleasant Sundays, visitors often saw them walking, hand in hand, on the beach in Santa Monica.

So why would Myron Bournewell, powerful, wealthy, and generally beloved, jump to his death?

Or did someone help him take that awful flight?

Chapter Nine

When I got home, the answering machine was blinking furiously. Fine left a message telling me to "trawl the Internet tonight and prepare to write something on Myron Bournewell first thing in the morning." My mother called to tell me Bournewell had died "in case you hadn't heard it. Don't worry about calling me back—I'm going to Boston for three days with Barbara; we're helping your cousin move into her new place in Cambridge. We're at the Copley Plaza if you need us. Otherwise I'll talk to you when I'm back." I sort of wondered whether my young cousin Cecile would need two seventysomething ladies to help her move into a high-rise apartment with an elevator, but that degree from Harvard Law says she's way smarter than me, so let her figure it out.

Aunt Edith called to remind me we were on for dinner on Saturday, and to say plans had changed; Instead of the W, in Westwood, she'd be at the Regent Beverly Wilshire. "It's farther from the Getty, but closer to the shopping." That Edith—always has her priorities straight.

And Signe called. "Girl, they didn't go for a story on your boy's murder after all, but I got the deal of a lifetime at the Mondrian and two days' comp time for doing that Venus-Serena thing. So I'm coming anyway. You and Paul can come over and drink at the SkyBar and we can look out over the city and be hip and happening."

I didn't need to call Fine back; I'd just keep working. I could leave a message at Edith's hotel, confirming dinner. And I suppose at some point I'd have to tell Signe that Sky-Bar was actually on the *first* floor of the cooler-than-thou Mondrian, and that the only view she was going to get was of size 4s and 6s sucking down apple martinis and whatever else the drink of the moment was. I made a mental note to ask someone who'd know. Signe liked to order the drink of the moment.

And since she was going to be here, I'd need to make a place for her on Saturday night. I know she wasn't going to want to stagger back to the hotel after a few bottles of wine. Driving was out of the question—*I* certainly wouldn't be in shape to take her, I was going to help her drink the wine. Paul might be able to get her there, but he'd get lost getting back. And Signe would probably come help *cook*. That would definitely be worth granting her the sofa bed, even if the bathroom thing was going to be dicey. Things were looking up.

I spent the evening with a pastrami sandwich I found in the back of the fridge—I think it was only a couple of days old—and washed it down with a glass of leftover red. That kept me going while I scrolled through Myron Bournewell's life since the profile I did of him. Nothing amazing—just more accolades, more stuff about how he was the backbone of the city. So much for the official spiel. I picked up the phone and called Georgie.

"Speak," the voice at the other end said.

"It's me. I'm on Bournewell duty."

"Poor you. Poor Lydia Bournewell." Georgie sighed.

"Did you know her?" A sixtysomething socialite and Georgie didn't seem part of the same world. But you never know—Georgie gets around.

"I met her a few years ago at the L.A. Opera fund-raiser, and later at the Will Rogers Park Foundation polo benefit. She was quite nice."

"Too bad. They seemed very fond of each other."

"That's what Mother says—she was on the Arts Center board with Mrs. Bournewell."

"Whoa—Mummy must've written a *big* check," I teased. Mummy Marks is married to a Bajan businessman who made enough money from his Island Chutney Enterprises to retire ten years ago, at age sixty, to a lovely spread on Hilton Head Island. They stay there when he and Georgie's mother aren't living in their London or New York pieds-à-terre. When they're out and about, the Markses—Madame and Monsieur—cut quite a dashing figure through several cities. Including ours. Mostly because the baby of their family, their beloved Georgie, is here. I imagine that had Georgie decided to move to Cleveland (about as likely as her shopping at -Wal-Mart), it would be *that* city's symphony that would be getting the ducats. As that won't happen in my lifetime—or Georgie's—I hope the CSO remains well endowed.

"They have their little favorites," Georgie said.

"So do you think she'd share her impressions of the Bournewells with me?"

I could practically hear Georgie rolling her eyes skyward. "You know what the price is going to be. Are you sure you're up to it?"

The price, if history is any guide, will be a long lunch someplace splendid when Mummy Marks gets to town. And since she always pays, and we always have a good time teasing Georgie, I can definitely stand it.

"Tell her I'm up for it. There are three good restaurants here she hasn't been to yet, so find out when it would be convenient for me to call, so I can get my investigation on."

Georgie tapped her pencil against her receiver and laughed. "Oooohhhh, so we're an *investigative* reporter now, are we?"

"Just temporarily. I want to know why, if the Bournewells had a happy marriage and Myron Bournewell liked his job and his life, he'd do something like jump from one of the tallest office buildings in Los Angeles."

"Maybe because he could," Georgie said affably. "It *was* his building, after all . . ."

"All the more reason it's suspicious. I mean, if you love your work and you're proud of it, do you want people saying 'that's the building Myron Bournewell jumped to his death from'?"

There was a brief silence as Georgie pondered that point.

"Male menopause? Bipolar, and he wasn't taking his meds? Men are bad about following doctor's orders."

"Dunno. But we have some asking around to do, and I'd like to start with your mother."

"What do you mean 'we,' white man?" Georgie laughed. "Tonto is far too busy with his day job to get involved in this mess . . ."

I sighed. "Okay, be like that. But at least give me the number of where your mother's going to be in the next couple of days."

I heard rustling, probably Georgie fishing through her bag for something.

"Looking for your PDA, aren't you?" I teased. "Can't find it because your bag is so big."

Big bored sigh. "Honey, don't say that out loud to anyone you know, okay? PDAs are *so* last year . . ."

"Then how do you find the numbers you need?"

"The phone, honey, the phone. If you'd get a decent cell, you could store goo-gobs of numbers right on your little phone."

I *have* a decent cell phone—I've just never bothered to input the numbers.

"How twenty-first century of you. So what's the number?"

Georgie gave it to me, and agreed to come to dinner on Saturday night.

"Low carb, no carb, South Beach, Atkins, what are we on at the moment, so I'll know what I can and cannot serve?"

"You can serve pickled pigs' feet for all I care, you know I eat almost everything. Just be sure to have plenty of wine."

That I could do.

I did manage to reach Georgie's mom a few hours later. She sounded a little out of breath.

"Did I catch you at a bad time, Mrs. M.?"

"No, darling. Howard and I were just coming in from a round of golf." She chortled. "Want to hear our scores?"

"SHOWOFF!" a booming voice shouted. "Shame on you. That's why we end up with white women—you Sapphires keep emasculating the brothers."

Regina Marks burst into laughter.

"Oh, that's the reason this year? So we should always just, what, let you win? Do you hear that, Alex?"

Howard Marks grabbed the phone from his wife.

"Alex, you aren't married yet. Don't listen to my wife, or you won't be. Assuming you *do* want to be. Or maybe you're like my daughter, just happy to *date* for the rest of your life . . ."

"Hey, Mr. M. Georgie told me she would marry whenever she found a man who treated her as well as you treat her mother. So she might be waiting for a while."

"Don't change the subject. Darlin', you got to let a black man feel like he's in charge, *that's* what keeps us happy."

I couldn't resist. "*Are* you in charge, Mr. M.?"

Howard snorted. "Honey, I'm not crazy—or stupid. I said you got to let a brother *think* he's in charge. We'll let you do anything you want as long as we *think* we're running the show . . .

"It's true." Regina Marks grabbed the phone back, as Howard yelled, "Bye, Alex, pay attention, now. Hook that boy Georgie tells me you're running from. Or is it the other way around . . ."

I heard ice cubes rattling in the background. Which meant he was at the wet bar in the den.

"He's not drunk—yet." Regina Marks laughed. "I whipped him so bad, emasculating Sapphire that I am, he will be soon, though. But seriously, Alex, there *is* some truth in what he said. How else to explain our home here on Hilton Head, or the little place near Regent's Park—"

"Or that damn sable-lined raincoat you just *had* to have," Howard hollered. "You live in South Carolina. *When* are you going to need a sable-lined raincoat?"

"We travel a lot," Regina said smoothly. "And *need* was never the point. Need hasn't been the point for decades."

"Uh, speaking of *point*—"

"Poor Alex. We didn't mean to be rude, but some things you just have to address at the moment—*don't you, sweetie?*"

Lots of purposely audible good-natured grumbling in the background.

"But you wanted to ask about the Bournewells, didn't you? So unbelievably sad. It just goes to show you: you never know what's happening inside a person."

"When was the last time you saw them?"

"I saw Lydia Bournewell a few months ago, when the Caritas Center was rededicated after the new building was opened. You know we worked for several years together to raise the money for that facility."

Pediatric AIDS. Got it.

"Did she seem at all stressed to you? How was the marriage?"

"How is *anybody*'s marriage? It seemed fine. I think it *was* fine. Myron adored her. He sent her flowers for no reason, they were always going away to romantic places for the weekend. Well, sometimes it wasn't romantic—sometimes they took their grandchildren. Lydia said it was like having her own kids little again—but with a huge benefit: she could enjoy them, then return them to their parents. I imagine your mother will discover the joy of that soon enough." Regina chortled. I ignored that last part.

"So outwardly, at least, you can't think of any reason he'd have had to take his own life?"

"Not a one. But as I said, who ever knows what's going on in another person's head?"

We pondered that for a moment, then she gave me the numbers of a couple of other mutual friends. And Lydia Bournewell's number.

I was working up my nerve to call her and leave a message when my phone rang.

"Alex Powell," I responded absently.

"This is Lydia Bournewell, Ms. Powell. I understand

you're writing a piece about my late . . . about Myron for the *Standard*."

That was a statement, not a question.

"Yes, ma'am, I am."

"I would think you would need some family details not included in the public record, and I am willing to provide those for you. I'll be busy with arrangements soon, but if you can come now, I can talk with you for about twenty minutes."

I assured her I could, and got directions to her home in the Pacific Palisades. If I hustled this time of day, I could probably get there in a half hour.

Chapter Ten

The Howe home, perched on its Los Feliz hill, was imposing, but the Bournewell home was awe-inspiring. Most people in Los Angeles who cared about such things knew that Lydia Bournewell and her late husband had commissioned their home from one of the country's most revered modern architects—who happened to live just down the street from them. Sterling Good had a whole genre of modern American design named for him. He was in the same league as Phillip Johnson, I. M. Pei, and Frank Gehry. Good's use of glass to maximize light and space was his trademark—his residential designs seemed to float above the ground.

The Bournewell house was no exception. To get to it, I'd had to turn off the Pacific Coast Highway and wend my way up several increasingly quiet streets. Lydia Bournewell's directions landed me on Via Portofino. Halfway between PCH and Sunset, the street was lined with graceful trees twisted by the ocean winds. Huge homes sat comfortably on meticulously landscaped lawns. The Bournewell home looked in real life exactly as it did on the cover of *Architectural Digest:* the series of large white cubes and rectangles seemed windowless from the street. I wondered how much light filtered into the interiors.

I got my answer soon enough. Lydia Bournewell answered the door herself, and smiled wanly at my astonishment: she was dressed in a blazing orange silk caftan that was studded with tiny mirrors and metallic braid. Her short silver hair was tousled in a fashionably boyish cut. She was pale, and her lack of lipstick made her look even more so.

"Miss Powell?"

"Alex, please."

"Then thank you for coming . . . Alex. You'd make a pathetic poker player."

I raised my eyebrows.

"There you go, doing it again. When I opened the door it was obvious you were expecting someone dressed in mourning."

I could feel my face getting red.

"Don't worry about it. I'm not wearing black because Myron hated black clothing. He always said it had become a cliché, a bad habit L.A. and New York started and the rest of the country picked up. And he designed many projects in South America and India, so he loved white, and bright colors. So . . ." She looked down at herself. "So I'm trying to honor that, even now. Although I would probably be excused for wearing black under the circumstances. And of course I'll wear it to the service tomorrow night.

"But here I am, leaving you standing in the doorway. Please come in."

She held the door wide, and I stepped into . . . light. The sun was starting to set on the Pacific, and the foyer and living room were awash in coral light. Light poured from skylights strategically placed in the ceiling. The glass walls in back gave an unimpeded view of the mansion-dotted hillside and the ocean beyond. Pale marble floors reflected back yet more light.

"How beautiful," I murmured.

"Yes." Lydia Bournewell smiled, tearing up just a bit. "My husband did good work. Of course, I'm not the most objective critic, but there are others who've said so, too. We moved here when our children were in junior high school. People thought the design was crazy, but we've always loved it. We've been here for twenty-five years, and I've never tired of the view."

She turned and faced me squarely. "You must come back sometime in the near future, and we'll have lunch out on the terrace. But now I need to tell you some things about Myron. Sit, please."

She gestured to a deep leather sofa with an Islamic prayer rug thrown over the back. "Would you like a cup of tea? I'm going to have one . . ."

"If it's no trouble, I'd love tea. Thank you."

I took out my microrecorder and my notebook.

"Yes, go right ahead. I want this remembered correctly. You see, I know your paper will do a news story about Myron and all that he has accomplished. But I want people to know who he was as a human being."

She didn't say so, but I knew that she'd called the publisher to press for an additional article that would do just that. In fact, three Bournewell articles would appear eventually: straight news; a Style piece that was a kind of retrospective of his work; and my column.

Lydia Bournewell went on to tell me how she and her husband had met (as UCLA undergrads), and what their parents had thought of their respective dates when things had gotten serious. ("Nice Jewish girl, nice Jewish boy—my parents weren't so strict about that, although of course they would have preferred that I have a Jewish husband. But his mother was *delirious*—so many Jewish men were marrying out back then, you know.") And how he had been one of the first fathers allowed in a California delivery room when their oldest child, Celeste, had been born.

"My doctor tried to talk him out of it, told him men fainted even at the birthing movies—and those were sanitized versions of the process. You know what Myron told him?"

I smiled to encourage her.

"He said, 'If she's woman enough to carry and deliver my child, I'm man enough to catch it when it's born.'"

"Wait—they actually let him *help*?"

"Did you ever meet Myron?" she asked with a laugh.

"When I did the magazine piece on him."

"Of course. Then you probably learned that nobody *lets* my husband do anything. Myron does what he wants."

The present tense hung awkwardly in the room.

"Or, I should say, he did what he wanted."

Lydia Bournewell swallowed hard.

"Miss Powell, I don't think my husband killed himself. He had no *reason* to. His business was in great shape. He had just gotten to the point where he could take days off here and there to spend with our grandchildren. He was part of a design consortium that had signed a contract to make well-designed tools and household instruments for a European version of Target. And just this morning, this came . . ."

She reached over to the glass coffee table top and handed me a large, square envelope.

"Please open it."

I pulled out a deep cream parchment card with a blue and gold seal placed prominently at the top.

> *The President and First Lady*
> *Request the Honour of your presence*
> *At the*
> *Investiture of*
> *Myron Aaron Bournewell*
> *The American Academy of Arts & Design*
> *5 May 2004*
> *The White House*
> *Washington, D.C.*

"This is a big deal, isn't it?"

"A very big deal. And I had no idea until this came. Myron's assistant says he was planning to tell me in a week or so, but she wanted it to be as much of a surprise as possible. We were supposed to have a lunch date at the Getty on Friday. I wouldn't be surprised if that's when he was going to break the news . . ."

She looked away, and quickly wiped at what I knew would be tears.

"You should put this in your article."

"I will." I made a mental note to call the White House in the morning and see how big a deal this investiture thing was. Meanwhile, it was clear Lydia Bournewell had run out of steam.

"Mrs. Bournewell, it was so gracious of you to see me, especially now. But I think we should stop. I know you have a lot more to do . . ."

She patted my hand and sighed. "I do, and thank you for understanding—and for setting the limits. I'm probably prattling on because I don't want to go on to the next part, but I'm afraid I have to."

As if on cue, the doorbell rang. Someone called, "I'll get it."

In a moment, two people walked into the room. One was obviously the rabbi for tomorrow's service, and not just *any* rabbi, but the venerated rabbi for the city's Holocaust Museum. Clearly the Bournewells weren't a family to have just any old cleric marry and bury them.

Lydia Bournewell crossed the room to meet him halfway.

"Hyman," she began.

"Darling Lydia," the dapper man crooned, taking both her hands in his and squeezing them tightly. "How horrible for you. For us all. But he was a greatly loved man, and may it comfort you and the children to see how *much* he is loved in the next few days."

Lydia smiled through her tears and turned to me, still holding his hands. "Alex, this is our rabbi and dear family friend, Hyman Silverberg. Hy, this is Alex Powell, from the—"

"Yes, I know Ms. Powell's byline. From the *Standard*. How do you do?"

We shook hands.

"I don't approve of your editorial board's position on Israel and the settlements, but I usually enjoy reading your columns. We don't see eye to eye on foreign policy, but you're right on the social justice issues."

"Um, let's talk about this another time, shall we?"

Saved by a pretty woman about my age in a simple black turtleneck and camel slacks. "Don't mind Uncle Hy—he can't resist fresh meat wherever it appears. *Whatever* the circumstances, I'm Celeste Bournewell."

"Celeste Bournewell *Hirsch*," the rabbi interjected emphatically.

Both Celeste and Lydia laughed with genuine amusement.

"Celeste is married, Alex, to a very nice young man. He's part of a progressive law firm downtown, but you'd never know she's anyone's wife from her name."

Celeste Bournewell Hirsch laughed again, showing teeth that were the result of good genetics and orthodontics, or good cosmetic dentistry. It was hard to tell, but in moneyed Los Angeles, natural teeth were like natural breasts: one encountered them infrequently.

"Alex, another time, I'll bore you with the list of Things That Impossible Celeste Has Done."

"Another time, we can swap lists," I promised. "I know you have more important things to do this evening."

"I wish we didn't, but you're right."

The sun had gone down, and light sensors had somehow signaled the hidden lights in the room; the darker it became outside, the brighter it became inside. Even with the soft, indirect light, it was obvious that the Bournewells had a long night ahead of them. I turned to Lydia Bournewell.

"Thank you again for letting me come."

"Don't be silly—I asked you." I said good-bye to Celeste and the rabbi, and Lydia walked me to the door.

"Remember," she said as she opened it. "A man, not a mausoleum. There will be enough of that from people who think they know him."

I nodded.

"I hope you're available to come to the services on Friday. One P.M. Temple Beth Shalom, in Brentwood."

"I'll be there."

The door closed behind me.

Instead of going down to the ocean highway, I went uphill, to Sunset, turned right, and was happy I wasn't rich enough to be driving in the direction I'd just left. Sunset westbound was bumper to bumper with Jaguars, Lexi, Mercedeses, and luxury SUVs. All with spotless bodies, pristine chrome, and one white person apiece, most of whom were driving and talking on their cell phones. They were making their way toward multimillion-dollar real estate with live-in help, gourmet kitchens filled with the latest appliances they never used, and temperature-correct wine cellars. Some of the stored bottles cost more than they paid their Central American nannies in a week.

The chasm between these people and the ones like the angry brother who urged Simp Hastings to "reconsider your utility to the community, *brother*" would never be joined. Black and Hispanic L.A. doesn't even pop up on their maps, except when it blows up as it did in '65 and '92.

And now one of the few bridges over that chasm was gone, for reasons still undetermined. Myron Bournewell, as rich as he was, had irritated a fair number of the city's establishment by insisting that poor neighborhoods be paid attention to. What if Lydia Bournewell was right? What if her husband had irritated someone to the point that he was "helped" out of his window?

And if he wasn't, how were the Bournewells going to explain why Myron wasn't buried in the family crypt? What if the Jewish faith looked at suicide as an abomination? Maybe that meant Myron Bournewell would have to be buried ignominiously, as close as possible to the cemetery fence.

Or maybe that was the rule for Catholics. Maybe Jews didn't care if you killed yourself, as long as you did good works while you were on earth. I suppose we'd find out soon enough where Myron Bournewell's final resting place would be. And wherever it was, it would only be one of many memorials. The real testimonies to his work and life were scattered all over Los Angeles, from soaring towers to low-slung upscale shopping malls to the gleaming metal building on the downtown hill that had only been completed because Myron Bournewell raised the money to make sure that happened.

It made me wonder. If, as Lydia Bournewell maintained, he hadn't killed himself, who would be interested in removing him from a scene to which he'd contributed so much?

Chapter Eleven

Even going in the opposite direction, traffic was heavy. By the time I'd gone across town, it was dark, I was hungry, and trying to figure out what, if anything, was in my refrigerator. If worse came to worst, Sally would let me rummage around in her kitchen; there was always too much food there, and she was always sending Tupperware over to me that had something good in it.

But when I pulled up to the house, there wasn't a spare parking space in front—there were even strange cars in my driveway. All of Sally's lights were on, and the casement windows in the front were thrown open. I could see light spilling out onto the lawn, gilding the white blossoms on the camellia trees. The guide lights on the front walkway twinkled a cheery welcome. I could hear feminine laughter, and the tinkle of Sally's baby grand. Jazz tunes.

Usually, Sally lets me know she's having a party, because sometimes a guest or two will park in my spare space. And indeed there was a convertible in the space next to mine. And a note on my door.

I got out and squinted at the note under the overhead light—Sally had insisted that the wattage be upped after my attack—and saw immediately it was in Sally's loopy socialite penmanship. (Why did they all write that way, I wonder? You could immediately tell who was inherited-money kind of wealthy by that penmanship. Probably they taught it at Rich Girls' School, along with needlepoint and dressage . . .)

Alex [the note read], impromptu party—you must come. Mostly the usual suspects, and a few out-of-towners who are dying to meet you. Very informal. Just slip in, have some dinner with us, and leave. I know you have to work tomorrow. Josefina made the halibut you love . . . Sally.

Well, that cinched it. Food bribes almost always work on reporters, and this was the food equivalent of a tip from a Saudi oil prince. Josefina made a splendid dish: seared halibut in a sublime sauce of butter, white wine, garlic, chopped tomatoes, green olives, and capers. Even people who didn't like fish liked this dish. She usually served it with a lemon risotto and a big salad, but sometimes, in the winter, she did potatoes gratin. I didn't need to be told twice.

I walked through my darkened house, dumped my reporter's gear, and ran a comb through my hair. A little blush and that was that. (What was the point of working hard through the day if people didn't know that you had? How were they going to be impressed, or feel sorry for you, if you showed up all bright eyed and pink cheeked? And maybe Josefina would feel sorry for me and give me extra dessert to take home. I hoped it was tres leches cake . . .)

The door opened before I could even knock hard.

"Oh, Miss Alex. We think you not coming, but here you are. Come in, come in . . ."

Josefina, in a gray uniform and crisp white apron, stood smiling a genuine welcome. I caught a faint whiff of her scent—something ladylike and powdery she'd been wearing for decades; it came in a bottle shaped like a fan, and she brought it back from Mexico on her annual trips home. She closed the door and smoothed her apron.

"I must back to the kitchen—my niece Flora is here, to help, but not to cook. I don't let. But she's okay with passing the trays . . . I make her take out that thing in her stomach first." She made a face.

Flora Bienevides was a pretty girl who went to USC, and who helped Josefina out from time to time. I suspected Sally was paying her tuition—her family had practically built half the campus—but Sally and Josefina go back to before I was born, and some things you just don't ask. Josefina was actually Flora's great-aunt, and she didn't hesitate to exercise her great-aunt prerogative. Which, in this case, meant ordering Flora to remove "that thing"—her little gold navel ring—before she passed the trays. Not that anyone was going to *see* her navel: Josefina had made sure Flora's white polo shirt covered her belly right up to the waistband of her black jeans.

"You go in. Mrs. Sally is waiting for you . . ."

I walked up the hall and into the living room, and immediately lowered the median age by about forty years.

A room full of handsome, platinum-haired people were laughing, chatting, and drinking. *Lots,* from the look of the drinks cart. Sally was deep in conversation with a good-looking guy whose long legs were encased in gray flannel slacks; the upper half of him was Rich Guy Casual—cashmere turtleneck, navy blazer. Sally looked up and saw me.

"Oh, here's our Alex! Darling, come, let me introduce you. This is Hamilton Smith. Ham is visiting from Florida."

"You should come down and see us in Palm Beach." The tall man winked. "We're always glad to see another pretty girl down there. And"—he gestured with his vodka gimlet—"you'd get a head start on your tan."

"Oh, my God, Ham, don't say that," Sally stage-whispered. "That would indicate she actually can *get* darker, and she thinks she's the African Queen."

Hamilton Smith looked confused.

"Jeez. How many martinis has she had?" I rolled my eyes.

Hamilton Smith laughed. "Not enough. I'm trying to get her to come to Barbados in a few weeks . . ."

"*Go,*" I urged Sally. "Torture someone *else* for a couple of weeks. It'll be fun." Ham Smith looked like he could be a fun guy. "For me, anyway."

We all laughed.

"Well, I might as well introduce you to everyone at once. Stop the piano for just a moment," Sally instructed whoever was behind the raised top of her Steinway. Monk's "Round Midnight" stopped 'round 10:55.

Sally clanged a spoon against an empty martini glass, which obligingly gave a musical little tinkle.

"A lot of you do, but for everyone who doesn't know her, this is my tenant and dear friend I've been telling you about, Alexa Powell. She's the one who caught the killer last year. Everyone's always asking about her . . ."

(Oh, great. Geezer groupies.)

". . . and tonight I'm delighted to say I finally got her to stop working for a moment and come to a real party. A little last-minute party, but that's the only way to get her to come to these things. And of course, you've already met her other half, Paul."

What?

A very familiar face peeped around the top of the grand piano.

"Hey, Einstein." He winked. And began playing again, quite competently. Not well enough that Brad Meldhau would have to watch his back, but well enough that Monk wasn't spinning in his grave.

"Surprise!"

Sally clapped her hands delightedly as everyone laughed and raised their glasses, pleased that they'd put one over on Sally's antisocial tenant. I smiled a "yeah, you got me" smile, and they went back to their chatter.

I slipped through them to the piano. Paul scooted over a

bit and kept playing. Now it had segued into "It Might as Well Be Spring."

"What are you *doing* here?" I hissed. "You're not supposed to come till Thursday night."

"It *is* Thursday night, Einstein. At least by Gregorian calendars. Which calendar are *you* using?"

He looked so good I forgave him for poking fun at me.

"Damn . . . I lost a day somewhere."

"Don't sweat it; I hear you've had your hands full."

"I didn't know you could play the piano."

"Been doing it since I was about eight. Hated it till I was about sixteen."

"Then what happened?"

"What happened was the realization that some girls really *like* a brother who can play. Worked pretty well in high school." His smile made me wonder how far he'd been able to take that skill. Then the grin widened. "Worked *great* in college."

Wasn't working too bad at the moment, either. I watched his strong, copper-colored hands dashing across the keyboard, and imagined them playing other things, later.

"What are you thinking?"

"I was wishing I could play something, too . . ."

His mouth quivered in a badly suppressed smile.

"Oh, no—if you offer to let me 'play the mouth organ' for you later, you can stay here and sleep with Sally." That is such a fifth-grade joke.

He burst out laughing, a full-bodied whoop that turned heads and had the old folks smiling indulgently in our direction.

"Doesn't have to be Sally. You should hear some of the offers I've had so far this evening. All couched in "honey, if I were forty years younger, or you were forty years older . . .""

Fortunately, we were both spared those scary visuals, because Sally chimed her martini glass—empty again—and caroled, "Dinner, everyone!" Someone had filled the CD with bossa nova. Strains of Rosa Passos and Bebel Gilberto followed us into the dining room.

Sally was old-school: she didn't mind buffet service, but insisted that every diner have a seat at the table. None of this big-napkin-in-your-lap kind of stuff. "All that *balancing*—I can't stand it! When you're my age, you should set a proper table for your guests."

So we all sat. To my left was one of Sally's neighbors, a banker. His wife was on the other side. (Sally wasn't into that gender alternation for casual dinners; but if this had been formal, it would definitely have been boy-girl-boy-girl.) Interestingly enough, they were discussing Myron Bournewell's death.

"I was telling Selwyn, I was just shocked. I mean, we'd just seen Myron and Lydia at the Young People's Symphony fund-raiser at the Disney Center last week. There was no indication that anything like this could ever happen." Darcy Shannon shook her head in disbelief.

"Did you know the Bournewells very well?" I asked, tucking into my salad.

"Oh, quite. Sel and Myron played tennis several times a month at Riviera, and Lydia and I sit on the YPS board, and on the Children's Hospital Capital Campaign." That meant the Shannons were loaded. Membership in the Riviera Country Club ran in the five figures each year; half the city's power brokers belonged. The other half were waiting for someone to die, so they could be asked to join. I looked at Selwyn Shannon and wondered just how chatty he could be induced to be . . .

"Any kind of business deals that might have soured, something that might have made him despondent?"

Shannon shook his head.

"Are you kidding? The man was in the real estate business in the middle of one of the biggest housing booms in Los Angeles history. He was making money hand over *fist*. No, if Myron were going to kill himself, he would have done it in the late eighties or early nineties, when the bubble burst with a vengeance."

In the early nineties, Westside mansions that had trebled in value suddenly went down to half that. People who'd bought or built multiple homes to flip a few months later, when prices went up again, found themselves stuck with multiple mortgages and no buyers. Contractors, architects, and realtors sang the blues behind that for a good three years, and then, slowly, the market began to creep up again. Myron Bournewell's company, BroadBranch Development, was large enough to have been shielded from the worst of the housing recession. He built throughout the West, although his major holdings were in California, so several areas shared the burden. He lost a fair amount, but not as much as some of his competitors who had chosen to focus solely on Southern California.

"So if the housing recession in the early nineties didn't do it, if he was happily married . . ."

And here the Shannons exchanged discreet glances.

"Are you telling me they *weren't* happily married?"

Darcy Shannon smiled slightly. "Have you ever been married, Alex?"

"Nope."

"Well, you will be soon, I imagine." She smiled and nodded at Paul who, several seats down from me across the table, was blissfully unaware that a complete stranger was planning his nuptials.

"Here's the thing. We've been married for forty-two years, and it's work. It's not how they make it look on *Will and Grace*."

Okay, Darcy, I get it, you're hip—but *nobody* is happily married on *Will and Grace*. *Father Knows Best* would have been a better example. My face must have given me away again.

"I probably got that wrong; I don't watch much television. But what I'm trying to say is this: every long-term marriage has a rhythm of its own. It's like a bird's flight; sometimes you ride the thermals, sometimes you're beating your wings for all you're worth, trying to stay above the turbulence. Happily ever after means that sometimes there are a few strained interludes. Anyone who tells you they haven't had them, that they've had unmitigated bliss the whole time they've been married—if they've been married for longer than a couple of years—well, they're not telling the whole truth."

I contemplated this as my dinner plate was removed. Flora was circulating with a big silver tray covered in little white dishes. On each dish was a golden square sitting in a glistening puddle. Atop each square was a generous spoonful of whipped cream, and fresh berries were scattered over the whole thing. Tres leches! I silently gave thanks for having a landlady rich enough to afford berries out of season.

Darcy Shannon waved away dessert with a "just coffee, please" to Flora. "I'll take hers," Selwyn Shannon offered. Flora grinned and gave him both plates.

I turned to Darcy Shannon again, who was watching her husband enjoy his dessert without a trace of envy. Guess she's a size 6 for a reason.

"So you're thinking the Bournewells were going through a patch?"

"Not a *patch* exactly. But there'd been a little strain recently. Lydia was actually considering making an appointment with Dr. Palmer—just for a consultation, she said. But for her to even go *that* far . . ."

Preston Palmer was a plastic surgeon to the very rich and very famous. A lot of women in Los Angeles who seemed to be aging with extraordinary grace would thank Palmer for fooling the rest of us into thinking that was so. His trademark was subtlety: "If you want that Michael Jackson look, you'd do better to look elsewhere," he'd been known to tell patients in his office. His faces were fresh, not freakish. His breasts were full, not fanciful. His scars were nonexistent, and he cost a mint. The city's Ladies Who Lunch swore by him.

And Lydia was thinking of submitting herself to his knife? What would drive her to it?

"Another woman? Younger?"

Darcy Shannon regarded me for a moment. "Maybe. Maybe it was just maintenance to insure that wouldn't happen. Preventive measures."

Her look seemed to say, *"live long enough and you'll find out one day."*

People were starting to take their leave. Sally nudged me.

"Go home. Take poor Paul; he must be exhausted. See Josefina on the way out; she has cake for you."

Cake! Oh, boy!

So I thanked my hostess, waved good-bye to Sally's guests—Hamilton Smith was apparently hanging around for after-dinner drinks—and stopped in to thank Josefina and Flora. And to pick up a very generous square of leftover tres leches. It would make an excellent quick breakfast . . .

And then we were gone. Paul was rolling his suitcase over the noisy gravel to the guesthouse's front door, where the porch light winked welcome.

I gave him the key.

"Remember how to use this?"

He shimmied it into the lock, clicked and pushed. The door swung open. I could hear the beep of the alarm system—something else Sally had insisted be installed after last year.

We stepped inside, and I pushed the security code to disarm the alarm. Paul looked around and whistled.

"You mean you forgot I was coming and it's this clean? You must not have been here much the last few weeks . . ."

"Go ahead, laugh. I told you I could turn over a new leaf."

"Can I open a closet to stash my bag, or will I be killed by all the falling stuff?"

"Try it and see."

Clean closet, too.

He walked into the bedroom and peered under the bed.

"What are you looking for *now*?"

"The *real* Alex Powell. Obviously aliens left someone in her place."

"Perhaps an inspection is in order?" I suggested.

Paul looked up from his position on the floor and grinned lasciviously.

"Indeed, I've always had great respect for the scientific method . . ."

"Would the scientific method be compromised if we injected a variable or two?"

Paul got to his feet and dusted off his knees.

"What kind of variable?"

"Vanilla shower gel. Signe gave it to me. It smells good enough to eat."

Paul pulled me toward the bathroom.

"See, that's the beautiful thing about science, Einstein. It allows one to investigate things like that. In this case, I think it's of paramount importance to discover whether that bath goo actually *does* make you smell good enough to eat."

"Well, if it's for science . . ."

"Can't deny the potential benefits to humanity. Wouldn't be right."

So in the interest of science, we made the sacrifice.

Chapter Twelve

Paul took his rental car and left early the next morning for a series of meetings downtown. I went back to bed after he left, and took the papers with me. Because I needed to be across town in a couple of hours, it wouldn't make sense to go into the office first. So instead, I caught up on my reading, and read all the Bournewell tributes that had been published so far. My column would run on Sunday.

Sally and I had decided to go to the Bournewell service together. I'd offered to drive, but she'd waved me off. "Don't be ridiculous. Michael is sending a car for us. Just come up at noon, and we'll go together."

Michael Riley was the oldest son of Sally's retired chauffer, Colin. Sally mostly drove herself around town, when she drove at all. She keeps a little Audi sedan that her daughter left for her when she moved to New York a few years ago. But when parking looks to be a problem or when she doesn't want to drive, she calls Michael and orders a car. Colin Riley drove Sally's husband for years, and after Neville died, he continued to drive her. Michael was one of three Riley boys. All three of them went to college, courtesy of their dad's savvy dabbling in the stock market and Neville Fergueson's will, which, with Sally's blessing, provided funds for each of the boys to go to college. Michael had gone from a B.A. from UCLA to an M.B.A. at Pepperdine, and now ran one of the city's best limousine services, which provided a fleet of town cars for everyone from visiting heads of state to rock royalty.

When I walked into Sally's from the back door, she was pulling on her gloves in the foyer. She was completely in black—high heels, stockings, crepe de chine suit, and a small pillbox hat. The only color came from her red lipstick and her gumball-sized pearls. She looked me over.

"Very nice. Very appropriate." And snapped the clasp to her black clutch. I had on a navy bouclé suit I'd bought at one of those designer thrift stores that send all their sales money to charity. It had belonged to someone grand in earlier life, I'm sure, but now it belonged to me. Both the jacket and skirt had lengths of chain sewn into their linings, "so everything hangs right," the saleslady pointed out. I, too, was wearing pearls, but they were several millimeters smaller than my landlady's. And you could not have found a hat or unlined glacé gloves in my closet if you'd looked all day.

The doorbell rang.

"Right on time, as usual," Sally said as she opened the door.

Devin Riley, Michael's younger brother, grinned and made a little bow.

"Gorgeous, as usual."

"Oh, get on with you." Sally blushed. "Alex is coming, too. You've met Alex?"

"Ah, no. I definitely would have remembered if I had. Nice to meet you, Miss Alex."

"Just Alex."

"Not while I'm on duty." He laughed. "Company rules."

Michael Riley, taught chauffeuring essentials by his father, ran a tight ship. No first names, even for entertainers. No illicit substances in the cars, no matter what the rockers' advance people begged, pleaded, and threatened for—and no stretch limos. "The last word in vulgar," Michael declared.

A navy town car was idling in Sally's drive. Devin helped Sally down the stairs—a service I declined—opened the door, and ushered us into the back seat. Then he climbed into the driver's seat and gently pulled off.

It was a good thing I hadn't driven—we would not have been able to get anywhere near Beth Shalom. After driving across town, we joined a long line of dark cars on San Vincente. All were pulling up and disgorging similarly soberly dressed passengers. Most had on dark suits or dresses and dark glasses, to guard against the midday glare that bounced off the pavement. When our car pulled up, the door opened before Devin could come around and get it.

A face very much like Devin's, but fuller, came into view.

"Ladies. It's a zoo out here. Let me escort you in the side door." Michael Riley's black-clad arm extended toward Sally.

"Michael! You're working today?"

"Had to, Mrs. F.; we needed all hands. Everybody's here."
He reached back and pulled me out, too, and smiled briefly.

When we squeezed past the paparazzi, the local television
news reporters, and the print reporters, I could see exactly
what he meant: everyone who was anyone *was* at this service.
The mayor and his wife were sitting just behind the still-
empty family seats. Our new governor came. Close up, he
was much smaller than his outsized personality as a former
movie star would suggest. His wife, a wraith with knife-sharp
cheekbones and long, reddish hair, was impeccably dressed in
a size 0 couture suit that overwhelmed her teeny figure. The
chief of police and his movie-star wife were here. The chief
was in his dark dress uniform, complete with firearm. While I
gawked, he handed the gun to an aide at his wife's prompting.
She was discreetly looking through her dark glasses to see
who else was there and where they were seated.

Myron's board members from the Community Foundation all sat together, as did a huge contingent of people from
BroadBranch.

Farther back, things began to get more diverse. Members
of many of the community organizations to which Myron
had contributed or for which he'd volunteered were in the
pews—kids from South Central L.A., the city's Mexican and
Salvadoran barrios, and what looked like half the residents
from a low-income housing complex in Koreatown for which
BroadBranch had received several prestigious awards.

"This place must hold two thousand people, but it's
bursting at the seams," Sally whispered.

It was true: a lot of Los Angeles had turned out to say good-bye to Myron Bournewell.

In a waterfall reaction, heads began to turn as the family walked in. Lydia Bournewell walked steadily between her son and Rabbi Silverberg. Celeste Bournewell Hirsch leaned into her husband, Andy. Silver-haired people who looked as if they could be Bournewell siblings walked in their wake.

Behind them, though, came a slender, black man who was visibly upset. From photos taken in happier times, I knew this was Hiram Walker, the architectural protégé with whom My-ron Bournewell had become very friendly in the past few years. He wore a wedding ring, but there was no wife appar-ent. Selwyn and Darcy Shannon were a few steps behind him.

The funeral was uneventful. Lots of remembrances that honored Myron for being a pillar of the community, for hav-ing knitted Los Angeles together when many others couldn't or were not interested in doing so. There was a moving trib-ute from a Vietnamese mother who said Myron's building near MacArthur Park had given her family a new start at a time when they'd thought that America had run out of new starts. Some people wiped away tears.

Hiram Walker read an Old Testament passage, the fa-mous one by Micah. " 'God has told every one of you what is good, and what God requires of you: only to do justice, love goodness, and walk modestly with your God.' " He started to add something at the end, but clearly didn't trust his voice, so he just nodded to Lydia and her family. Lydia smiled at him as if to say *"don't worry about it . . ."*

A choir from a local youth club Myron Bournewell had quietly and consistently supported over the years sang an inspirational song, and a string quartet comprised of the first and second violin, first viola and first cello from the Los Angeles Philharmonic played a beautiful piece by Schumann.

Rabbi Silverberg spoke of Bournewell as a personal friend and member of his congregation. He talked of Bournewell's work "as a builder of homes, and of bridges. Myron understood that community is a fragile thing, built of more than bricks and mortar. And although Los Angeles is a huge place with many different communities—an assortment of sometimes-fractious villages and tribes—Myron traveled comfortably through most of them. His philanthropy drew us closer together as Angelenos, as neighbors, as humans. Many of his mitzvahs were done anonymously, as Maimonides advised us. His gift to us was a stronger, more human Los Angeles. And the greatest gift we could give to him is to continue that work to the best of our ability."

And soon it was over. The family, pale but tearless, filed out. And the schmoozing that always accompanies this kind of gathering began.

Sally rolled her eyes, even as she was nodding politely to illustrious citizens who were waving at her from across the temple. "I've seen enough, haven't you? Let's go speak to Lydia and then we can leave."

We made our way to a comfortable room at the back of the synagogue, where several close friends and family members were gathered around Lydia Bournewell. The police chief nodded at us as he left Lydia's side. I was surprised to discover he wasn't much taller than I was. He looks more imposing in photos. He crossed the room and talked briefly to the Latino councilman who was rumored to be challenging the mayor for his job this fall. No one ever loses the opportunity to cement political alliances in this city, even if there's a casket in the room.

"Oh, Sally, so good of you to come." Lydia smiled, holding out her arms to her old friend.

"Oh, but my dear. I wish the circumstances were different . . ." Sally whispered as they hugged, hard.

Then she turned.

"I understand you've met Alex? We came together."

"Of course. Thank you, Alex, for coming. Celeste will be happy to see there's someone her age here—she swore she'd be the only person besides her brother who didn't need a daily dose of Metamucil."

I barely suppressed a giggle, even though I tried to stop.

Lydia saw me and touched my arm.

"Darling, laugh if you want to. Myron would not want us all to stop living because he died."

She squeezed Sally's hand. "You all are coming to Valentino for lunch?"

Apparently the family had decided to invite people to one of Myron's favorite restaurants instead of dragging everyone over to the house afterward.

"No, darling. We have out-of-town guests coming later this evening. But we thought perhaps we could get you and

Celeste out in a few weeks for a girls' luncheon someplace fun. What do you think?"

Lydia Bournewell smiled. "It's a date. I'm sorry you're having to rush off, but I certainly understand."

"Lunch will be after you come back from Grohman's?" I asked.

Lydia Bournewell looked surprised.

"Why would we be going to the memorial park now?"

"Yes, why *would* we be going there now?" Celeste Bournewell had come up behind me and repeated the question. "Didn't you tell them, Mother?"

Lydia looked a little uncomfortable.

"Tell us what?" Sally asked, curious.

"There's no need to go to the cemetery," Celeste said, linking her arm through her mother's. "We had Daddy cremated late yesterday. His ashes will rest in our library."

"I thought it would be best," Lydia said gently. "I talked with Hy, and he agreed there was no prohibition against it, so we did."

"But Jews don't cremate," I blurted out.

"*These* Jews did," Lydia said firmly. "It was a last-minute decision."

Her tone indicated she didn't want to discuss it further. And who would press, at her husband's funeral?

So we said our good-byes and went out to look for Michael. But while we waited for Devin to come around with the car, a small drama unfolded before us. Hiram Walker, who'd been speaking to a knot of developer types, was approached by the chief of police, who was looking especially grim. Shortly into the conversation, Walker dropped to his knees in agony. "No, *no!*" he sobbed. The chief motioned to two of his deputies to help Hiram Walker up. The chief himself kept his arm around Hiram, and continued to talk to him in low tones as tears streamed down the younger man's face.

I edged a little closer so I could hear.

"We're going to find out who did it. This is unconscionable," the chief was saying.

"How could this happen?" Walker wailed.

"Same way it always does." The chief sighed. "Those dogs should be outlawed, period."

"Alex." Sally was waving in my direction, so I had to leave, unsure of what all the drama was about.

I got filled in soon enough, though.

After Devin handed us into the car he settled into the driver's seat, replaced his sunglasses, and nodded in the direction of the now-larger group around Hiram Walker and the chief of police.

"Poor bastard." Then he looked back at us. "Sorry."

"What happened? Has there been an accident?" Sally inquired.

"Worse. He just found out his wife's been killed."

"Oh, no—that's why she wasn't with him at the funeral." Devin nodded, his mouth set in a thin line.

"Call came in on the scanner. We keep one in each car to know what to avoid—traffic accidents, police chases. Stuff like that. I was listening while I was waiting for you ladies.

Seems Lenora Walker was leaving some community center she's worked at for years when three pit bulls, unleashed, came down the street and jumped her. The people at the community center tried to beat them off, but they wouldn't budge. She died of multiple dog bite wounds. By the time the EMTs came ten minutes after they were called, she was dead."

We sat in silence for a moment.

"Do they know where the dogs came from?"

"That's the strangest part: a witness swears she heard a whistle first, then the dogs appeared. They stopped attacking when they heard a second whistle. Just ran through the yards and vanished into the neighborhood."

Which meant that Lenora Walker's death was not an accident or even a random attack. It meant someone, somewhere, had targeted her.

But why?

Chapter Thirteen

After Devin dropped us off, Sally and I parted for a few moments. "I have to get out of these widow's weeds," Sally complained. She looked over at me. "And I know it just killed you to be in stockings for four hours, Alexa, but you looked very nice."

"Oh, well, then in that case my agony counted for nothing. I'll be back in a bit, after I change clothes and check the answering machine."

Which was, of course, blinking a welcome when I came in.

Message one, the mechanical guy on the voice mail intoned: "Alex, I'm getting on the plane in a minute. I'm figuring you're still up under that man, so I'll see y'all tomorrow night. I'm going to catch up with my homeboy at CBS. He be comin' over on expense, so you know we're going to be right at my hotel, downstairs at Asia de Cuba if you need me. Call my cell when you get this and leave a message, so I'll know when y'all come up for air. Bah." Of course that was Signe, who'd been living among the Yankee heathens for more years than she's spent in the South, where she was raised. Despite that, her *bye* would forever sound like "bah."

Message two:

"Alex, darling, it's your aunt Edith. Just wanted you to know I'm here, and am looking forward to seeing you tomorrow night. I just ran into Melissa Silver—you know, that young curator at the Harlem Museum. She's in for this meeting, too, so we're going to go to this dinner together this evening. I have to ring off and check my wardrobe. Missy is very sharp and you know we New Yorkers have to show the rest of the folks in this cow town how it's done. We're going down the street, to Spago. Talk to you tomorrow, and you can let me know when someone will be over to pick me up. Ciao."

Edith knows Los Angeles hasn't been a cow town for at least fifteen minutes, but it never stops her from sneering at us. New Yorkers can be so provincial, can't they? And of course a diva of Edith's magnitude couldn't suffer the indignity of traveling down Wilshire in a taxi. Oh, no. I made a mental note to see if Georgie was coming that way; maybe she could save me a trip.

Message three:

"Yo, Einstein. I think I've about finished over here in West L.A., so I'm going to slowly make my way back to your place. Call me on my cell if you need anything en route. And let's go out to dinner tonight . . ."

Isn't that sweet? I thought.

"You cooked for me once last year, and if you do it again tomorrow night, that's probably the limit for the rest of the decade. Don't want you to strain anything you might put to better use later this evening. I'm leering, but you can't see it 'cause you're too cheap to spring for a picture phone. See ya."

Sigh. I waited for the next message, which turned out to be the last one.

Message four:

"Powell, call the Style desk and, if there's anything from the Bournewell funeral that you're not using, give them your leftovers. They're doing the *Entertainment Tonight* aspect: what politicians and celebrities came, probably who came with who, and what they wore, for all I know. You know I don't care about any of that stuff. But I *do* expect to see a column for Sunday. We're holding space, so send it tonight if you can, tomorrow morning if you must."

Fine, of course. As usual, no "How are you, Alex? Must've been a hard day, Alex". Nah. Why waste time inquiring after your staff if you don't care, right? No hypocrisy. I liked that in a boss.

I slipped into jeans (hey, *I* wasn't eating with Aunt Edith this evening . . .), a turtleneck, and suede flats, and left a note for Paul telling him where to find me.

Sally was casual, for Sally: tan trousers and a toast cashmere turtleneck. Her version of a track suit. She was waving her remote at the television.

"The news is just coming on . . . good timing. Sit."

I sat on a hassock in her library and looked at the television

tucked into a wooden armoire. The multiculti anchor team—
a brother and a Latina—were giving a preview of the day.

"Good evening. I'm Al Washington . . ."

"And I'm Leticia Legado. Our top story tonight: the city
mourns one of its most prominent citizens in Brentwood . . ."
She looked at Al, who smoothly read the teleprompter.

"And a shocking murder in South L.A. We'll tell you what
connects the two when we come back in a moment."

A laxative commercial was running when Paul appeared,
in a sport jacket, but no tie. Casual Friday for East Coast guys.

"Don't you wonder, when you see these commercials,
why that Raymond guy and Clarence Thomas are never in
the same room?" He hugged Sally and gave me a noogie.

"How'd you get in?" (We'd now moved on to the commercial promise that whatever happens in Las Vegas stays in
Las Vegas. Four women were just *hollering* about something
that the fifth one had done. Apparently it had been a wild bridesmaids' party, and the bride had been the wildest of the bunch.
She was just rolling her eyes in mortification, while the chauf-
feur drove stoically, eyes straight ahead. Looked like something
had happened that *needed* to stay in Las Vegas . . .)

"Josefina let me in as she was leaving. Sally, she says to tell
you the water guy shouldn't come next week—you haven't
used up the four kegs he left the last time."

"Who needs water when you can have a martini?" Sally
snorted. "Speaking of . . ."

"I'm on it. Where's the bar?"

"Push that panel, the one with the Cassatt hung on it."

Paul pushed, and the gilt-framed painting of maternal devotion swung back to reveal a fully stocked bar.

"Don't want the revenuers to see your stash?" Paul teased.

"Well, I don't care, but you know that's exactly why it was built. When Mr. Williams did this house for my husband's parents, Prohibition was still on—a gift from *another* stupid administration." Sally rolled her eyes. The house had been designed by architect Paul Williams, who was known for his elegant neoclassical interpretations for Los Angeles's gilded elite. In one of his signature touches, Mr. Williams had cleverly hidden the bar of Sally's house, built in the 1920s, so that only the residents and their intimates knew where to find the liquor they weren't supposed to keep, back in the day. Paul not-Williams walked to the alcove, pulled out the vodka bottle, and poured a generous amount into a silver shaker. He rinsed two glasses with vermouth, then tossed the extra into the bar's tiny sink. He shook the shaker, poured the vodka into the vermouth-lined glasses, and turned to Sally.

"Lemon, or olives?"

"Olives. A girl has to have her vegetables."

He put three olives into the glass and passed it to Sally. She gestured to me.

"Alex will have a Lillet, Paul. I've given up trying to get her to drink like a grown-up."

"Look, just 'cause y'all like to drink those things that taste like nail polish remover smells, don't be hatin'."

My maligned vermouth was passed to me just as the

interminable string of commercials was finishing up. Apparently women with stress incontinence no longer had to worry about leaking pee-pee when they went ha-ha. I think I'm a few years away from needing that technology, but I'm glad they got it down, nonetheless.

"Our top story today," Al Washington intoned, "is the memorial service for one of the city's most powerful men. Late Wednesday, real estate developer and arts patron Myron Bournewell fell to his death from the twentieth floor of the BroadBranch Development building in West Los Angeles. Bournewell is considered one of the city's Medicis, a pivotal patron of the arts community, and the guiding force behind the city's new and architecturally significant Performing Arts Hall." Leticia picked up from there.

"Today, at Temple Beth Shalom in Brentwood, the city's rich and powerful as well as its regular citizens turned out to say good-bye to Myron Bournewell."

The tape showed plenty of dignitaries going into the temple. We watched the mayor enter with his wife, the chief of police with his wife, the governor's oddly Blutoish profile (huge shoulders and arms, narrow hips that rotated in exact opposition to the shoulders . . . left, right, left . . .), and his elegantly dressed wraith of a wife.

The televised coverage was useful because it showed a number of people I'd missed at the service. For instance, Kwaku Halstead had come with a group of young black children. Cameras showed him gently ushering a sober clutch of middle-school-aged kids up the steps and into the synagogue.

He was dressed in a dark suit, and his dreadlocks were pulled back into a ponytail that was constrained with a black cloth band.

"Interesting," I told Paul and Sally. "See this guy right here? He was at the reading on Monday. He came up to Simp afterward and said something nasty to him."

"Really?" Sally sat up. "What did he say?"

"Actually, thinking on it, it wasn't nasty, but at the time I thought it was kind of threatening. He told Simp he really should reconsider his social utility to the community."

Paul shrugged. "I would guess that a whole lot of people had similar sentiments. In fact, I know they did. Remember Sinclair McCabe's column in the *New York Daily News*? He said almost exactly the same thing. So why did this guy worry you?"

I shrugged, trying to figure out why it had been worrying me since I'd heard the exchange.

"I guess it wasn't *what* he said," I admitted finally. "I mean, I'm not all that far off the same sentiment. It was *how* he said it. He kind of leaned into Simp, got right up into his face: 'you really ought to rethink your utility to the community, *brotha.*' He kind of hissed it, like it was a message meant only for Simp."

"Did Simp know him?"

"Didn't act like it."

"What happened immediately after that?" Sally asked.

"Eso Won ran out of books, Simp offered to use some extras that were in the trunk of his car. He walked out to the parking lot . . . and never came back."

"And where was this Halstead guy?" Paul wondered.

"Well, nobody noticed right away, because of all the confusion. But he just disappeared. And no one can say whether he left before or after Simp was killed. But I don't think he had anything to do with Simp's death."

Sally and Paul looked at me, waiting.

"Come on, the police have probably already been to visit him. I've already made an appointment—to go see him tomorrow morning; allegedly to tour the Center. So if he was responsible, don't you think he'd have been taken in for some serious questioning right now?"

"Maybe." Paul shrugged. "Is Jim coming for dinner tomorrow? We can ask him—"

He cut himself off to turn his attention more fully to the television. They were showing a clip of Hiram Walker being held up by the chief of police. Leticia Legado looked into the camera.

"And in a startling, possibly related development, architect/developer Hiram Walker discovered just after the Bournewell funeral that his wife, Nora, a lawyer known for her work with community nonprofit organizations, had been viciously attacked by three unleashed pit bulls outside the Central Avenue Community Center . . . our Beverly Banfield has the story."

The camera showed a small building with CACC stenciled on an awning above the door. People were milling around nearby, talking in agitated tones. Then it panned to a blood-stained section of sidewalk. Police analysts were packing up their gear, while beat cops and detectives were talking to some area residents. The reporter, a meticulously dressed sister with a throaty voice, came into view.

"Leticia, just before noon today, Lenora Walker had finished her work with the Central Avenue Community Center and was rushing to join her husband, architect Hiram Walker, at the funeral service for their good friend Myron Bournewell in Brentwood. As Mrs. Walker approached her Lexus SUV—you can see it here behind me—witnesses say three huge pit bulls rocketed out of this alley . . ." A slim, brown finger pointed across the street, a few houses up.

"And made straight for Mrs. Walker. Domenica Sifuentes was here in the center, and described how quickly it all happened."

A young Latina holding a toddler tearfully told the rest.

"I was coming in with my baby to sign up for the Mami y Mi class they run here every Friday and we was almost knocked down by these big dogs. I just had time to pick up my Aurelio, but they wasn't interested in us—and those dogs kill little kids all the time. But they went straight for her." She paused to cross herself quickly and clutch the squirming toddler tighter.

"It was terrible, *terrible*. They just jumped [it sounded like *yumped*] on her and started biting. She was screaming. I was screaming. The people from the center, they came out, and when they saw what was happening, they went in and came back out with brooms and a shovel and tried to beat those dogs off. But nothing could stop them.

"And then we noticed she wasn't screaming no more. Just still. And there was blood everywhere."

The reporter looked into the camera. "According to witnesses, Leticia, all three dogs attacked Nora Walker, knocking her down and biting her indiscriminately. As Ms. Sifuentes said earlier, neighbors immediately came to her aid, and tried to beat the dogs off with rakes, brooms from the center, and spare lumber that was piled up at a house being renovated nearby. But Maceo Higgins says it was impossible."

The camera panned to two men, both thin, with scraggly Vandykes. The taller one spoke while the shorter one nodded agreement.

"Me and my brother, we tried beating them dogs to get them off that lady—my brother slapped one upside the head with some lumber. They would *not* let go. It was like they was programmed or something. At first she was screamin, then after a minute, she didn't scream no more. She just lay there. And there was hella blood."

Beverly Banfield again: "Higgins says the dogs stopped as suddenly as they started."

"There was this whistle, and all three of em raised up their heads, looked at each other—and just took off. They ran through yards, and down the alley there, on Ninetieth, and that was it. Couldn't nobody catch em."

Banfield's somber face appeared again. "Walker was pronounced dead on arrival at King Drew Medical Center. Police are not releasing details to the public, but one witness told *Eyewitness News* that the dogs stopped when they heard

a distinct, three-note whistle. Young Diego Alvarez repli-
cated it for us."

A boy about ten years old looked at Banfield. "Am I on
TV, like, *now*?" She nodded.

He straightened. "See, the whistle went like this . . ." He
demonstrated; it sounded familiar, but I couldn't remember why.

"Finding out what that whistle means may be the key to
this horrible death, as authorities continue to search for the
owner of these killer dogs."

Leticia Legado asked, "Beverly, is this the first time something like this has happened in this neighborhood?"

"Leticia, residents on the block where this horrible maul-
ing occurred say there have been frequent complaints about
dangerous dogs running loose. Mrs. Sadie Samuelson says
what happened to Lenora Walker was destined to happen to
some innocent bystander."

A heavy, older black woman was on screen now, shaking
her head in indignation.

"We have told them and *told* them: these children walk
around with these pit bulls and these other big dogs, what do
you call them? Rottweilers, that's it. Those. And it scares us
to *death*. No leashes, just walking with these baggy-pants-
wearing boys. It's outrageous! Two little children almost got
bit to death last year, and now this. The police know it's a
problem, I know they know 'cause we call every time one of
those dogs is loose. So why can't they stop it?"

"Why *can't* they stop it? That's a question that will be
repeated over the next several days, as authorities seek to

discover whose dogs killed Lenora Walker, and why they have been allowed to terrorize this neighborhood. Reporting for *Eyewitness News,* from Central Avenue and Ninety-second Street, I'm Beverly Banfield."

Sally looked at Paul and me. And held up her martini glass.

"I don't know about you all, but I could use another one of these. And maybe some dinner. There are leftovers in the kitchen, but how about I take you out?"

Paul stood up. "Absolutely not."

Sally's face fell. "Oh, of course, I was being presumptuous. You all go ahead, you don't have much time to spend together."

"No, no, I meant let *me* take *you* to dinner," Paul insisted. He turned to me. "You can come, too, Einstein."

Oh, gee, thanks.

Sally was radiant.

"Except," Paul continued, "where can we go that's good that will take us at the last minute on Friday night?"

"I think I know a place. Sally, may I use your phone?"

"Why are you even asking? You know where it is."

So I called G Garvin's. It was one of the city's hottest restaurants, but Georgie and I had been there together a few times, and the way he was grinning at her led me to believe I had a chance of getting squeezed in if I said the magic words *"Georgie told me to try . . . "*

Two minutes later, I was grinning, too.

"He had a cancellation. C'mon, I told him we'd be there in fifteen minutes."

G Garvin's was just what the doctor ordered to counter our macabre cocktail hour. The food was great—Sally and I split the rack of lamb, Paul had the roast chicken. The handsome crowd was lively. And as Sally noted, even if the food had been crappy (my word, not hers), it was always fun to look at the chef, who came out to check on all his diners.

"Did you notice, Alexa, he looks just like LL Cool J?" Sally asked, as we rode home. Paul almost ran through a stoplight.

"How much wine did you have with dinner, anyway? And how on earth do you know who LL Cool J *is*, let alone what he looks like?"

"Well"—Sally blushed—"after I watched Katie Couric drool all over him on *The Today Show* one morning, I went out and rented *Deliver Us from Eva* that afternoon. He is the *cutest* thing. Those dimples—to die for!"

Paul was speechless.

I turned to Sally, who was riding in back. "Wonder if he's as ripped under those chef's whites as LL Cool J is?"

We pondered in silence for a moment. LL's six-pack was legendary. I knew 'cause he liked to flash his abs in the action movies he was starting to favor.

"Quite possibly. Don't *you* think G Garvin looks like LL Cool J's brother?" Sally asked me.

"Fa shizzle," I agreed.

"I think you're *both* a little ripped—and *not* like LL Cool J," Paul muttered, as he drove down Third Street, toward home.

Chapter Fourteen

Early Saturday morning, Kwaku Halstead greeted me at the door of RVC. I knew from articles the library had dug up for me that RVC was the acronym for Rise, Vision Coming. It was a center that mentored at-risk black and Latino boys. Especially black ones. Halstead was very specific about where his center of interest lay.

"The young brothers, they're always getting left out, left back. I don't mind taking in the Hispanic brothers, too, as long as they're okay with hanging with the brothers. We got some out there that think they're better than us 'cause they don't have nappy hair . . ."

"Some are just afraid," I offered. "They've been victimized in neighborhoods in transition, and they think all black people feel the way the folks who attacked them do."

Halstead looked at me for a moment over his granny glasses, and conceded the point.

"True, that. I'm not interested in anyone getting victimized, which is why we're doing this."

RVC was on a shady street just off Central Avenue, in the early Nineties not far from where Nora Walker was killed. The neighborhood was a mixture of busy main streets lined with light industry, junkyards, and mom and pop stores. The side streets were lined with graceful old trees. The bungalows had tended grass and often side gardens that were filled with trellises for the tomato vines and snap beans that would come later, in warmer weather, and borders of cabbage and kale. Most every house was rimmed with a strong iron fence, and all of the windows—at least on the first floors and often on the second—were barred.

Kwaku Halstead's kids came from this neighborhood, and the housing projects a five-minute drive away. They'd gone to overcrowded classrooms in L.A.'s most neglected public schools. Many had dropped out by eighth grade or age sixteen—whichever came first—to look for jobs.

"Much good that did them." Halstead snorted. "See any black people, any at all, in entry-level jobs in this city?" He went on to answer his own question.

"The Latinos have the hotels and restaurants sewed up, and they only hire their own. Used to be, it was *brothers* serving at all those fancy downtown hotels. No more. The white folks think the Latinos are more pliable. But they'll find out. See, they're taking their cues from what we did in the sixties. *We* struck the template for them."

"What about over on the Westside?" I asked.

"Are you kidding? Ain't nobody over there going to hire a young brother when they can get a white boy who's waitering between acting gigs. They have to pay them more, but they don't have those pesky accents. And they look like the clients. No," he concluded sadly. "There's no place for a young, marginally educated brother in today's Los Angeles. That's why there's so many of them out here selling dope."

It was a bleak picture, to be sure.

"But there are people who want to help," I pointed out. "Like Nora Walker."

He shuddered, probably remembering Nora's grisly end.

"That was some shit, wasn't it? Nora was good people. She worked with us here and at the center for years. She wasn't one of those bourgie Negroes."

"I know you don't have much patience for bourgeois black folk in general, and she was certainly that. So why did Nora get the exemption?"

"It's not the *bourgie* part I despise—I don't begrudge anyone the right to live well. Hell, I'd like to do that myself someday. It's the *distance* from poor black people. The derision I see aimed at them all the time: 'That's so ghetto.' 'Don't let those Shaniquas into this place'. 'That welfare mentality.' I'm sure you've heard variations of it."

"I have," I admitted, running my hand over an African carving on his desk. "And I don't like it, either. But it seems to strike a particular nerve with you. And I'm wondering why."

Silence. I knew why.

142

"That was you at Eso Won, wasn't it? You were the brother who came up to Simp and hollered that he should consider his social utility to the community—"

"Yeah, that was me," he admitted. "I didn't holler, though. And I didn't kill him, either. But I straight-up hate the snotty bullshit he's selling, and that so many people—including black ones—are buying."

"There is something else, though, isn't there? A missing piece to the backstory. I can feel it."

He paused for a moment, as if trying to decide whether to say anything to me.

"Oh, hell. It's going to come out at some point anyway. What I tell you, I don't expect to go farther than this room."

"Like the Las Vegas commercials?"

"*Exactly* like the Las Vegas commercials."

"As long as it's not illegal, fine."

"It's not illegal, but it *is* complicated."

I waited. Sometimes people tell you things if you let the silence stretch on long enough. And he did.

"My name is Wilfred Halstead *Howe*. Sheila Howe is my first cousin. Our fathers were brothers."

Whoa.

Satisfied that my jaw had dropped as far as it was going to, Halstead continued.

"Ever hear of the Nu Afrika Movement? It was before your time. Pretty much before my time, too."

It *was* before my time by a few years, but certainly I'd heard of it. Nu Afrika was part of what some people referred to as

"That Sixties Craziness." A former bodybuilder with strong political convictions had changed his name from Samuel Johnson to Samu el-Simba Johnson—his middle name came from the Swahili word for *lion*. His trademark was a huge lion's mane of an Afro. Samu el-Simba (somewhere the "Johnson" got dropped) mobilized large numbers of black students into Simba chapters throughout the state on all the University of California campuses, and their Cal State counterparts.

A few years after Nu Afrika started, it clashed head-on with a chapter of the Black Panther party.

Tensions over who owned L.A.'s black political hearts and minds had been rising for about a year. Finally, there was a fierce shootout between the two on UCLA's campus, in 1969, and when the smoke cleared, five people lay dead. Three of them were Panthers. And one of them was . . .

"Will Howe was your dad?"

"He died before I was born," Kwaku said briskly. "Never knew him. Only through photos. Moms and me, we stayed in L.A. after he was killed. She worked with the Party here. Sometimes other people from The Party would drop by and visit with my moms. I remember they were always fierce-looking brothers, black leather, berets, shades—the whole nine. Clean as a hound's tooth. They looked fierce, but they were always kind to me and Moms. I looked up to them, 'cause they were doing something for the community. When I was old enough, she would have some of my pop's friends talk to me about him, try to fill me in. Give me some male role models." He paused and smiled tightly. "Just like the social workers said she should—but she didn't need them to tell her that. She did all right on her own."

"If your dad and Sheila's dad were brothers, didn't you spend lots of time with him?"

Halstead shook his head.

"Oh, no, Miss Thing. That wasn't ever going to happen. My moms told me the story." And it was something out of a novel:

"She came from Chicago," Kwaku said, stretching out his legs and settling in to tell the tale. "Her family was blue-collar: her dad worked for one of the big meat packing companies. There aren't any left today, but there were a whole grip of 'em almost until the early sixties. Then there were just a couple. It wasn't fancy work, but it was steady work. So her pops worked for Hormel, and her mom worked in the cafeteria at Du Sable High. She was really beautiful, my moms."

"What was her name?" I figured asking might keep him going. He stopped, looked at me, and squirmed a little. Obviously something made him uncomfortable.

"Velvet. Velvet Halstead."

"That's pretty. Like *National Velvet*? Was she named after Elizabeth Taylor's character in the movie?"

He smiled slightly. "Depends on who you talk to. My *father's* mother says that's where it came from, that forties movie. But my *mother's* mother used to tell people 'when I saw that baby in the hospital, I said to my husband, she's beautiful, got skin just like black velvet! And that's what they named her.'"

"So was it a tension between mothers-in-law thing that made the two stories so different?"

He laughed, showing nice teeth, and twirled a lock.

"Uh-uh. It was a 'who you callin' BLACK?' thing. My grandma's back was *totally* up when Grams made that 'black velvet' statement. Even though they were all pretty much my color"—he lifted his deep brown arm—"calling anybody black in the nineteen-fifties was fightin' words, unless you were racially progressive." He chuckled. "Grams was real progressive. Grandma was not. So they agreed to disagree, and they named Moms Velvet."

Something still didn't make sense, though, and I realized it was the last name.

"But your dad is Howe and your last name is Halstead . . ."

"I'm getting to that. Moms and Pops met on the campus of UCLA. She'd gone to the Lab School in Chicago, and had a scholarship to one of those fancy women's schools back East. I forget the name. They're all alike to me." (I didn't correct him.) "But she didn't want to go. She went to the University of Chicago for two years, but she *hated* it. Back then, there were very few black folks on campus—even fewer than there are now—and she just found it elitist and repressive. Her parents had a fit, but she transferred to one of the California schools. She'd never been to L.A., but she'd seen it in movies and thought she'd like it. So she transferred to UCLA for her junior year."

"That's where she met your dad?"

"Yup. He was a year ahead of her. He'd been a big man on campus before he got so political. Debate team star. Cross-country. Tennis. Majored in philosophy. He left the summer between sophomore and junior years and worked for some community-organizing outfit not too far from here, came back all radicalized. Wasn't interested in debating about anything other than the oppression of the masses and class stratification. All his political science classes turned into guerrilla theater—almost gave his professors nervous breakdowns."

"Why?"

"'Cause he *argued* so damn much. About everything. And he was *good*. And they were freaked that their prize Negro, the one they'd had such hope for, had turned left on them, literally."

I can imagine. It's always so hard on optimistic white people when the next Ralph Bunche or the next Marian Anderson doesn't go along with the program . . .

"So he was a senior when he met your mother?"

"Yup. Apparently, he'd blown off the light-skin long-hair he'd been dating and was almost engaged to for a year. Symbol of the oppressor, blah, blah, blah. She was crushed. Her family was furious—and so was his. They'd expected him to settle down with the appropriate kind of girl."

Not atypical of the times.

"How did they know your mother wasn't?"

"For one thing, she was black. I mean, identifiably, deep dark bittersweet chocolate colored."

Oh, nooooo! I held my hands to my face, like the little character in Edvard Munch's *The Scream.*

He yelped with laughter, pleased that I got it, and wasn't offended on behalf of yellow people everywhere.

"You got that right! And for another, her people weren't anything in particular. A meatpacker? A cafeteria worker? *Please.*"

"Not good enough?"

"Let's just say this was before the days when *any* damn body ended up in the *New York Times* wedding pages. Which are still the only wedding pages that count. In newspapers, anyway." He smiled wryly at my amazement. "Oh, yeah. I know what the pecking order is on the society pages, and which society pages count. I'm not into all that, but I know what time it is. I also know the *Times* wedding pages count less now, since they've gotten all democratic and whatnot. So to get a colored girl onto the wedding page in the sixties was a *big* damn deal. And if Will Howe had stayed on track, that woulda happened, and both families would have been in heaven."

"But falling in love with your mother kind of blew that out of the water?"

"Like a U-2 to a troop transport—*ka-boom.*"

"What attracted them to each other?"

"She was fine—stayed fine till she died about five years ago, from breast cancer. Moms told me when my pops first met her, he told her he liked how she carried herself. I have some of their old letters to each other, and he just goes off on how she's so different from the usual college coed. 'You can think for yourself, you care about larger society, you see past the wedge of privilege the man is trying to use to separate black people by class . . . ' "

I smiled, imagining how attractive a thinking, articulate, politically astute courtier must have been to this strong-headed young woman.

"Guess that's heady stuff when you're in college."

"Oh, he told her other stuff, too, but I ain't going there. Anyway, They became inseparable. And first semester of senior year, after they'd both turned twenty-one, they borrowed a car, drove to Vegas, and came back Mr. and Mrs Wilfred Howe."

"How did the families react?"

"The same way, but for different reasons. The Halsteads just wanted to make sure Velvet stayed in school, and didn't get pregnant before graduating. She'd married sooner than they would have liked, but they could live with it if Pops was good to her and she did those two things—got the paper before getting pregnant."

"But the Howes had a different reaction?"

He shrugged.

"You could say that. After they finished pulling out their hair, they disowned him. Stopped paying his tuition for his last year. He went to work in a bookstore so they could make ends meet. She had a job in the afternoons pulling espresso. They were doing a'right."

"They were happy?"

"Quite. He'd just been admitted to the law school—full freight—and she'd done so well, she was going to graduate a semester ahead of time. Then later that spring, everything happened."

"By 'everything,' you mean the Simba-Panther shootout."

"Yep. My dad died on the steps of Royce Hall. By the time my mother got there, he'd already been taken to UCLA Medical Center. DOA. Gunshot wound to the chest."

Poor Velvet. Married and widowed in the same year. "She must have been beside herself."

"She was. She said she would have thought about taking a gun and going to find Sammy's thug ass, or maybe even just put it to her own temple. But she'd just come from Student Health. When they found her, she was trying to locate my pops to tell him some news. She was pregnant. With me."

Ah, so Velvet Howe was keeping one of her two promises to her parents, but had slipped with the other one . . .

"She didn't return to Chicago?"

He shook his head firmly. "Nope. She stayed here in L.A., to be near her husband's body. He's buried in Inglewood Memorial Park, and she said she just couldn't make herself leave."

"How did she survive?"

He looked at me levelly. "Without Howe help, that's how. They just turned their backs on her. Figured if she hadn't been in the picture, he never would have gotten killed. Which is stupid, because he'd been political before they met. But they needed somebody to blame, so Velvet Halstead Howe was it."

"How did she feel about that?"

"Hell, it hurt her, but she was a proud lady. Her people weren't in much position to help unless she returned to Chicago."

"Which she wouldn't do, because it would mean leaving your father?"

"Exactly. So she worked as a Head Start assistant in Watts. Because she left school after Pops was killed, she didn't have a degree. So she couldn't teach in the public school system. That required paper. But Head Start didn't mind. Didn't pay much, but she was happy, and it meant I got to go to pre-school for free."

Free preschool was no little deal back then, before it was offered to everyone.

"Where were you all living?"

"Right where the program was. We got free housing as part of the deal. So I grew up in the Howe Homes. Yeah, Ms. Powell. The great-grandson of Elijah Howe, the son of Wil-fred Howe, and the nephew of Horace Mann Howe is a project kid."

Not only that, the projects he grew up in were named for the family that had spurned him and his mother. *Wow.* We were getting into Terry McMillan territory.

"Your mother didn't use her married last name, did she?"

"Never did. She figured if they were so ashamed of who we were, she was ashamed of them for being ashamed. She went by Velvet Halstead. And that's what I went by, Halstead, even though my birth certificate was never changed from Howe."

"Ah, so *that's* why you were so sharp with Simp Hastings at the book signing—the class stratification thing."

He popped off his stool and began pacing, running his hand along the top of the desk.

"Fuck, yeah. I spend my professional life trying to erase the hurts that big-timey Negroes have inflicted on the poorest of us, and here comes this fool ripping the scab off all over again."

" 'Ripping the scab off.' That's what Mrs. Elton said the night Simp read from his book."

"So what? It's a common enough expression."

The look on my face must have indicated I didn't think so.

"Look, I didn't kill Simp Hastings. He's not worth spending time in Q behind. I don't know anyone else who thinks so, either. But I'll have to tell you something, my sister: I ain't crying that he's gone."

"Any thoughts as to who got him gone?"

Kwaku Halstead pushed his glasses up on his nose and wrinkled his brow in thought.

"A lot of people might have wanted to; he was not popular outside his own circle. He was a snotty, prissy, 'I got it and you don't' kind of guy. And that book he was working on about pretender types? Oh, yeah, Miss Alex, I know all about his little book. Well, it's books like *that* that get a brother killed. People don't like it when you mess in their business, much less when you *publicize* their business. He was doing both. So it was just a matter of time . . ."

"Interesting, isn't it, that just a few days after, there's a suicide, and a few days after that, an alleged accident involving vicious dogs."

He stopped and straightened up. "What are you trying to say? They all died for different reasons. That brother got offed. The rich white boy jumped from his window. And Nora . . . I'm thinking that was a gang mistake."

"*A gang mistake?*"

"It sounds like they were targeting someone, but maybe not her, I don't know."

"That doesn't make sense—three big dogs appear out of nowhere, jump on this one-hundred-pound woman, maul her to death, and stop as soon as they hear that three-note whistle? That's no accident."

He pondered that for a moment. Then: "You said a whistle? What kind of whistle?"

"Don't you watch the news? It was all over television."

"I don't watch TV a whole lot: the programming is mostly bullshit. I was in San Pedro at a public health conference and then I went straight to the Bournewell Service. So I didn't hear about Nora's death till late that night. What kind of whistle was it?"

"Like this . . ."

I blew the notes.

Kwaku Halstead was brown, but he paled considerably when he heard my imitation of the whistle the lady on the news had used.

"That's a standard street signal for training aggressive

dogs. I hear the young brothers around here using it sometimes."

"When they're training their dogs?"

"Yeah. They're training them to fight. To the death. For *money*. If someone used that whistle, Nora Walker's death wasn't an accident. No way."

Chapter Fifteen

M y meeting with Kwaku Halstead was so interesting, I'd totally forgotten I was having people—how many people was it?—to dinner this evening. I'd done some quick thinking and figured out I'd do paella. That's good food for a crowd.

Paul had been in meetings—again—but had promised to do whatever I needed for the evening, so I left a message on his cell about what I'd decided to cook, and asked for wine. That would be one less thing I'd have to deal with.

By four o clock, I'd been to the fish market, the grocery store, the florist, and the bakery. I had three hours before everyone got there, so I chopped all the vegetables, rinsed the lettuce and packed it, dried, in paper towels in the fridge. The chicken had been rinsed and patted dry, and the sausages (turkey sausages, for the pork-averse), were waiting on a plate.

I spent an hour arranging flowers and setting the table, and putting little guest hand towels and scented candles in the bathroom, so Georgie wouldn't crack on me. Paul came in at five with a case of wine, and stuck the white in the fridge to cool. While he laid wood in the fireplace, I hauled the huge paella pan out of the closet.

Yeah, the closet. When you live by yourself, why do you need a pan that serves a dozen people more than once a year? In the interim, it's perfect for holding the big bag that stores all my Rollerblading safety gear. Something else, Georgie would point out, that gets used about once a year.

By six-thirty, the whites had cooled, the reds had breathed. Paul, showered and freshly shaved, was looking through my CD collection and muttering to himself. I didn't ask him to speak up, because I didn't want to know his assessment of my collection. It was show-tune-heavy, and I was pretty sure the likes of *Gigi, Guys and Dolls,* and *Hair* were not going to be floating through the living room this evening. Everything was done. I was getting out of the shower when the first guests arrived. I knew it would be somebody who wasn't black, because my peeps know that when they're invited for dinner at seven, I don't expect them till, say, seven-thirty. After that, they're on CPT. Using that Socratic logic, I had deduced that the folks at the door were not Colored People. (Hey, they don't call me Einstein for nothing.)

I could tell from the voice it was Sally. She had called earlier to ask if it was okay to bring a friend, and I'd said of course. The friend turned out to be her dinner guest of a few nights ago, Hamilton Smith. Hmmm . . . was this their first date? I'd have to do some nosing around.

By the time I walked into the living room, Paul and Smith were comparing notes on Brazil—sparked, I suppose, by the music. Sinatra doing Joabim.

About fifteen minutes later, as the first martinis were almost gone, all the air got sucked out of the room: Signe arrived with Jackson Fisher, her Memphis homeboy from yesterday evening. He's a correspondent for CBS who'd gone to Wesleyan with Signe's phantom steady, Otha Barnes. CBS had just transferred him from Mexico City to Los Angeles. "I wanted him to meet some real people in L.A." And right behind her came Aunt Edith—courtesy of Georgie and Jim Marron. They'd come together and stopped in Beverly Hills to pick Edith up. She, too, had called to see if she could bring a guest—a very distinguished-looking gentleman with flowing white hair and a bottle wrapped in silver paper.

"For the gracious lady who was so kind to invite a stranger to dinner this evening with Mrs. Edith," he said, sounding very much like Fernando Lamas. "I am, madame, Diego Arturo Sánchez y Coronado." He bowed deeply and kissed the air over the back of my hand. Wow.

"Diego is on the Prado's board, and he's the head of the fine arts department at the University of Barcelona," Edith explained, as Paul took her coat. "He's very interested in launching an exhibition of African-American art at the Prado in two years, so we've been putting our heads together. He's been on the road for weeks, so I thought it would be nice to offer him a home-cooked meal." She turned to me as if a thought struck her. "Or did you call the caterer?"

"No, I actually did cook." I laughed. "But poor Mr. Sánchez y Coronado—"

He held up his hands. "Please, Diego is quite enough."

"All right, then, Diego, you may wish I had called the caterer. It's certainly not what you'd be used to at home."

"I shall partake happily of the meal, because it has been prepared with love."

Whew. This guy was *good*.

And it all worked out. After the olives and cheeses had disappeared, I had Paul place the huge pan on the pass-through, and told my guests to grab a plate from the stack next to it and help themselves.

I must say, it looked great. The rice had absorbed its saffron-infused broth and glowed richly yellow. Pink shrimp, chunks of sausage, and browned chicken sent up heavenly aromas, and the color from roasted red peppers and fresh green peas set everything off just right.

Signe was contentedly filling her plate. "Girl, you have *burned* tonight! Jackson, you'd better not be shy, 'cause Lord knows when sistawoman is gonna feel the urge again." Jackson, right behind her, didn't need telling twice. He heaped his plate, until Signe admonished him to leave room for the salad. "'Cause apparently there ain't gonna be no *proper* salad plates on the table."

"I said it was going to be *casual*—that means no salad plates."

"Uh-huh." Signe just rolled her eyes and waited as Jackson pulled out her chair.

Diego had no complaints. In fact, he looked like he'd hit the lottery.

"Paella! *Dios mio,* this looks spectacular!" It sounded like "spack-TACK-u-lar." He passed a plate to Edith, who began spooning up, before taking one himself.

"Well, it's a *version* of paella—an *American* version," I cautioned. He made a shushing noise, and filled his own plate.

I'd squeezed us all in at my dining room table. When I first saw it, years ago, I thought, *This is huge—I'll never need all this space.* But over the years, it had shrunk—or I'd gotten used to it. We were all quite cozily tucked in, and the tight quarters meant there was actually one conversation going on. (*"Perfecto!"* breathed my Spanish guest. Yay, me.) And as the glasses were refilled, and the group began on seconds, the talk drifted to the recent deaths.

"Those dogs should be illegal. Any citizen should be allowed to shoot them on sight, no questions asked, leash or no leash," declared Jim Marron, taking a sip of red wine.

"No trial, no quarantine, nothing?" I teased.

"Nope. They're ticking time bombs. You don't want to know how many times I've taken statements in the ER from some idiot parent who just doesn't understand why the dog didn't get that he's only 'sposed to bite people they *don't* know, not, like, Junior, who's learning to walk." He shook his head in disgust. "Dogs like that see little kids as appetizers. But there's no teaching some people."

Diego Arturo Sánchez y Coronado looked puzzled.

"Very vicious dogs got loose yesterday, killed a lady here in L.A.," Marron explained.

"*Un accidente? Qué horrible!*" Diego whispered, crossing himself with the hand that wasn't holding his wine glass.

"Maybe not an *accidente*," I said, "and that's the problem."

"Who would want to impose such a dreadful death on a lady?" Diego wondered, munching a slice of bread.

"Yeah, who? Inquiring minds, so on, so forth," Signe prompted.

I looked at Marron. "All yours. I just nose around as an amateur," I pointed out.

He sighed.

"I don't want to go into details—we *are* at dinner, after all—but yes, Nora Walker was mauled to death by three pit bulls that nobody can find. And there's some thought that it could have been an odd sort of gang hit."

"Crips or Bloods?" Edith asked brightly. Paul choked slightly.

"I'm okay," he gasped. Signe thumped him on the back.

"Can't say, for definite, but where it happened is the known territory of a certain set, so that's a definite possibility."

"Why *can't* they find the dogs?" Hamilton Smith asked, refilling Edith's and Sally's glasses with white wine. "Three marauding pit bulls can't just disappear into thin air."

He looked at Jim as if to say *why aren't the police doing their job?*

And apparently Marron thought Smith's tone was critical, because his response was a little defensive.

"Seems they were responding to a signal, and the signaler was out of sight. It's being looked into."

"What was the signal?" Smith persisted.

"A whistle," Sally told him. "We heard it on the news."

"What did it sound like?" Diego wondered.

"Like this . . ." And Georgie demonstrated. "It actually sounds like something I've heard before."

"Me, too," Jackson said. "It's been bugging me since I heard it on the news, but I can't for the life of me figure out where it's from."

"You said three deaths?" Diego prompted. "This is but one."

"Myron Bournewell—you remember the real estate developer I mentioned?" Edith turned to him. "He jumped to his death on Wednesday. Alex went to his funeral yesterday."

"We don't know he jumped," Marron cautioned. "We know he fell from the terrace of his penthouse office on the Westside."

Paul looked up from his third—yes, third—plate. (Where does he put it?)

"There's a question that it could have been something else?"

"There's always a question, unless there's a note. And even when there's a note, there's *still* a question," Marron responded, finishing off the last of the salad. I made a mental note to do the romaine and orange sections with jicama again.

"You mean he could have been pushed," I pointed out, as I started to clear the table.

"I mean we're still looking into it, and there's not much more I can say about that at the moment."

"Man, I hate it when you turn all cop on me," I said, pouting. Sally made as if to assist with the clearing.

"Sit," I instructed Sally. "Georgie, you never do an honest day's work—you can help."

"All right," she grumbled, "but don't tell anyone outside this room I did it. I have a reputation to maintain, you know."

While we cleared, Marron brought the table up on the third death, Simp Hastings.

"We need to finish and get back in there," Georgie whispered, as I shoved leftovers down the disposal. " 'Cause you know your aunt knows everything we don't."

"True, that," I conceded, as I put decaf in the coffeemaker. George heated the milk in the microwave, and poured cream in a small pitcher, for purists.

When we trucked out the plates and the platter with the tres leches cake, Marron was just winding up what he knew (or what he would tell) about the Hastings murder.

"So we know where and we know how, but we still don't know why. And it's gonna be hard. A lot of people didn't like the guy."

"Ain't that the truth," Edith agreed, and motioned for me to give her the cake cutter.

"You know, when he started writing that book, he called a number of friends and they were all asking each other, 'who *is* this kid, anyway?' They'd never heard of him. And they were hardly going to speak to him about something they only discussed with their closest friends."

"What book?" Hamilton Smith wondered. "And why should it cause such a fuss?"

I was so afraid Aunt Edith was going to say something like *"you white people wouldn't understand,"* but to my relief, she didn't. Instead, she filled him in.

"Hastings was writing a book about the black upper class," she explained. Hamilton Smith nodded for her to go on, but he didn't look amazed. (If he had, she would have declared him hopeless and stopped right there.)

"A lot of people were very upset with him for writing it. Class remains a sore point within the black community, so for someone to talk about class stratification so openly—who is from a grand family, who is not and so forth—is a very touchy thing."

"It's like rich people talking about money," Hamilton Smith mused. "It's one thing to do it on your boat with your friends, another to do it in mixed company. *Economically* mixed company."

"Exactly," Edith said approvingly. "Although you may be interested to know that there is a stratum of black society that doesn't like to talk about it at *all,* so this book really stirred the pot."

"These would be your black cliff dwellers, the old families," Smith stated. "That doesn't make them any different from the white ones."

"But," said Sally, passing the cake as it was cut, "it's probably a novelty for a number of whites. The notion of black people who live in closed circles."

"Closed to whites, too, generally—present company excepted," Edith reminded Sally.

"Of course. So all this hoo-rah must be mighty intriguing to what Alex calls the WP."

Now it was my turn to choke, and Georgie absently hit me on the back.

"Of course I know that lingo, Alexa. I may be old, but my ears work just fine. And it's a perfectly serviceable nickname. Unless one considers calling white people white an insult. Always best to call a spade a spade."

I thought wine was going to come shooting out of Hamilton Smith's nose.

Jackson yelped with laughter, and Sally turned crimson. "Oh, my Lord, I didn't mean—"

"I don't care if you did—that was priceless," Jackson panted, as he wiped his eyes. The rest of us were grinning, too. Except for Diego Sánchez, who looked completely lost.

"In America," I told him, "*spade* is a derogatory term for *los negros*. Kind of like *mayate*."

"Ah." The museum man nodded. "*Now* I understand."

"So a brother wrote this book and riled up the hincty"— he turned to Diego—"*fancy* Negroes, and you think *that's* why he was killed?" Jackson asked. "By the way, Alex, this cake is slammin'. Totally."

I took a little bite of mine. Damn if the boy wasn't right.

"Thanks. And we don't know why he was killed. Or I don't. The assumption is that's the reason. Although I hear he was working on another book about the crème de la crème that will be even more incendiary."

Marron looked at me quizzically. "I thought the crème de la crème wouldn't *talk* to him."

"The rumor is that's why he's doing the second book. It's kinda payback to certain people for not having cooperated the first time around," Georgie explained. "But also, he's been able to research a bit more, and now he doesn't need these people to cooperate—he'll just write around them."

"If I may—and Jackson is correct, my dear Alex, this tres leches is *muy delicioso*—this is not so new, this old families versus everyone else. In Spain, it is the same thing: the truly noble speak of some things only among themselves. If someone who is allowed into the inner circle speaks, then he is allowed in no more. He is an outsider forever after. So why was this Mr. Hastings not cast out?"

Everyone looked to Edith for an explanation. Which she was only too happy to give.

"That's the point—he was never *in*. He was on the shakiest margins of everything, and always made his family sound more grand than it really was. The people who knew better just stayed silent. And the people who wanted to be thought of as grand took advantage of that, and spoke."

"So one of the Big Negroes could have killed him," Signe said.

"Or one of the little ones who'd been masquerading as a Big Negro."

"Well, being unmasked as being less—what was that word?" Marron turned to Jackson again.

"Hincty."

"Yeah, less hincty than they'd been supposed to be actually provides a pretty credible motive."

"But someone who was publicly prominent would have a harder time doing it, wouldn't they?" Paul asked. "I mean, if you're a Really Big Negro, people notice when you come and go. And if you mess up and kill somebody, you'd have more to lose than you did to gain by killing that person. Business interests, your place in society, your family shamed." He held out his plate and Aunt Edith put another slab of cake on it, while I looked on, speechless.

"Well, you clearly don't feed this poor man enough, Alex," she said. "Look at him—skin and bones." Paul gave me a beseeching look, like one of those kids in the ads that say for two dollars a day you can save them—or turn the page.

I left the Kwaku Halstead information alone for the moment—I needed time to roll it around in my head and see where it all fit in, and I'd promised it wouldn't become public knowledge immediately. So without that, the group drifted into general gossip: the latest over-the-top celebrity wedding, whether a new presidential appointee would help or harm the quality of black life, who was going to be in New York in May when the annual booksellers' convention descended upon the city.

By about ten-thirty, the last Spanish brandy—Diego's gift—had been consumed, and Marron pushed away from the table.

"I hate to be the first one to go, but I have to be up early tomorrow—" he began.

"And I'm on East Coast time, so it's the middle of the night," Aunt Edith agreed.

"For me, it is about breakfast in Barcelona." Diego smiled. "But for some reason I, too, am a little tired."

"Well, we'll take you back, of course," Georgie pronounced. "As soon as the hostess with the mostess brings our coats."

"Alex, pick up mine while you're at it," Signe called from the table. "C'mon, Jackson, we can go back to the SkyBar for drinks, on me. Well, on the *New York Times*. I hear Usher is staying in the same hotel, so you can watch the groupie parade."

"*Excellent.*" Jackson was showing all thirty-two of his teeth.

"Just make sure they're all legal," Marron cautioned. "No R Kelly action. We don't want to be reading about you in the *Jet*." *Jet* magazine was still the official chronicle of black goings-on.

We all laughed.

And then, amid a flurry of hugs and handshakes, they were gone.

Paul took the snifters to the kitchen while I dumped the dessert plates in the dishwasher. The CD player had gone into another round of Brazilian music, and I walked over to put something new in. I was scanning my collection, when it hit me.

"Paul," I called, putting a CD in the player. "Come in here for a minute. I figured something out."

He came in, wiping his hands. "You figured out there is other music besides show tunes? Congratulations."

"Very funny. Listen to this. Sound familiar?"

And the opening strains of Leonard Bernstein's score to *West Side Story* floated out. The three notes that had been haunting us for days was suddenly in my living room.

"That's the whistle the Jets used to see if the coast was clear. That's the whistle that little kid said he heard calling the dogs."

"Yup," Paul agreed. "So now we know what it is—but we still don't know what it means. And we probably won't figure it out tonight." He went around the rooms and turned out the lights, then took me in his arms.

"Sometimes these things become more clear when you sleep on them."

I kissed him. "So we're going to sleep now, are we?"

He kissed me back.

"Eventually, Einstein. Eventually."

Chapter Sixteen

Y ou know when we walk in there the entire ceiling is going to fall down, don't you?" Paul grumbled as he straightened his tie.

"I told you before: you totally do not have to go. And I won't be gone very long—the service only lasts about an hour."

He studied himself in the mirror and picked an invisible hair off his coat.

"It'll take longer. All your media brethren will be there, wanting a quick two-way so they can tell their respective public the inside story on 'Why Alex Powell Showed Up in Church' after staying away for umpty-odd years." He ducked calmly as my hairbrush sailed toward his head.

"You throw like a girl."

"It was just a hairbrush. My aim with knives is excellent."

"Want me to wait while you go get one?" He smiled.

I looked at him and smiled back. "And nick that jacket? No way. Where'd you get it, anyway?" It was dark brown tweed, with flecks of moss green and lavender in it.

"Ireland. I went over to do a piece on reverse Irish migration about five years ago, and one of the villages that had a knot of high-tech businesses was about nine hundred years old—and it had a mill. The manager gave me a tour one afternoon. There was a bolt of this and I just liked it. So I ordered a jacket made before I left."

"Well, well. Who knew there was a fashionisto lurking just beneath your staid surface?"

He cinched his belt and raised an eyebrow. "Funny . . . you didn't call me staid last night."

I'd have thrown my hairbrush, but it was still on the opposite side of the room.

"But seriously, why *are* we going to church this morning?"

"*I'm* going because I heard Lenora Walker belonged to Good Shepherd before she married Hiram and they moved to a fancier one. At his insistence."

"Where'd you hear that?"

"Colored club-lady network. Georgie told me she'd heard from one of her Smart Set sisters after Nora's death."

"So then why go to the one that she *used* to belong to, instead of the one she goes to now?"

"*Went* to. She's no longer with us, remember?"

"Right." He was tying up chocolate-colored suede shoes. "Ireland?"

"London. Same trip."

"An *international* Negro. Anyway, Georgie heard that when Hiram was working or gone, this is the church Nora would return to. They went to his haut Negro church to keep him happy—he seemed to think his high-profile black clients would expect him to be someplace like St. Andrews—but Nora was more comfortable at Good Shepherd. So that's why we're going there."

"And where is this church, 'cause you know we don't want to be late, not when you haven't walked through the doors in so long . . ."

"About twenty minutes away, so drink the last of your coffee and let's git."

Everybody thinks Los Angeles is so open—and while it might be more so now, it certainly wasn't before or after World War II. As Norman from Eso Won likes to point out when something occurs that is, in his words, "particularly out," Los Angeles isn't in the South, "but it *is* below the Mason-Dixon Line, and some of the towns and neighborhoods around here are just as full of crackers as any little Southern town you want to name. You aren't any safer in Glendale than you are in Inglewood, and don't even *think* of going to places like Brea and Fullerton. We'll be reading about you in the paper."

South L.A., the region that faithfully reflected the racial practices of the people who had helped to expand it from the twenties to the late fifties, also had parallel institutions. The

Dunbar Hotel had flourished for years on Central Avenue, with nightclubs and black-owned businesses that were patronized by the whole community, from doctors to dope sellers. And the churches were just as segregated as the rest of the city. Which perhaps made it understandable that greater Los Angeles had not one but five black Episcopal houses of worship. One had been closed a few years ago because of a dwindling population and the archdiocese's unwillingness to prop it up with funds that could be used in more vibrant parishes. Which left four more: the oldest black Episcopal church west of the Mississippi was in deep Southeast L.A., and was struggling to avoid the fate of the Compton church a few miles away that had closed. The parishioners were older, the ranks in the pews thinner each year, as the children of the elderly attended church—if they went at all—closer to home. The cliff dwellers' church was a little architectural gem on Adams. It, too, had a small congregation, but it had always been small, catering as it did to the crème de la crème of black Los Angeles. Small, in their case, meant full enough of the Right People.

The church Hiram had insisted Lenora attend with him was huge—a real cavern of limestone and stained glass. The floors were polished marble, brass chandeliers hung from the ceiling, and the silk velvet altar cloths were encrusted with gold embroidery. The city's black business elite, most of its fancy doctors, and socialites attended this church. If an architect needed to be seen mingling in the milieu that would support him, I suppose this was a rational choice for Hiram.

Good Shepherd was like people described Nora Walker: small and homey. It was at the edge of Leimert Park, a neighborhood off Crenshaw that had been alive with pedestrian traffic and commerce when it was white, in the forties and fifties. Then when racial covenants were broken in the sixties, black people moved in, and white residents began to flee. By the late seventies almost all of the businesses were black. By the time Rodney King had become a household word, the neighborhood was filled with art galleries, jazz joints, Afrocentric gift shops, and a couple of coffeehouses. It had become even more upscale since the riots that singed the edges of Leimert, but the neighborhood was now synonymous with hip and artsy.

Except for Good Shepherd. It was traditional, but not stuffy, I explained to Paul as he parked on the street outside the church lot.

"Why'd you do that? There's plenty of space in the lot."

"You might need to make a quick getaway, after the service," he said, laughing. "If we're stuck in the lot, you might actually have to sign up for the ladies' Auxiliary."

Good point.

And of course, in a church this small, there is no escaping notice. I thought we'd get there in plenty of time, but I forgot how Father Holywell likes to start things on time. So of course the processional was lining up at the doors to the church as Paul and I took programs from the greeters near the entrance. Father H. had finished whispering instructions to the acolytes, and straightening one little boy's surplice, when he turned and saw us. His eyebrows arched in delight, then he rolled his eyes upward.

"Should I warn people now that the roof is going to fall in?" he chortled.

Paul coughed behind me.

"See, it's observations like that that keep a sister away from this place," I whispered as I became enveloped in his scratchy, brocaded hug. "Your Grace, this is my friend Paul Butler. He's visiting from the East Coast." I call him Father H. when we're in church—everyone does—or there's only two of us, but in front of people he doesn't know, he gets his props: he's the Right Reverend August E. Holywell.

"Welcome, welcome. And thank you for convincing Alexa to come this morning." He winked at Paul.

"She's not here *every* Sunday?" Paul asked in shocked tones. He turned to me. "You mean you've been ignoring my e-mails that tell you to get right with the Lord?" He looked at Father H. and shook his head sadly.

"One step at a time, dear Paul, one step at a time. And now, if you'll excuse me, I've got to get to work." The Right Reverend August E. Holywell settled his miter at the correct angle, made sure its ribbons were cascading down his back, and accepted his crook from an older acolyte, who had been regarding our conversation with interest.

"Showtime, children."

Paul and I slipped into aisle seats about two thirds of the way back as the organ struck up the processional hymn.

Between all the standing and sitting, I looked around.

The small church was built like a ski chalet—modern A-frame with blond wooden pews, recessed lighting, and clean, simple lines. When it was built in the early fifties, there was no pretense about making Good Shepherd look as if it had been erected two hundred years ago. There were only two obvious concessions to tradition: the baptismal font was carved stone, and the stained-glass windows that illustrated scenes from the Bible could have been in a far less modern building.

The congregation was a mixture of old and new, too: old-school Episcopal ladies still came with hats, even though hats were no longer mandatory. There were still a number of fair, straight-haired types who had traditionally been thought to populate black Episcopal churches. But there were as many immigrant congregants, mostly from Belize, but also from other predominately Caribbean countries. The children of both mingled in a noisy, vibrant Sunday-school population.

The Prayers for the People part had included, per usual, blessings for the ill and dead. When they got to the point where the congregation was urged to make individual peti-tions for people they knew—"we ask that you remember our dearly departed, and welcome them into eternal joy and the company of the saints"—I heard Nora Walker's name whis-pered several times.

Father H. was winding up his sermon, which had been about sacrificing for others, even when they are ungrateful for the sacrifice—or unaware that it had been made.

"... in the name of the Father, the Son, and the Holy

Spirit," he intoned, making the sign of the cross, as we did the same and responded, "Amen."

"Now, are there any visitors who are with us this morning? Please stand so we may welcome you." Oh, no. I *hate* having to do this.

A lady from San Francisco stood and noted she was visiting her sister. A couple on the other side of the room had come to help celebrate their friends' anniversary and had come to church with them this morning. A family from Belize announced they would be here through Easter to visit the family matriarch.

"And we have another visitor, although she is declining to stand. But I'm going to point her out to you anyway." I could feel my heart thudding in my chest.

"How many of you read the *Los Angeles Standard*?" Hands went up all over the place.

"Does anyone read Alexa Powell's column, on the Metro page?"

Lots of murmuring assent.

"Of course we do, because in a city like Los Angeles, as African-descended people, we often feel lost in the rising tide of newcomers from other countries. And while it is right and good to welcome *all* newcomers as God's children, it is also very human to feel somewhat . . . overlooked. *Deserted*, even."

More murmurs of agreement.

"That is why we are especially blessed to have someone like Alexa Powell as a voice for the voiceless, especially the African-descended voiceless in this city. To do what many journalists have forgotten to do over the decades: to, in the words of Saint Paul, comfort the afflicted and afflict the comfortable."

"Yes, *indeed!*" one old lady breathed.

"It is good to have a voice like that in times like these, so I am especially pleased to introduce you to this young woman, whom I have known since her childhood on the Other Coast. Alexa Powell, please stand so we can welcome you. And then you may introduce your friend."

Sigh. I slowly rose to a very warm welcome. I knew my cheeks were the color of peonies—two big, pink spots of color that flashed I AM MORTIFIED loud and clear.

"Good morning, and thank you for having me. It's nice to be here—even if Father H. did make me stand up and say so." Kindly laughter erupted through the church. I felt my face cool off.

"And per his instructions, I'd like to introduce you to my friend Paul Butler, who is visiting from the Other Coast this weekend."

Paul stood gracefully and nodded. More applause. We both sat.

"Paul is here to do what his saintly forebear instructed— afflict the comfortable," Father H. laughed. "And to look at Alexa's face, it seems to be working quite nicely."

More laughter.

"All right, then, you will have a chance to inspect all our visitors at tea after service. In the meanwhile, may the peace of the Lord be always with you."

"And also with you," we responded.

Then a free-for-all broke out. Everyone left their pews and wandered around greeting friends with the outstretched hand of peace, as intricate harmony from the choir's song, "Sweet Heav'nly Spirit," floated down from their loft to settle on the milling crowd like a melodic benediction.

I was watching Paul do his usual magic with a bunch of little old ladies when someone grasped me by the wrist. I looked down to see a bishop's ring on the fingers curled around my wrist. *Uh-oh.*

"Peace of the Lord be always with you, your grace," I offered.

"And also with you, dear Alex," the prelate said smoothly. "Now look here—no, don't go off yet, I have a task for you."

"For me?"

"Yes. I'd like for you and Paul to be my oblationers this morning."

"Your what?"

He sighed. "Oblationers, Alexa. Those would be the people who carry the elements to the altar."

Elements? What on earth?

Paul came up behind us. "Wine and wafers, Einstein. Sacraments? Your basic communion materials?"

"Exactly," Father H. said with satisfaction. "Paul, you will show her what's what, since it's been a while?"

Paul nodded. "Happy to, your grace."

"Very good." And in a swirl of robes, the prelate turned and went up the aisle.

"Suckup," I muttered.

We waited in the foyer—or whatever it's called in a church—while collection plates were passed. One of the greeters handed me a heavy, covered chalice, and gave Paul two silver pitchers.

"Grab them around the neck, like this," she instructed. "That way, the LEMs can take them from you by the handle."

"What's an LEM?" I whispered.

"Lay eucharistic minister. They help the bishop distribute communion."

"Ah, like acolytes, only old."

She smiled wryly. "Close enough. Now scat—you're on."

"C'mon, heathen," Paul said. The greeter winked at him.

We lined up behind the ushers, who were returning the filled collection plates. After the ushers secured the communion rail, we handed over the goodies, bowed, and beat it out of there.

The rest of the service passed in a pleasantly recognizable blur. I people-watched as lines of folks went up to receive communion. I was trying to remember when was the last time I'd actually *taken* communion—college? High school?—when I felt myself pulled up and propelled forward.

"Why'd you do that? I'm not taking communion," I hissed to Paul.

"Looks like you are," he responded blandly.

"I haven't done it in years. You probably have to be recon-firmed to do it after all this time," I whispered.

"So don't do it. Bow your hard head and receive a blessing instead—certainly *that's* something you can do." Paul inched forward.

"Why do *you*, of all people, even care?" I asked, as we drew closer to the altar.

"Tell you later." And that was all he'd say.

So I dropped to my knees, crossed my arms over my chest so my hands rested on my shoulders, and bowed my head. Through my slitted eyes, I could see Paul kneeling perfectly still, with hands outstretched for the wafer that was supposed to symbolize Christ's body.

"The body of Christ, the bread of Heaven . . ." the LEM whispered, as she placed a wafer in Paul's palm, which remained outstretched. Father, no, Bishop H. came behind her.

". . . the blood of Christ, the cup of our salvation," he said softly, as he plucked the wafer from Paul's palm, dunked it in the silver chalice, and placed it in Paul's mouth. The pleasant smell of sweet wine drifted toward me.

Then a heavy hand descended on my head, and a thumb made the sign of the cross on my forehead. "May the Lord bless and keep you, may His radiance shine upon you and give you peace, in the name of the Father, the Son, and the Holy Spirit . . ." He touched my cheek gently and was on to the next person.

I arose, feeling strangely light, and followed Paul down the aisle.

•   •   •

After church, we mingled a while in the parish hall, so the congregation could, as promised, inspect us up close and personal. Two people from the paper identified themselves ("we work in ad sales—you're not supposed to know us because of that business-edit separation thing," the wife winked. I promised if I saw her in the elevator, I'd stare straight ahead so neither of us would get in trouble, and we both laughed.)

A young woman with an inquisitive toddler urged us to come again; Paul promised he would, when he was in town. "And she'll come with me when I do."

An older woman in a coral suit walked up to me while Paul was talking to one of the LEMs.

"I understand you're trying to make sense of Nora Walker's death," she said.

"I don't know that anyone can *understand* it," I told her. "But yes, I'm trying to figure out how it happened, although discovering *why* would be even better."

"I'm Demetria Chavis. Nora was a lovely young woman. She raised funds for the tutoring program we run for the community here. It's important work, because some of these children have no role models at home. And they adored Nora. We all did."

Her eyes grew watery.

"I understand she didn't attend services here very often?"

"After she married, her husband asked that she attend his church, and she did. Reluctantly." Demetria Chavis looked over her shoulder to make sure no one was listening.

"I shouldn't say this, but she didn't like his church very

much. She said it was too focused on show-and-tell. She liked a more intimate atmosphere."

Church rivalry. Guess that doesn't change no matter what city you're in.

"She came back here from time to time?"

"Whenever he traveled or was gone for the weekend, she was here. She always came for midnight services on Christmas Eve—ours are actually at eight o'clock, so the older people can get home safely. Then she'd go across town and attend the eleven P.M. service with her husband."

"That's a lot of church in one evening."

"That's Nora. Loyal. And wanting to keep the people who loved her happy." She sighed. "I'd better go. I'm supposed to be supervising coffee hour this morning and my cosupervisors are looking daggers at me because I'm not behind the punch bowl. Of course," she continued with some asperity, "I'm the person who collected all their raffle tickets at the March Madness raffle last month—but memories are short." She gave me a tight smile and prepared to go join her friends at the long table where Paul was being plied with yet another piece of coffee cake by a group of adoring old ladies.

They looked up with dismay as I drew near.

"Oh, dear, now I suppose you'll have to go," one fretted.

"Don't want to wear out my welcome," Paul told her.

"Well, you come back real soon, and bring Alexa with you," another instructed.

"She will definitely be coming with me when I return."

Our good-byes made, we swiftly walked out the door and

waved—from a distance—to Father H., who was having an involved discussion with a vestry member.

As we drove up Crenshaw, past the Baldwin Hills mall, and the throngs of people greeting each other outside the new cathedral for West Los Angeles Church of God in Christ, I said, "Okay, you said 'tell you later.' *Now* is later. What was all that business at the communion rail about?"

He drove in silence for a moment. "That's why you *go* to the communion rail, to take communion, right?"

"*You,* maybe. Why did *I* have to go?"

We were stopped at the light on Crenshaw and Adams. A line of well-dressed people from the Foursquare Church on the corner were crossing. Most toted their own Bibles; the women had on astounding hats. A block south, the lines were starting to form outside Chef Marilyn's for soul food. I turned to Paul, indicating I was still waiting for an answer.

He shrugged and spoke: "Because as nosy as you are, and as weird as these murders are getting, it doesn't hurt to have somebody trying to keep you safe when I'm not here."

"So God's like, what, my personal bodyguard?"

"God's the Big Enchilada. I'm just an instrument. And remember what JFK said: 'here on earth, God's work must truly be our own.'"

This was creeping me out.

"That was his speechwriter, Dick Goodwin." Writers are always getting screwed out of their credits. "And are you telling me you're a deeply religious person and I'm just finding this out?"

He turned to look at me. "Would it matter if I were?"

I thought for a moment.

"Not as long as you don't try to convert me. And you don't give me that strict biblical-interpretation stuff, like man was meant to rule woman and so forth."

He laughed out loud. "Not a chance. Here's the deal. I grew up going to church, as we all did, and a few years ago, I decided to go back when I could get there."

"Do you go every Sunday?"

"Many Sundays. I'm not a fanatic."

I pondered this in silence.

"And while going many Sundays is a good thing in general, going *this* Sunday was particularly good."

"And that would be because . . ."

"That would be because the ladies who were urging me to come back had some *very* interesting information."

"Don't make me beg you, boy."

"Maybe later. But listen to this: guess who changed her will a couple of months ago to ensure that if she died, her services would be at Good Shepherd and not the fancy church uptown?"

"Nora Walker? Did her husband know?"

"Apparently not. But he does now, and he's beside himself that she'll be buried from the 'wrong' church."

"So Nora Walker will be coming home . . ."

"Yup. The Lord does, indeed, move in mysterious ways, Einstein. Now let's go find some brunch."

Chapter Seventeen

After brunch, we went to a movie at one of the big, deluxe theaters that had sprung up over the past few years. Paul was impressed with the amenities.

"I could get used to having a martini before a show," he allowed, as we lounged in the bar a half hour before the show started.

"Pick the wrong movie and you'd need a martini to get through it," I pointed out.

We'd picked the right movie, though—a digitally remastered version of *Rear Window*. Hitchcock and martinis seemed to go together well.

Paul left for some meetings in San Diego that night. He wouldn't elaborate on what he was doing. He just said he'd be back in a few days. Signe was staying on for a couple of days. We were going to meet for dinner tomorrow night. "I'm catching up with some of my sorors this evening," she told me.

"Have fun at your Delta dinner."

"We always do. We're going over to drool at G Garvin. Sally tells me he looks just like LL Cool J."

"Don't forget to eat—everything's delicious. If you can stop panting after him long enough."

"I'll try, sisterwoman, I'll try. See you tomorrow."

I was just looking around thinking how much I hate Sunday evenings. When I was younger, it was because Sunday night meant homework checks, and signified I was only a few hours away from the school week. I'd gotten beyond the homework stage, but work loomed large on the horizon—just a few hours away. And I would have to figure out what to wear. And, once again, since I'd forgotten to go to the cleaner, my options were becoming more and more limited.

Just when I was giving up and going off to sort the darks from lights, the phone rang. A little cheery voice chirped in my ear.

"Hi, darling! My Sunday night has a horrible cold, so she begged off. Which is just as well. But I was wondering if you'd like to come down and have a quick bite, just us girls. And I may have some news for you."

Aunt Edith definitely knew how to get my attention.

"Sure. Shall I come get you, or do you want to eat at the hotel?"

"Oh, come get me and let's go someplace fun—my treat."

We agreed I'd be there in about forty-five minutes. But what would a New Yorker think was "fun" here in L.A.?

Westwood was a straight shot from Beverly Hills, so we went to the Napa Grill. My persnickety aunt approved. "Very nice. The ovens are a nice touch." Pause. "Of course, we've been doing that in New York for years." Of course.

Over drinks, as meat roasted on spits in open ovens, Edith gave me what she calls the 911.

"You know Nora Walker is being buried on Wednesday from Good Shepherd?" she asked.

"I found out today that's where services are going to be, but how did you know?"

"I had lunch today with Augie Holywell—you know he's an old family friend; he used to be the priest at St. Philip's before they made him a big shot and transferred him to the West Coast—and he told me how delighted he was to see you in church this morning. You and Paul," she amended.

"Yeah, we went. It was . . . interesting." I took a sip of my wine while Edith spread a piece of bread with tapenade and took a delicate little nibble.

"What else did the right reverend tell you?"

"That Nora was preparing to return to Good Shepherd. She missed it too much, and had decided that was one thing she wasn't interested in giving up just because she married a social climber."

"Aunt Edith!"

"Well. He *is*. You know that as well as I." She took a sip from her own wine glass. "Anyhoo, Augie's wife, Marcella, says that Hiram had been trying to micromanage Nora ever since he set eyes on her and decided she needed to marry him."

"Love at first sight?"

"Or love of her *credentials* at first sight. She has two graduate degrees—law and public administration—from very prestigious schools, and worked for the Ford Foundation before she left to come out here to marry him."

The waiter drifted by, dropped another bread basket, and a new bowl of tapenade, and drifted away.

"Couldn't Nora work for a foundation out here?"

"They don't really have a West Coast office, but she sort of functioned like a West Coast bureau. She was like a community liaison between the foundation people and the grass-roots organizations they funded. Did a lot with low-income housing, and community stuff like jobs programs for gangsters. They say she loved it."

"That's a pretty cushy job. Why would she leave it?"

"Well, what I heard from Grace Elton—she was at lunch, too—was that Lenora Walker got tired of being told what poor black community organizations needed by well-fed white people who didn't spend any time in those communities. She wanted to cut out the middleman and let the groups speak directly to the foundations." She wrinkled her upper lip. "You know how white folks must've reacted to *that*. So when she couldn't make them listen to reason, Grace says, Nora quit the foundation and went out on her own. As a consultant for, among other places, her old foundation."

"Kind of the best of both worlds," I mused. "Kept the status of foundation work but remained independent. Did they say how her husband felt about that change?"

"Well, she was still making good money and had retained her association with the big foundations, so that made him happy. White man's ice."

Before we got off on the "white man's ice is always colder to some Negroes" riff, I wanted to know something else.

"Kwaku Halstead says Nora had some atypical street cred. So why would somebody want her killed?"

Edith cooed with pleasure as her lamb chops and mashed potatoes were placed before her. "Oh, these look delicious," she told the waiter. "And look, Alex, asparagus." She turned back to the waiter. "We don't get it this early in New York."

"These come from an organic farm up near Gilroy," he informed us. "Very hard to get this early on. But our chef has a connection."

He lowered his voice, as if he were helping Edith score crack, not spring veggies: "The asparagus farmer is family."

Of course he is. Everybody's got an angle, everywhere, all the time.

Having given us the provenance of our vegetable, the waiter retreated.

"So about Nora?"

"Well, the Holywells and Grace were just saying that they were detecting a growing strain of independence in her, and were wondering whether Hiram was going to tolerate it."

I looked up from my roast chicken and frites. "*Tolerate* it?"

"You know how husbands are . . . Oops, no, you don't, do you?" (This said completely without irony.)

"Anyway, they can be sulky sometimes when they don't

189

get their way. Even my Harmie was. So Grace and the Holy-wells were trying to figure out how Hiram was going to take Nora's defection from his church."

"Frankly, I don't see what the big deal is. So you go separate places on Sunday morning, and meet for lunch after."

Edith looked at me sympathetically. "Oh, Alex. It's about *image* with some people. And for most architects, image is everything. Remember, they socialize with many of their clients, so it's completely necessary to be seen a certain way if you want to be taken seriously. How can you build homes for your clients if you aren't intimately aware of how they live?"

I allowed that there was a certain logic to that, but still.

"And it gets more complicated with children," Edith continued.

"The Walkers didn't have any," I pointed out.

"Oh, that's the other thing I found out: Grace was pretty sure Nora was pregnant."

That little bomb was dropped while Edith was perusing the dessert menu.

"*Really?* Who told you?"

"Grace. Her daughter is an ob-gyn. And all the young female doctors in her hospital have just been shaken by Nora's death. They're all about the same age, you know."

Wow. That *was* an interesting piece of news.

"Did Hiram know?"

Edith dipped a spoon into the crème brûlée we'd chosen to share. "I think she wanted to surprise him."

And so she had—but not in the way that she'd planned, obviously.

I dropped Edith off and promised to try and catch up with her before she left for the Other Coast on Wednesday. When I got home, I called Ben Porter, the media liaison for the coroner's office. And was flabbergasted when he picked up.

"Ben, it's Alex Powell, at the *Standard*. What are you doing in your office on Sunday night?"

"I suppose I could ask you the same thing—what are you doing in your office on Sunday night?" Ben teased. "And for the record, I'm not at home, packing for that conference I mentioned the other day. My calls are being forwarded."

Forensics. Dallas. Right.

"Oh. Well, I'm calling from home, too. But I was going to leave you a message so you could get back to me on Monday morning. I forgot you'd be traveling."

"About?"

"Nora Walker."

"Alex, you know I can't tell you a thing about her death. We haven't released a statement of confirmation yet."

"Number one, I wouldn't expect you to tell me anything you're not supposed to. Number two, you've already announced that primary cause of death is exsanguination."

"So then what can I do for you? You know what everybody else does."

"Actually, Ben, I know something that hardly anyone else does, and I wanted to run it past you."

"Shoot—although you realize I'm not promising to tell you anything."

"Right. But here's the thing: I had dinner with someone this evening who is pretty sure that Nora Walker was pregnant when she died."

Blank silence.

"Are you telling me that's incorrect?"

Blank silence.

"Are you confirming that this *is* correct?"

Silence, then: "Alex, we've had a good professional relationship, you and I. And I have never lied to you, and I'm not going to start now. I can't tell you what to do, but I can tell you that if *my* wife had died under the circumstances Nora Walker did, the *last* thing I would want is some reporter calling up to inform me I'd lost a child I didn't know I was going to have. Think about it."

"I don't plan to say anything to Hiram about this."

"I hope the hell you don't. Nothing's official yet. He should hear this from her doctor, or from someone in my office. Preferably both."

"Then you should call him soon, Ben. Because if enough people know about it to tell me Nora was pregnant when she was killed, word will leak out sooner or later. *You* think about *that*. Have a safe trip."

And then we both hung up the phone. It would probably be a while before we had that lunch we kept putting off.

Chapter Eighteen

I spent the night wondering if Nora Walker's assailant had known she was pregnant. Probably not, if her husband didn't. Ben had said two people knew—him and Nora's doctor. He didn't mention the doctor's name, but I didn't think it would be too hard to narrow down. I knew Grace Elton's daughter, Allison, practiced at Cedars Sinai Medical Center—I'd run into her in the Medical Towers elevator as I was coming from my allergist. And Edith had said the group of female doctors who'd been shocked to hear of Nora's death were all about the same age.

I picked up the phone.

"Speak."

"Georgie, do you have a female ob-gyn?"

"Is there any other kind?" Georgie drawled. "You can trust a man to set a broken bone or give you an eye exam, but I draw the line there."

"Is your doctor young and black?"

"She's about my age, and of course she's black. Why, do you need a referral? I don't think she's taking new patients, but I'm sure if I call I can get you in."

I'm sure she could. If she could do it for four-star restaurants and hotels, why wouldn't I believe she could do it with gynecologists?

"Oh, by the way, she's only a gyn, not an ob. Her partner is the ob."

"Don't they usually do that together?"

"Yeah, a lot of them do, but I didn't want my schedule to be inconvenienced by someone needing to give birth, so I specifically searched for someone who doesn't deliver babies. Why, are you telling me you need an obstetrician?"

I crossed my fingers while I poured juice into a glass.

"God, no! No, I want you to do me a favor. I want you to call your doctor and ask her who Nora Walker's doctor was."

"Phew. I wasn't ready for that shower thing. All those stupid games. Okay, I'll call you back in a moment."

While Georgie was making her calls, I had a chance to get dressed. As I was pulling a brush through my hair and silently thanking whoever was responsible for inventing covered rubber bands, the phone rang again.

"Leslie Seaver-Smith. Cedars Towers. Here's her number. Use Marguerite's name, so they'll put you through. And Marguerite says call her office 'cause she can bet you haven't had a Pap this year."

"Last year, either. I was busy."

"Yeah, get busy enough and your womb will rot and fall

out while you're not looking. It only takes two minutes. Get your ass in to see her, Einstein."

"Thanks, Georgie. I guess my ass is the pertinent part in this case, huh?"

But she'd already hung up.

Georgie's name was the magic password, because ten minutes later, Dr. Leslie Seaver-Smith told me she'd see me before she began seeing patients, if I could get to Cedars on the double. It was maybe fifteen minutes away from the house, so that was no problem.

Dr. Seaver-Smith's office was on the eighth floor of the Medical Towers that housed many of the Cedars doctors. The waiting room was done in soothing tones of bamboo green, beige, and brown. The magazines were current and plentiful—*Essence* and *Town and Country* and *Vogue* for women patients, *GQ* and *Esquire* and *Fortune* for whatever men might accompany them. And *National Geographic* for the rugged individualists. A small fountain tucked away in the corner burbled cheerfully.

At eight-thirty, the waiting room was empty. Seaver-Smith's staff was sipping coffee and lining up the files of patients who'd be expected in a few moments. One office administrator, in pastel pink scrubs, opened the door to the back and motioned. "Dr. Seaver-Smith will see you now." She pointed down the hall. "All the way to the end, last door on your left."

I entered and Leslie Seaver-Smith, M.D., looked up from her desk. "Ms. Powell? Leslie Seaver-Smith."

I wondered if Dr. Seaver-Smith made her patients insecure. I'd certainly be insecure if the person looking up my . . . you know . . . looked like Thandie Newton. Same tawny skin, fine bones, and big doe eyes. She wore a simple V-neck top and skirt under her white doctor's coat. Her only noticeable jewelry was a gold watch on her left hand. No rings.

"I understand you're interested in my former patient Nora Walker," she began.

"I know you can't tell me very much . . ." Dumb move. Why not give her an out from the jump?

"That's right," she said crisply. "Doctor-patient confidentiality."

"Even for dead people?"

"Yes," she said. "If someone comes in here with a subpoena, that might change things . . . it *might*. But for the merely curious, no."

I looked at this steely young woman. Was she always this cold a fish, or was this how she coped with losing a patient and friend?

"I'm not merely curious . . . although I confess this is a puzzle." Leslie Seaver-Smith's look said "about what I figured" loud and clear.

"Three people have died under very strange circumstances in a short period of time. I'm trying to discover if there's any connection between them."

Seaver-Smith looked out of her large window to the panoramic view of the Hollywood Hills. The famous sign was clearly visible in the early morning air.

"What kind of connection would there be?" She faced me squarely. "That writer from Boston was murdered. Myron Bournewell committed suicide—"

"Maybe, or maybe it was an accident. Or maybe he was pushed."

"Whatever happened, none of it has anything to do with Nora's death."

"I've heard she was pregnant at the time of her death."

She didn't blink an eye. "The coroner's office will have to confirm that. I cannot tell you a thing."

"The coroner has pretty much confirmed it already, although the official report hasn't been released yet."

"So why are you here, Ms. Powell? Nora's still dead. Asking questions won't bring her back."

Tough cookie, this woman.

"Don't you want the people who killed her apprehended?"

Seaver-Smith thought for a moment, as she absently rolled a mail opener back and forth on her desk blotter. It looked like a scalpel, only it was silver plated. Probably some kind of doctor in-joke. Ha ha.

"Is there anything else you could tell me that might narrow down the search?"

Leslie Seaver-Smith looked up, hesitated, then looked down again.

"Not a thing. As I said, there is the aspect of confidentiality . . ."

I rose and collected my notebook and tote bag. No sense in wasting more time here.

"Then I won't keep you any longer. Thank you for seeing me, Dr. Seaver-Smith."

I left my card on her desk, next to the silver scalpel.

"If something else occurs to you that you can share, please feel free to call me, anytime."

She looked at me intently for a moment, as if gauging whether I meant it.

"I will do that, Ms. Powell. And now I'm afraid I have patients I must attend to."

On the way out, I saw a man's briefcase propped against a chair in the waiting room. It was dark brown leather, and was stamped with the initials H.R.W. on one side. As I was trying to think whether I knew anyone with those initials, the door opened and Hiram Walker and I looked at each other in surprise.

"Hello," he began hesitantly. I probably looked vaguely familiar to him. Too bad I'd have to blow my own cover, but Journalism 101 says reporters have to identify themselves as such before they start to ask questions. We can't just lurk. It's not fair. I took a deep breath.

"Hello, Mr. Walker. I'm Alexa Powell. I work for the *Standard,* and I'm so sorry about your wife's death."

He walked swiftly over to his briefcase, looked at it, then

at me, as if assessing whether I might have been snooping through his things, and nodded at the receptionist.

"I'm ready," he told her, handing her back the big key ring that contained the key to the men's room.

He turned to me.

"No offense, but I don't talk to reporters. I've said everything I care to about Nora. Now if you'll excuse me, I have some loose ends to tie up."

And he walked through the door without looking back. Made me wonder what he'd look like when he emerged. Leslie Seaver-Smith was almost certainly going to inform him of Nora's pregnancy, so when he exited the doctor's office, he'd probably look like a man who had lost everything.

Chapter Nineteen

Work was uneventful until after lunch, when I returned to find my voice mail notification blinking. The voice on the machine sounded like an older black woman. The exchange on the caller ID came from somewhere south of Slauson.

"Ms. Powell, I read your column yesterday about Lenora Walker's death. I don't know if this is related or if these are the same dogs, but you should know that there is a young man in this neighborhood who keeps a lot of vicious dogs as part of a dog-training business. We have been complaining and complaining for *months,* but the police don't do a thing. I can't tell you his name, because we've never been introduced. But one of my neighbors says his uncle is Samoo el Simba. [That's how she pronounced his first name.] You know, the one who started all that mess over at UCLA in the sixties? I don't know where he is now, but maybe he had something to do with this. I'm not leaving my name because these children have no respect for anything. I live alone and I can't afford to make anyone angry, but I hope you will look into this. Thank you."

Interesting. Twice in the space of a few days comes the name of a guy who hasn't been seen or spoken about in years. Time to find out what Mr. El-Simba is up to these days.

I immediately delved into Nexis to see what came up, but it only went back to the mid-1980s. I'm usually pretty good at this, but clearly it was time to call in a professional. So I called the library.

In about half an hour, a few articles had been e-mailed to me with a note:

Alex . . . he didn't disappear into thin air, but damn near. This is as much as I could find after 1986. Hope it helps. Call if you need anything else. Sylvie.

Sylvie the librarian had sent a couple of clips. One noted that Samu el-Simba had gotten off when tried for the UCLA murders that had claimed, among others, Will Howe. The jury had been split, so the judge had had to dismiss. There had been rumors of at least three cases of juror intimidation, but that couldn't be proved, either. Apparently, Mr. El-Simba had wide reach outside the courtroom, and no one wanted to be on the receiving end of his wrath.

Another clip, from the late seventies, had a brief interview with him in the Metro section. The headline said " 'THOSE WERE CRAZY TIMES:' COMMUNITY ACTIVIST LOOKS BACK

ON SOMETIMES VIOLENT PAST." It was a catch-up interview with El-Simba, implying he was still committed, but had cooled down considerably from the guy who once had turned the plaza before Royce Hall into Dodge City.

The third clip was actually from the library's tracer service. It's amazing what a librarian can do if you give her an approximate spelling and date of birth. There was no Samu el-Simba listed—but there *were* six Samuel Johnsons with the same approximate birth year scattered throughout Southern California, with addresses and phone numbers for each.

I got busy.

The first Samuel Johnson, in Fullerton, was clearly white. And suspicious.

"How'd you get this number?" he snarled.

"Directory information?" I lied.

"I ain't been in a directory for years—too many damn people calling *wanting* stuff, either money or to know something ain't none of their business. You take my name off your list, you hear me, missy?"

"Yes, sir, and have a pleasant day." I hung up with new sympathy for telephone solicitors. But not enough to take my numbers off the do-not-call list.

The second Samuel Johnson was white, too, and British. And way different from the first one. When I apologized for having the wrong number he said, "No bother at all; it's a very common name. Good day."

The third Johnson's voice had the lilt of the Caribbean. Just to be safe I asked if he'd been in Los Angeles in the early seventies. "No, dearest, I was livin' back in Bridgetown then. Dat was back when Tortola was a nice place to stay . . ." I'd visited Tortola once, and it felt pretty heavenly to me, but maybe it had been even better back in the day. Or maybe people in the British West Indies had higher standards than yours truly.

The fourth Samuel Johnson was actually a junior—he lived in South L.A., near Watts. His father had died a year ago, he told me, but he'd never spent any time in West Los Angeles, as far as he knew.

"Why? Somebody leave him some money?" he asked, hopefully.

I told him no, but if I discovered otherwise, I'd call back. He gave me his cell number just in case.

The fifth Samuel Johnson sounded about the right age and race. A husky voice that I imagined could have belonged to the one-time activist came through the phone:

"You have reached the household of Sam and Angie Johnson. We're not in at the moment, but leave a message and we'll get back to you. Peace."

I looked again at the area code, then clicked on my area code guide, which told me 951 was in Norco. I had never heard of it, so I called the State desk.

"Hey, Mick. Alex Powell. Know where Norco is?"

Mick Franklin not only knew *where* it was, but *what* it was.

"Cow town. Actually, *horse* town, in Riverside County."

Huh?

"It's a city that's zoned for horses. No sidewalks or

asphalt driveways. Residents gotta have enough acreage to allow 'em to keep animals safely. And everybody has one."

"*Horse?*"

"Hell, yeah. It's why they move there. So they can keep horses. Its nickname is Horsetown, USA. If you're planning to go, go soon."

"Why? Are they going to disappear it in a couple of months?"

Mick laughed. "Nope, but if you go in hot weather you'll wish *you* could disappear. *Stinks.* Horses—remember?"

Oh, yeah. Because of course with every horse comes several pounds of horse poop. Daily.

"How would I get there if I wanted to go?"

He gave me directions. I decided the thing to do would be to go without calling. Right after rush hour tomorrow morning.

Which is exactly what I did. Even after rush hour it took a bit over an hour to traverse the three freeways needed to get down to Norco. Mick had been right—people rode right through town on horses, and nodded a cheerful hello. As he said, the houses—many with appropriately horsey split-rail fences and wagon-wheel motifs—were set back on huge lots, which legally allowed the residents to keep large animals. There were hitching posts in front of some of the stores, and corrals in back of some restaurants. I pulled into the town

McDonald's on the main street for a cup of coffee, and to ask around. People always tell you more if you buy something.

"Welcome to McDonald's. How may I help you?" The pink-cheeked girl behind the counter sounded as if she actually wanted to help.

"Small coffee, please."

"Just coffee? Sure you don't need anything else?"

"Well, I *am* trying to find Angie Johnson. Her husband's name is Sam. You wouldn't happen to know her, would you?"

The girl placed my coffee before me. "Cream?" I nodded. She gave me two.

"Course I know Angie. Everybody with a sweet tooth knows Angie."

"Really? Why's that?" I stirred my cream and decided to live a little and put sugar in, too.

"'Cause she owns the best bakery in Riverside County, that's why. Good thing you're only having coffee here." She leaned forward, and whispered, "'Cause if I was going over to see Angie, I would not be wasting my calories on *our* pastry. It's pitiful by comparison."

"Would you mind telling me how to get there?"

The young woman whooped with laughter. "How 'bout walk out the door and turn right? They're about half a dozen steps east of here. Tell her Sarah said hi, okay?"

"I'll do that. Thanks a lot."

And Sarah was as good as her word. I could have thrown an apple from where I was standing and hit the side of the

Hitching Post Bakery and Café. I walked up to the window—a sign in it read SPACE FOR OUR FOUR-LEGGED FRIENDS OUT BACK. Curious, I walked around back just to check. Sure enough, a big brown horse was standing placidly tethered to a rail while his human cohort was inside having coffee.

I walked back around front to inspect the window. A glass bakery case had samples of the day's offerings—huge cinnamon rolls dripping with white icing, thick slices of banana bread, and an overly generous square of sour cream coffee cake.

Walking into the cheery space, I was embraced by the smells of vanilla, cinnamon, and butter. I quickly ditched the McDonald's coffee in a trashcan standing sentinel by the door—no sense in advertising my stupidity at having stopped in a fast-food joint when the real deal was right down the street.

Sarah's clone was behind the counter.

"Hi, what can I do you for?" she bubbled.

"How about a cinnamon roll and a small coffee?"

"Sure thing. For here or to go?"

I looked around. The breakfast clientele had mostly cleared out, and the mid-morning crowd looked small and friendly. There was a stack of newspapers on a stand in the corner, and a bunch of dog-eared horse magazines that had clearly been thumbed through many times by people with sugar-sticky fingers.

"For here, definitely," I told the Sarah clone.

"Good choice," she whispered. "If you stay, we can offer you fresh whipped cream for your coffee."

Yay for good choices.

I spent the next half hour contentedly sipping good, strong coffee with a whipped-cream head, and trying to put a dent in that obscenely huge cinnamon roll. The cake part was buttery and cinnamon-scented. The thick icing wasn't too sweet, and had a hint of almond flavoring. The combination literally melted in your mouth.

I'd convinced myself I was downing two days' worth of calories in one sitting for investigative purposes: I was waiting for the café's owner to come in. But the two people I saw helping—the Sarah clone and a young guy barely old enough to work—didn't look as if they could have any connection with her.

When the Sarah clone came back to freshen my coffee for the third time, I figured it was time to be more direct.

"You didn't like your cinnamon roll?" she asked curiously. "It's the house favorite. People drive all the way down from L.A. just to pick 'em up and drive back."

"Are you kidding? It's fabulous—but it's way too generous for one person. That's why I haven't finished it . . . um, what's your name, anyway?" (Full of finesse, moi.)

"Amy. I'm the day manager."

"Amy, I'm Alex, and I came down here from L.A. for two reasons: number one, I'd heard about these cinnamon rolls." Okay, I was lying through my teeth. "And number two, to try to see Angie Johnson."

Amy nodded. "Angie doesn't usually get in till noon, but you might could find her at home at this hour. Here's the address. And if she's not there, Sam can tell you where to find her." She scribbled down an address that looked to be maybe five minutes away, and a phone number.

"You don't think they'll mind if I just stop on by?"

Amy regarded me with something like scorn.

"I don't know how they do it out L.A. way, but everything down here is *real* informal. You just tell 'em you were in the bakery and asked after Angie, and that I sent you over to their place."

Trusting folks, these people.

"Okay . . . thanks. But how do you know I'm not an axe murderer, or somebody who wants to rob their place?"

She chuckled. "You look okay to me. And we hardly ever have any crime down here. A lot of us don't even lock our doors. Last time the sheriff had to be called, somebody's horse was stolen. But it turned out that wasn't really the case."

I waited expectantly.

"It was this guy I used to go to high school with." She rolled her turquoise eyes at male stupidity. "Him and some friends had a few too many beers and smashed up their VW on the way home. So they sneaked in back of the steakhouse and 'borrowed' someone's horse. Turned out to be the *mayor*'s horse. So it got returned the next morning."

"What was the punishment?"

" 'Bout what you'd expect for horse-wranglin'."

"They were *hanged*?" That's the only punishment I'd ever heard of for horse-rustling.

That laugh again. "Oh, heck no! But they had to shovel out a lot of horse manure from the corrals in back of the steakhouse—and the mayor's barn—for a week. That'll cure just about anybody. Y'all should try it in L.A. sometime."

I left smiling, thinking the manure that usually gets slung in city council meetings was more bull than horse, but the same principle probably applied.

The Johnsons' home was a low-slung ranch with a brick foundation and white siding above it. There was a white-washed split-rail fence and a winding gravel driveway that was apparently as far as Norco city rules would allow home-owners to deviate from dirt. I drove up and parked to the side of the drive, near a big red pickup with hay and feed bags in the back. You could hear the front door ring throughout the house.

"Out back!" a voice hollered.

I followed around the side of the house. "Hello?"

"This way. I'm in the barn."

And there on the first floor of a picture-perfect red barn, a burly black man with close-cut gray hair and a bushy mus-tache was mucking out a horse stall. The weight-lifter physique that had been so famous back in the seventies had gotten a little softer, but not much. Gone were the beard, Afro, and dark glasses that had shielded his eyes from the flash of television cameras. In place of the dashikis he'd be-come known for were a flannel shirt and well-worn jeans.

And the ominous shades were now wire-rimmed grandpa specs. He looked like an old Charles Dutton. With hair.

He wiped his hand on his jeans and came forward and offered it. I shook.

"Samuel Johnson. How can I help you, miss?"

"Alex Powell, Mr. Johnson. I'm a reporter for the *Los Angeles Standard.*"

He stepped back and regarded me coolly.

"If you're here for one of those 'Where are they now' pieces, I'm not interested. And if you're here to dig up the past, I'm not interested in that, either. The Bible says, 'let the dead bury their dead.'"

"So to speak," I murmured. He looked at me sharply, but chose not to comment.

"But I'm not here for either reason," I explained.

"Then why *are* you here?" he asked, pushing back his tractor cap and massaging his forehead.

"Have you been reading the papers lately, Mr. Johnson?"

"L.A. papers?" He snorted. "Nah. Haven't read 'em in maybe a decade. I read the farm report, the Riverside papers. Every now and then the *New York Times,* on the computer. But I have to say, when I left L.A., I stopped caring about what was happening in that city. I gave up on it."

"Really? Why's that?"

He returned to shoveling the last bits of poop out of the empty stall. Idly, I wondered where its occupant was. "'Cause it's a city that has gone beyond the pale, Ms. Powell. You should know that. You report on it. Rich keep getting richer. Poor keep getting poorer—only now half of 'em don't speak English and aren't even here legally. Despite that, black folk keep getting pushed to the bottom of the rung for services and political attention. And"—he paused, took out a bandana and wiped his brow, resettled the cap—"so-called black leaders in the city are only interested in getting their pictures in the paper with celebrities. They're not about any *real* work on behalf of their constituents."

"So you left because you were disgusted?"

He handed me an armful of hay. "Here, if I'm gonna answer this many questions you might as well make yourself useful . . . spread it out, like this."

So I did. And while I did, he told me about how he'd tried for years in the mid to late seventies to organize black Los Angeles politically. But it didn't work.

"Too much infighting. Everybody had to have his own little fiefdom. And the bourgie Negroes did not want to work with the grass-roots organizations that could have solidified their power. They just were not interested in sharing the power with people they thought of as their lessers. Meanwhile, those people were getting frustrated, and letting themselves find release in shit like crack, which was terrorizing the community. Black politicians weren't doing anything about it."

"So you gave up and moved out?"

He stopped shoveling and glared at me.

"I gave *out* and moved out. Had gotten myself a nice case of ulcers, hypertension. The doctors told me I'd better change my life or kiss it good-bye in a couple of years."

"That was back when?" I'd finished spreading hay. He nodded at the wire bin screwed to the wall about horse-head height. "Put some of this"—another fresh load—"in there, okay? Then you're done."

As I spread hay in the grate ("you don't have to fluff it," he said, laughing. "He's *eating* it, not sleepin' on it!"), the former Samu el-Simba Johnson explained he'd followed his doctors' advice and looked for something completely different from the stress-filled urban life he'd known. "I heard about this place, and liked the idea of living in horse country. My people come from Texas. I used to go visit my grandpa in the summers, he had horses. I had a little money saved up, so I bought a piece of land, built a little house." He nodded across the driveway at the ranch. "And been here ever since."

"Did you marry before or after you got here?" I asked.

A car pulled up in the driveway.

"There's the wife now. Ask her how we met."

"Anybody home? Where are y'all?"

"BARN!" hollered Samuel Johnson cheerfully. Clearly, getting married for him had been a good thing.

"Smells like horse in here," Angie Johnson joked, then stopped and stared at me in disbelief.

"You are *not* making her work! We don't treat guests like that." She turned to me and sighed. "Not when I'm home, anyway. You must be the young lady from L.A. who couldn't finish that little bitty cinnamon roll. I'm Angie Johnson."

I liked her immediately, and hoped I'd sufficiently hidden my surprise. I'd thought Angie Johnson was going to be gaunt and dreadlocked, one of what Georgie called "those Ujamaa sisters, the kind who wear clothes from the Motherland and walk three steps behind their Lord and Master." Instead she looked like she'd parachuted in from Indiana, or Iowa: medium height, slightly overweight. Creamy skin, naturally blond, shoulder-length hair, and delft blue eyes.

The former Samu el-Simba Johnson regarded me closely, waiting to see if I had any attitude about his white wife.

"Glad to meet you," I said, shaking her hand. "You make a hella huge cinnamon roll. If you sold them in L.A., you'd clean up."

Silvery laughter burbled out of Angie Johnson. Her husband relaxed, and smiled slightly.

"If I sold 'em in L.A., I'd have to live up there, which would take all the fun out of being rich," she chortled. "No, thank you, ma'am. Sammy and I have everything we need here. Couple of horses—that was Fig's stall you were mucking out—"

"She wasn't mucking, she was laying in feed," her husband corrected.

"She *should* have been sitting in my kitchen having a cup of coffee," his wife scolded fondly. He actually blushed.

"He didn't make me do anything—I liked helping," I protested. Johnson winked behind his wife's back.

"Well, never mind," she said. "What's done is done. If that stall's clean, I'll bring Fig in. Wanna come meet him?"

"Oh, definitely. Since I've already seen all his business, I should meet the source."

She cackled appreciatively. "Hey, Fig. We're comin' to get ya."

Fig turned out to be a handsome three-year-old chestnut gelding who'd gotten his name when the Johnsons bought him as a colt: when he was being broken to saddle, his favorite treat wasn't apples or carrots, but Fig Newtons. So that was his name: Fig Newton Johnson. He walked over and nickered appreciatively at the sugary smell Angie was giving off. Then he lowered his head and bumped around my pockets for a treat.

"Give him this," Angie instructed. "Hold your hand out flat, so he doesn't bite you by accident." She placed a crust of cinnamon roll on the flat of my palm, and it was duly snapped up. His muzzle felt like velvet.

"See? You made a friend," Angie said matter-of-factly, brushing Fig's forelock out of his eyes.

"More than one, apparently," her husband said.

"Can I ask how you all met?" I said, remembering Johnson's reference to it in the barn.

"He fell off his horse in front of my bakery." Angie giggled. "New in town. Bought a house and a horse and couldn't ride for spit. He was game, though."

"What about your grandpa's horses?" I asked Samuel Johnson.

"Those were workhorses," he clarified. "We didn't ride 'em. Had to learn to ride when I came out here."

I turned to Angie.

"You probably already knew who he was, right, since I didn't see a whole lot of black folks on Main Street."

"You got that right." Sam Johnson laughed. "When you rode in here this morning you increased the black population of Norco by one hundred percent."

"And when I go, it'll drop back down to just you?"

"Almost. It's pretty much always that way around here. You get used to it."

I looked around at the world they'd built for themselves out here, and wondered if race was ever an issue. Especially for an interracial couple.

"Nobody's ever had a problem that you all are a mixed couple?"

"Nope," Angie said stoutly. "If they did, they kept it to themselves."

"See, we don't usually talk race out here," the former president of Nu Afrika told me. "We mostly talk horse. That's what counts in this town—whether you're for or against horses."

"Why would anybody be against horses? What's not to like?"

"New people moving in sometimes don't like the smell," Angie explained. "It's not for everybody out here." She nodded at her husband. "We don't have kids, but Sam has a nephew who used to come out and spend part of each summer with us. When he was little, he loved it. When he got bigger, he didn't."

"Too slow?" I asked, rubbing Fig's side.

"Too slow, too white, too rural." She was pretty frank.

"Malik was my sister's child," Sam Johnson explained. "She died of AIDS when crack got to be a big problem in

South Central L.A. Malik was eight. His drughead daddy didn't step up to the plate, which was just as well. So he lived in Inglewood with my mother during the school year, but would spend summers out here."

"At first, he liked it," Angie continued. "Learned to ride, made friends with some of the local boys. But around junior high school, it stopped being fun for him. He'd stay in the city for most of the summer, come out for maybe a week or two. Wasn't interested in riding anymore. We'd have to bribe him to get on a horse."

"With money?" I wondered.

"With stories. Tales of the old days," Sam Johnson answered. "Malik wanted to hear over and over about community confrontations, Nu Afrika's glory days, the shootout at UCLA. He'd ride around town for hours listening to that stuff."

"Where is Malik now?" I asked.

"In L.A. somewhere," Angie said. "He's of age, so nobody can make him do anything. He is very bright, but he dropped out of high school to work with a dog trainer."

Ah-hah. My tip had been on the money.

"Dog training?" I made myself sound skeptical.

"Big money in it . . . people treat their dogs like they're children, and a lot of 'em—the dogs, I mean—behave like spoiled brats because they're given mixed signals," Sam Johnson said. "So if you can make a dog behave, and fit into the family's life, and cure him of bad habits like barking and pulling at the leash when he's on a walk, you could be in Fat City."

"So is Malik Johnson getting rich?"

"Malik Fereby," Johnson replied absently. "My sister was married when she had him—dude just didn't stick around. Liked smoking that crack better than he liked being married. And no, Malik's not rich. I don't think he's even working for the guy who started him out on training anymore."

"What happened?"

Angie Johnson picked up the story.

"He called up here a few months ago, all excited because he was going to go out on his own. Said he'd learned enough at the training center, all the clients were either bourgie or cops, and he wanted to bring his expertise to the People. So could he bring his dogs out to the country for training? We said sure, we were glad he was showing some initiative."

"We thought he'd come out here with some yappy pets," Sam Johnson said. "But he didn't. He came out with three of the most dangerous-looking canines I'd ever seen. And I know dogs. Ours wouldn't go near them. Neither would Fig, or our other horse, Silk."

"So what happened?" Angie and Sam looked at each other.

"He was pretty good about keeping the dogs crated in the far paddock, and they really did listen to him," Angie began, then stopped.

I waited, knowing sometimes people will talk more if you leave a void.

"We'd gone down to the steakhouse for dinner, and before the bill came, we got a call from the sheriff to come home immediately. We raced home, and when we came up the driveway, there was so much *noise*—horses neighing, the

217

dogs barking nonstop. The sheriff's SUV in the driveway, with the lights flashing . . ." She looked at Sam, and he put his arm around her, and picked up the story.

"The damn dogs had gotten out somehow, and they'd run into the barn. According to the vet, they ran into Silk's stall and just attacked her. Our dogs tried to help her, but they were outnumbered. Those killer dogs bit Silk all about the legs till she fell down, then tore her throat out. Vet had to put her down even before we got there. No way anybody would let an animal suffer like that."

"What happened to your dogs?"

"Poke, our shepherd, got some bites on the shoulder. He's okay now. Molly, our Heinz 57—she was mostly Australian sheepdog—didn't make it."

"What did Malik have to say about all this?"

" 'I'm sorry, it was an accident, I don't know how it happened' . . . the usual," Angie said bitterly.

"We told him those dogs were four-legged death warrants, and they needed to be put down immediately. He refused. He bundled them into his truck—where a boy with part-time jobs gets to drive a Chevy like that I don't want to know—and he drove off, mad. Haven't seen him since."

We were all silent for a moment, contemplating Silk's horrible death. Then a thought occurred to me.

"You wouldn't have remembered his license plate number, would you?"

Sam Johnson snorted. "Hell, yeah: A-DAWG."

A personalized plate. Easily traceable.

Chapter Twenty

I rode back to town with my sunroof wide open and the enticing smells of a dozen huge cinnamon rolls—which Angie insisted I take with me—doing battle with the less-than-enticing smell of Fig Newton Johnson. Why are rich people so attached to horses? You ride them, then you have to take half a day to get the smell off you. Just being in the stables had left me pretty pungent.

On the way back, I called a friend I'd cultivated at the DMV and asked for a favor. I don't ask often, I'm polite when I do, and I always send goodies at Christmas, so Mrs. Ting is happy to help. Quietly. Used to be anyone could run anyone else's plate at the DMV, but now things are a lot more formal. A young actress was tracked, stalked, and killed by a psychotic fan, so the whole system changed. You can still request a phone and address for a license from DMV Central, in Sacramento, but you have to have had, say, a hit-and-run, so you can pursue claiming your insurance or something. I didn't have that excuse.

But there are ways around it, and Mrs. Ting was my way. In about four minutes she had an address for Malik Fereby, but no phone. Which didn't surprise me: kids like Malik often used their cell phones as their central mode of communication, and cell phones aren't registered. Yet.

I thanked Mrs. Ting, asked after her family—her daughter is in law school at Berkeley, and she loves to brag about that—and let her get off the phone so her boss's suspicion wasn't aroused, if he was the suspicious type.

I took the 10 past downtown and got off at La Brea, and took it down past Slauson into Inglewood. The address for Malik Fereby was in the Hyde Park section of Inglewood. It was a mixture of small businesses—none of them glamorous—and apartment houses off Hyde Park Boulevard. Deeper into the neighborhood were small bungalows with trimmed hedges, green lawns, and lots of flowers. Every house had bars on the windows, and grilled security doors. Many of them had big, iron gates around the perimeter of the property.

Malik's house—or whoever he was staying with—had all three. The mailbox was on the outside of the front gate, which was about my height, and made of closely spaced black steel pickets. A generic sign like the kind you can buy in hardware and office supply stores warned would-be trespassers that a dangerous dog was on the premises—enter at own risk.

I pulled into a space across the street to contemplate my

next move. Clearly, going onto the property would be too stupid even for *me* to consider. How, then, was I going to discover if Malik did, indeed, live there? It wasn't like there was a Hitching Post Café I could pop into and make inquiries. And if I did, probably nobody would tell me a thing. People in this part of town haven't had good experiences with the media—it usually reports on these neighborhoods when something confirms their worst suspicions about black folks' depravity—so they're not all that interested in answering reporters' questions.

While I was pondering, a young man walked down the street in that loping stroll that black boys adopt to keep other folks from messing with them. It says *"leave me alone and you won't get hurt. Bother me and it's on."* He was dressed in a navy sweatshirt, black pants that looked as if they were going to fall off his butt if he sneezed hard, and too expensive sneakers endorsed by multimillion-dollar athletes who should know better. The sweatshirt was a hoodie, and it was pulled up over his head, so only his eyes peered out. A glint of something shone around his neck.

The flash of an expensive watch caught my eye as he turned the key in the gate's lock. As soon as there was a click—even before he opened the gate—the most ferocious barking started at the back of the house. Well, as long as the dogs were on that side of the fence, maybe I'd be okay. I got out of the car before I lost my nerve.

The kid watched me calmly as I crossed the narrow street.

"I'm looking for Malik Fereby . . ." I began.

He looked at me with blank eyes. "Why? Who you?"

"My name is Alex Powell. I'm a writer, and I'm doing a story on the history of the Nu Afrika Movement. I heard Malik has become kind of an expert on it, and I wanted to talk to him."

"I ain't him, but he stay here." He pushed back the hood, and I could see he was a handsome kid—maybe seventeen, eighteen. The gold watch shone in the setting sun. The glint around the neck, I now saw, came from a silver-looking chain with diamond chips on the links.

"Is he here now?" I asked.

"Naw. He over at his slave, in the mall. He work at the video game store. You can probably catch him if you go up there. They open till nine."

"Thanks a lot." I turned to go.

"Hey," he called out. "You want to sell that car? I bet I could get you good money for it. People like those real old BMWs. And that color's dope."

I smiled. "I like it, too—'cause it's paid for. But if I ever decide to sell it, I'll leave a note in your mailbox. What's your name?"

"Lequan."

"Thanks, Lequan. See you."

Something occurred to me. "Aren't you afraid to be left alone with Malik's dogs?"

Lequan looked at me like I was a total idiot.

"Naw. Me and Snoop, Nate, and Foxy, we unnerstand

each other. Ain't no problems with these dogs. Nobody don't bother them, they don't bother nobody. Want to see 'em?" He looked as if it might be fun to watch my reaction.

"Another time. I need to see if I can catch up with Malik before he gets off. Thanks again."

He waved, walked through the gate, and slammed it to make sure it was shut tight. Last I saw, he was walking around back to where the barking could still be heard.

The Baldwin Hills Crenshaw Plaza was supposed to be the revitalization of the old Crenshaw Mall, one of the first shopping malls in the country. The original had been built in the late forties. Ground had been broken for a three-story building of gleaming marble and a central atrium in the late 1980s. There were lots of speeches and articles about how this mall was going to keep the money in the gilded nearby neighborhoods of View Park, Baldwin Hills, Windsor Hills, and Ladera Heights "in the community"—never mind that it would still be going to largely white-owned chains. But nearly twenty years after the splashy opening, the mall had never become the community magnet developers had promised and local activists had hoped for.

Branches of national chain stores opened, just to close again a few years later. The variety that had once been envisioned for the mall—upscale clothing, bookstores, restaurants, and big department store anchors—had dwindled to what I was walking past now: a Korean-owned beauty supply store and a next-door beauty shop that did land-office business in weaves and manicures. Several plus-sized clothing stores for women. Two discount department stores. A Wal-Mart. A food court full of fast food. A bookstore that sold mostly black romances and fiction with titles that were mostly of the Urban Romance genre. Two jewelry stores that sold the kind of chains I saw on Lequan. And a large video-game store.

The people the mall was designed to lure in didn't usually stop there: they got in their nice cars and drove a few miles away, where the selections were better and more varied, the fibers natural, the merchandise crisp and not pawed over. Per usual, the people left to inherit the only partially leased mall were the people who could walk to it.

When I walked through the columns flanking the doorway to Phat Games, a loud bell dinged. A young Latino behind the counter looked up, and coolly cased my shoulder bag. Was it big enough to allow me to waltz out of there with a Game Boy or two? Apparently I didn't look like the type to be interested, because he returned to perusing *Nintendo Power*.

A door to the back opened and a young man came out dressed pretty much as Lequan had been. He spoke to the Latino.

"Hey, man, I put those extra Game Cubes up high, so don't forget they in there before you go ahead and order more."

"Whatever." The Latino kept reading.

The kid turned to me in exasperation. "He help you yet?"

"Actually, I was hoping to speak with you. Are you Malik Fereby?"

He squinted at me for a moment. "What if I am?"

"I'm Alex Powell. Your friend Lequan told me I might find you here tonight."

He sucked his teeth. "What you want me for?"

"I'm doing some research on a group that used to exist in Los Angeles, it was called the Nu Afrika Movement, and I heard you've become a real historian in that department. So I was hoping you might be able to fill me in." He relaxed visibly.

"What you want to know about Nu Afrika?"

"Well, I've been able to find out how it started, and who started it, but it's kind of a mystery why it broke apart. I'm wondering if you know anything you can share."

Malik puffed up. "Yeah, I can tell you some stuff. Hold up a minute." He turned to the guy still reading at the counter. "Alberto, I'm gonna take five, okay? I'll be right out there." He nodded at a mall-length planter with wide ledges that served as seating.

Alberto kept reading. "Whatever."

Malik rolled his eyes. "Pay attention, man, if a bunch of little kids come in here. They mess up all the displays, takes forever to put stuff back."

Alberto waved absently and kept reading.

We sat on the planter's ledge and watched Latino parents as they pumped quarters into the minirides lined up outside the beauty parlor: a helicopter that went up and down, a horse that went back and forth, and a train that shuddered from side to side. Over the mothers' cooing and the childrens' delighted screams, Malik began to talk.

"Nu Afrika was all about reclaiming our roots, speaking truth to power, and developing a black power base in L.A.— back when L.A. *had* some black people." He nodded in the direction of the rides and the un-black people clustered around them. "Samu el-Simba ran it, and when he talked, people listened."

"Did they stop listening?"

"Kind of. You know about the shooting?"

"Yeah, I picked that up in the library archives. Are you saying the shooting was a turning point?"

"I'm saying Samu el-Simba got fucked when that went down. There was this bunch of bourgie college niggas had been trying to organize the students at UCLA. Samu had been working with them first, but when this one smooth talker showed up, a lot of people switched to him."

"Personality thing?"

"Yeah. He was supposed to be like Denzel or something. Real good-looking, real forceful speaker. He was a Panther. They were into political stuff. Nu Afrika was into cultural-political stuff. Basically, they clashed over territory."

Sounded like a presidential convention, only with guns.

"Clashed enough that some people had to die?" We watched as two large women came out of Big 'n Gorgeous with full shopping bags, and walked down the hall to stop at the Fresh 'n Hot cookie counter. Special of the day was oatmeal chocolate chip.

"When you talk shit, you gots to be ready to back it up," he said simply.

"So you're saying Samu el-Simba was *provoked* into shooting those people?"

"Pretty much." He shrugged. "They was wolfin' at him, somebody pulled out a gun. Then somebody on the other side pulled out a gun, and it was on."

I watched as a gaggle of little boys cruised into Phat Games. Alberto never looked up.

"Seems like such a waste . . ."

"It *was* a waste," he agreed. "Lot of folks died. Black folks ain't been the same since that shootout. The bourgie nigga that died with everybody else was mourned like some kinda saint or something. His picture's up on a wall at UCLA."

"And Samu el-Simba?"

"Man, that nigga gave up a few years later. It's like black people broke his heart 'cause they didn't do right, so he just packed up and left L.A. Lives down in redneck country, with his redneck wife, and some horses." He looked at me, pained. "Can you believe that? He was a *hero* to black folk around here, and he went to Hee-Haw land and married Dolly Parton."

It was time to come clean.

"Actually, she seemed quite nice." His eyes widened in surprise. "I met her when I went down to Norco to look up your uncle. Who misses you, by the way. They both do."

Yeah, it was a lie, but it was a kind lie.

Malik shook his head, and the gold hoops in his ears swung.

"They don't miss me. I don't think they want to see me again after what happened."

"The dogs?"

He hung his head. "Yeah, their horse and their dog. It was an accident."

"Hard to control guard dogs like that," I pointed out, watching the hat lady cover her kiosk.

"I was new at it." He straightened up. "I know a lot more now. That would never happen now—unless I commanded them to do it. Not," he added hastily, "that I would."

Alberto was waving for Malik to come back. Just as he had said, the little boys had strewn stuff all over the place, and Alberto needed some help.

"Aw, no, *hell*, no!" Malik muttered. "I *told* him what would happen—didn't I say 'don't let no whole buncha little boys up in there, 'cause they'd trash the place?' " He blew his breath out in exasperation. "People *never listen*. Gotta go."

He got up and began to walk away.

"Malik?" He turned.

"Whatever happened to your dogs?"

He looked at me for a moment, and dipped his head. "They around. Why, you want a puppy? I can give you a good deal."

"You're breeding them?"

"Only Foxy. The puppies are real cute. I might keep one for myself."

"My landlord won't let me have a pet," I lied. "I brought one home, I'd get kicked out."

He nodded.

"Say hey to my uncle, you talk to him again. Tell him I'm doing a'right."

"Here at Phat Games?"

He shook his head. "That's just my day job. It pays the rent."

"So what are you doing that you think your uncle might be interested in?"

He paused, as if weighing his words, deciding how much to tell me.

"Let's just say I'm working to finish the work he started. He's gonna be proud."

Then he disappeared into Phat Games and started herding the ten-year-olds to the door. Alberto started picking up the mess.

Chapter Twenty-one

P aul's car was in the driveway when I got home. Inside, I discovered him rinsing off shrimp. Little bowls of chopped-up stuff were lined up on the counter, and a big pot of water was starting to boil on the stove. Next to it was a large, empty skillet.

"Hey," he said, coming to take the box from me. He bent to kiss me and stepped back quickly.

"Whew! Why do you smell like a barn?"

"Newfangled birth control," I told him, straight-faced.

"True, dat. For real, though, why *do* you stink? No offense . . ." He wrinkled his nose.

"None taken. I was *in* a barn for a good part of the day; that's why I smell like a horse."

Paul checked the stockpot. Still no boil, I guess.

"Actually," he said cheerfully, "you smell like a specific horse *byproduct*. Maybe you should leave your shoes outside."

"Wimp."

When I came back from depositing my shoes by the kitchen door, a cold glass of white wine was waiting on the counter for me.

"So, are you going to tell me about your adventures up and down the coast?" I asked, clinking glasses with him.

"Eventually," he promised. "It's still classified, until all the *i*'s are dotted, yada yada. But soon." I glared at him.

"Before I leave, Einstein, all will be clear. Meanwhile, about the eau de Mr. Ed . . ."

Clearly I wasn't going to get anywhere on the Mystery Mission, so I decided to cut my losses.

"All will be revealed over dinner—after my shower." I walked toward the bedroom, shedding horsey jeans, sweater, shirt, and socks.

"TAKE YOUR TIME!" he hollered, and went back to his pots and pans. Guess I was seriously stinky.

When I came out, twenty minutes later, the table was set, more wine had been poured, salad had been tossed and was awaiting homemade vinaigrette.

"Wow. You got skills."

"You haf no idea," he responded, arching his eyebrow like Claus von Bülow. "We're almost ready."

He swirled olive oil in the pan, and gently sautéed paper-thin garlic slices.

"Speaking of stink . . . we're gonna, if you put that much garlic in the dish," I pointed out.

"Not this way. There'll be just a hint of it in the sauce, and you won't taste it a couple of hours later. Promise."

"I'll be the judge of that, bub. You're doing a lot of promising tonight."

"Shut up and slice some bread. Make yourself useful."

"Yassuh."

In companionable silence, I sliced, he sautéed. The pasta went into the pot, the shrimp was added to the chopped tomatoes and garlic. He'd even swirled a couple of anchovies into the pan. I wasn't supposed to taste those, either.

Paul started to lift the linguine out of the pot with big tongs that had appeared from somewhere.

"Josefina lent them to me."

He dropped the wet linguine into the pan of sauce, and tossed it until everything was covered.

"I can feel you wondering from over there what's going on. Here's the deal, Einstein: if you put the pasta in with the sauce before the pasta is totally cooked, instead of absorbing water it absorbs what?"

"Sauce, Mr. Wizard."

"There ya go. Whyn't you bring me those bowls over there?"

The linguine went into the bowls, a few more shrimp were scattered around, and dinner was done.

And it was good. No, *excellent*. (And he was right: there was the barest hint of garlic, and I didn't taste the anchovies at all. Wonder how he did that?)

Over the meal, without interrupting, Paul listened as I explained how I'd found Samu el-Simba in Norco, how he'd changed, who he'd married, and how a visiting nephew had caused such bloody mayhem. When I got to the part about tracking down Malik's address and meeting Lequan, he put his fork down.

"Don't do that again," he said quietly.

"It was fine," I began, and he, uncharacteristically, cut me off.

"Maybe *this* time it was, but you make a mistake with dogs like that and you don't get a second chance. Anything could have happened. Promise me you won't put yourself in that position again."

I felt my face grow warm.

"It's my job, just like doing whatever it is you're doing is *your* job."

"Alex." He took a sip of wine and put his glass down very carefully. "If you were a war correspondent, it would be your job. If you were posted in any number of Third World cities where journalists are maimed or killed, it would be your job. It's *not* your job to find angry kids with lethal dogs. That's the *police*'s job."

"I wouldn't have had to if the police had been *doing* their job. That anonymous phone call I got on the voice mail tells me they aren't. So I should just sit by and let more people be killed, instead of getting those dogs off the street?"

Paul looked away for a moment, clenching and unclenching his jaw. Finally he said:

"It's not that I don't admire your tenacity—irritating as I sometimes find it—but you've lost sight of the main thing here, haven't you? You're supposed to be shedding light on who killed Simp Hastings and why. But you've allowed your-self to be sidetracked."

Now *I* was the one getting irritated.

"How do you know these deaths aren't connected? There's got to be a reason those dogs killed Nora Walker. And—"

"Stop! Listen to yourself. You're *still* sidetracked. Nora isn't the issue here, nasty as her death was. The issue is Simp. Do you see *any* way that they're connected? All I hear is about these dogs. And frankly, they might not even *be* the dogs you think they are. Every block in South L.A. has its own killer pit bull hidden away somewhere . . ."

"Sorry," I said stiffly. "I didn't realize you'd become such an expert on L.A. in such a short time." I rose. "Thanks for dinner. It was excellent. May I take your bowl?"

He looked at me for a moment. There was an uncom-fortable pause that neither of us made any move to fill. I waited with my plate in hand.

"Sure." He handed his over, and began to remove the salad bowl.

"I'll do that," I told him, probably more crisply than I'd intended. "He who cooks shall not clean, remember?"

He didn't smile. "In that case, I've got to go down to the bureau for a little. I shouldn't be too late."

"Tonight?"

"Has to be done before tomorrow morning, East Coast time. The overnight editor is in there, so there's no problem getting in." He gathered his laptop case and shrugged into his leather jacket.

"Probably better not to wait up for me," he said, over his shoulder.

The door was closed quietly before I could say anything in response.

I continued cleaning in silence. Was I wrong to press forward on the Nora connection? Was it merely a distraction? Or was there something underneath all the layers of . . . whatever that was slowly working itself to the surface, that would provide the link? I rolled it around and around my head, but no answer came. I figured things would happen in their own time.

My clothes had been run through the washer and the dryer. I'd tidied up and put everything away. It had been a long day and I didn't think I could stay up to check out the late news. Paul still hadn't returned. He must be good and mad.

The only other thing to do before going to bed was to check my e-mail. I'd put a forwarding mechanism on it yesterday before I left, so all today's mail would be delivered to my home box, just in case there was something that needed tending to before I got in tomorrow.

Thanks to the forwarding feature, my personal box was full. A lot of it was interoffice stuff that didn't much matter and could wait until tomorrow. A catch-up meeting with Fine in the late morning, deadline notification for those among us who thought we might get fellowships awarded in the next year. Reminders from building maintenance that parking spaces are first come, first served, not assigned, so people shouldn't get proprietary about their spots.

And an e-mail that said, "Re SIMP HASTINGS."
That caught my attention, as was intended.

Ms. Powell, I am a regular reader of your columns, and
a fan. And I have some pertinent information about Mr.
Hastings that might put things in a different perspective
for you. I wonder if you might be interested in meeting
for coffee sometime in the next few days? I cannot tell
you my name until we meet, and you must promise
to protect my confidentiality as a source, or there is no
point to our meeting, but I promise you if you can do
this, it will be worth your while. Please send your reply
to this mailbox, along with information on when and
where we should meet. I am in the general downtown
area, but can come to wherever you specify. With best
regards.

And that was all. No name. The reply went to VERITAS at a
common Internet service provider. I thought for a moment—
this wouldn't be like putting myself in danger with the dogs.
(And anyway, I hadn't promised, right?) This would be out
in public, in broad daylight, at a place of my choosing. Okay,
then:

Dear VERITAS: How about tea at the Biltmore at two-
thirty tomorrow afternoon? I will have a coral muffler
and a large brown tote bag. You will have to find me,
since I have no idea who you are or what you look like.

Your confidentiality will be assured. All best, Alex Powell.

I pushed the button and sent my message on.

Then, having done all I could do for one evening, I took a book of Anne Lamott's essays to bed, and read myself to sleep.

I woke when Paul slipped into bed.

"What time is it?" I whispered.

"Almost one-thirty. Go back to sleep," he urged.

"Your legs are cold." I snuggled up to him, and let him absorb the warmth of my body.

He turned to face me. "Einstein, about this evening—"

"I know, I was wrong."

"That's not what I was going to say." His now-warm body enveloped mine. "I was going to say you were right—you *do* have a job to do. But I worry about you sometimes."

"I know. I'll be careful."

He sighed. "No you won't. You'll *mean* to be, but you won't. So I hope you'll be lucky, because I don't want anything to happen to you."

That was so sweet!

"Because . . . do you have any idea how much trouble and expense it would take to break in a replacement?" he teased.

I bit him.

"*Ow!* That a trick you picked up from your dog excursion this afternoon?"

And again, but softer, "Ow!"

And softer, till there were only nibbles.

"I could get used to this," he breathed.

"You're lucky I have to get up early this morning," I growled softly.

"Really?" he asked, licking the side of my neck. "Or what?"

"Ooooo," I shuddered. "Or I'd get up and find the choke collar and chain I bought for you. I was saving it for your birthday."

He hollered with laughter. "Now, Einstein, let's see who makes whom sit up and beg first."

Jeez. For some people, *everything* is a competition.

Chapter Twenty-two

I arrived at the Biltmore with the promised coral scarf and brown tote bag. I'd told the hostess I was meeting someone, and needed a quiet table. She placed me practically in a potted palm on the perimeter of the area reserved for tea. For a moment I sat back and enjoyed watching the parade of people going through the lobby.

Because the dollar was at an all-time low in Europe, there were a lot of couples in the lobby speaking French and German. Italians—bronzed, casually elegant, and strung with fine gold chains—chatted away near the front doors, steaming to-go cups in hand, waiting for their car to pick them up, probably to take them shopping in places I couldn't afford. They stepped aside to let a quartet of meticulously dressed Japanese women through the doors. The group bowed to the hostess, who seated them diametrically opposite me, and produced long tea menus for each of them. I silently counted the myriad bags clustered around their chairs: Saks, Barneys,

Tracy Ross, Escada, Prada, Maxfield. These girls had blazed a path through West Hollywood and Beverly Hills in one day—no *wonder* they needed tea!

"It *is* a lot of shopping, isn't it?" a voice just behind me said. A man walked around the palm trees and held out his hand. "If you aren't Alex Powell, I will be horribly embarrassed."

He had a very cultivated voice, with the tiniest bit of a Southern drawl at the bottom of it.

"Mr. Veritas, I presume?"

He looked like a black thirties movie star—tall, slender, and café au lait, and dressed in what I guessed was a gray flannel suit that would have cost more than I was paid on any given week. Lustrous, hand-sewn oxfords, and a cashmere muffler of his own—gray and navy—thrown across his shoulders. He smiled widely, showing gorgeous teeth beneath his glossy moustache. "That would be me. May I?"

"Please." I indicated an empty seat. "I've already ordered tea, but no sandwiches. Would you like part of my Earl Grey, or would you rather have something else?"

The waiter appeared with a pot and my cup, turned before he reached our table and went back to the kitchen. He returned almost immediately with another cup and an extra spoon and napkin.

"Earl Gray would be fine, thank you."

The waiter poured, we gave our orders, and decided to add a glass of Champagne. It *was* approaching cocktail hour, after all.

"I'm glad you had them take the photograph of you out

of the paper," he said, staring at me frankly. "It didn't do you justice. You're much nicer-looking in person."

"Thanks," I said, laughing. "Actually, that wasn't my decision. The new editor decided the photos made us look a little more like the *Hooterville Gazette* and a little less like the *New York Times*, so we have him to thank for the absence of photos."

"Ah, the *New York Times*." Veritas laughed. "It sets the standard for everything, doesn't it?"

"Unfortunately, that's probably true."

The little plates of tea foods began arriving: cucumber sandwiches, open-faced whole wheat, thinly buttered, with salmon, delicate chicken salad on egg bread, scones, and tiny pastries.

Veritas and I oohed and aahed over the selection, then dug right in.

Then he wiped his moustache and placed his napkin on the table.

"This is the part in the book where I say, 'you're probably wondering why I called you here.'"

"And this is the part where I say, 'you're probably right.' Seriously, though, you have information on Simp Hastings?"

"I do, indeed. But before I tell it, you must reiterate your promise to keep my real name out of it."

"Is there a reason it would be inconvenient for your real name to be known, if what you're telling me is true?"

"There is, indeed, as you will see in the course of what I tell you." He took a sip of Champagne and began.

"My name is Herbert Marshall. I work for a large publishing house in New York that shall remain nameless for the moment, although a little digging could probably provide you with an accurate name. I am fairly high up on the editorial food chain. I have responsibilities in the acquisitions department. Where I happen to have received a book proposal from one J.S.L. Hastings."

"Ah, let me guess: the manuscript from the book that is supposed to out the social pretenders? That's not a secret. *Publishers Weekly* said it was going to be called Truly *Chosen People.*

He smiled thinly. "No, Ms. Powell, I'm talking about the *other* book, the one no one knows anything about, except me, and the president of the company, who had to sign off on its acquisition."

"He's writing two books at *once*? I thought publishers never allow that."

Herbert Marshall looked over the remaining pastries, picked a frosted brownie, and nibbled carefully. Then he dabbed his lips again.

"Normally, they do not. But this was a rather special case. He was actually doing research for both of them concurrently, and promised to write the second book first."

I looked at my Champagne glass. I had only had a few sips, but I simply could not follow this conversation.

"So, tell me again why they would allow him to do the second book first?"

He looked at me incredulously.

"Because they wanted it *more*. It was going to be a very explosive book."

"Nonfiction?"

"Yes."

"Are we going to play Twenty Questions on this, Mr. Marshall, or are you going to tell me why this particular book was going to cause such ripples?"

He leaned forward.

"*Ripples* will hardly describe what it was going to cause, Ms. Powell. Seismic reverberations would be more like it."

"One more time, Mr. Marshall: the book Simp Hastings was in the process of writing was about what?"

He paused for a moment for full effect. He really was a very handsome man, and you could tell he liked being admired. Then he told me what I'd come to hear:

"Let's just say his suggested title, the working title we used, was *DL: Undercover Brothers in America.*"

That was odd.

"He was writing about Down Low men? Why?"

And as soon as it was out of my mouth, it hit me: of *course* Simp Hastings was writing about Down Low brothers—he *was* one!

Herbert Marshall watched my ah-ha! expression with satisfaction.

"Exactly. Simp Hastings offered to do for Down Low brothers what he'd done for the gilded set in Negro society: name names, make connections, tell the provenance of certain people and things. All on the hush-hush, of course."

Another thought occurred to me.

"Did some of the names overlap? Were some of the Chosen also DL?"

"Go to the head of the class, Ms. Powell! That's exactly correct!"

"Wow. That *is* explosive information. If it's true. No offense."

"None taken." He reached into his oxblood satchel and pulled out a folder and handed it to me. "You may read it now, but I will have to leave with it, and I will have to ask you to refrain from repeating what you read here, which is, of course, highly confidential."

"Of course."

"Then please." He gestured for me to open it and read.

It was a shocking chronicle of visits to several major cities throughout the country. By day, Simp would sit in the salons of the black elite and record their family histories, and pore through private documents and photographs for possible inclusion in *Truly Chosen*, or whatever it was going to be called. But at night, after leaving his host families' dinner tables, things were quite different. There were meetings with married bankers at underground discos, quick furtive sex with professional athletes in their hotel rooms, a tryst with the head of oncology at one of the country's most prestigious cancer centers. And an on-again, off-again affair with one of the nation's most visible talk show hosts.

All successful black men. All married or universally seen as eligible bachelors who appeared in the social columns of several papers around the country, always with an adoring woman in tow.

I looked at Herbert Marshall, who looked grim.

"Wives and girlfriends are sleeping with these men. Some will get infected and some will die," I pointed out.

"Which is exactly why Simp was writing *DL*—he wanted women out there to know that what you see isn't always what you get. He was hoping some lives were going to be saved."

"What about his fiancée? Was he planning to save her life by telling her?"

Herbert Marshall squirmed a bit.

"We had a couple of conversations about this. He went back and forth about it. At one point, he was going to tell her immediately. Then he decided to tell her before publication, in case she wanted out of the relationship. But as time went on, I think it was harder for him to consider outing himself. He was very attached to the prestige of the Howe family, and he was starting to think maybe he could have it both ways . . . and of course he couldn't."

"Did he do a lot of this . . . screwing around, do you know?"

Marshall looked at me squarely. "Let's just say he was known in certain circles. But he restricted himself to DL circles, which meant his secret was safe—because they wanted *their* secrets to be kept, too."

Hmmm. "How far was he from being finished with the book?"

I reluctantly handed back the folder, which Herbert Marshall quickly took and returned to its safe place in his satchel.

"That's the interesting thing. We don't really know. He sent the proposal and the synopsis you just saw. He was writing from the road, whenever he was on the road. But it all went onto a small flash drive—one of those little memory-stick things—and it would seem that the drive has just disappeared."

"Maybe it just hasn't turned up yet?"

"No. I actually visited his fiancée's family to express condolences and to tell them that he was working on a book for us, and wondered if they'd seen the flash drive, or if it had been among his returned effects. It wasn't. Which they were sorry to hear about, because it would have meant we could have published posthumously."

"They couldn't have meant that if they'd known what he was writing," I said.

"True. The president of my publishing house and I are going to have a discussion about how to break that news when I return. The fiancée should be tested immediately."

"Because Simp was DL?"

"Because he was DL *and* HIV positive."

Holy shit. If the Champagne had provided an iota of a pleasant buzz, it was gone now.

"And how would you know that, Mr. Marshall?"

"One of the people he did was my stylist, who has been positive for quite a long while. He takes good care of himself, but he says he was diagnosed three years ago, after several encounters with Simp Hastings. I didn't realize they knew each other until I came in one day with a manuscript for *Truly Chosen People* and he told me the story of how they met. Somebody's bachelor party in Atlanta. Where things were, as Honoré—"

"Honoré?"

"The stylist. Mother named him after Balzac. Don't ask why. Anyway, Honoré says at the party, things got *beyond* totally out of control. He abandoned his normal insistence on a condom. He wanted to be with Simp. And Simp liked it raw."

"Did Simp *know* he was HIV positive?"

"Honoré says not. He says they were both shocked, none more than Simp. He kept saying, 'I only do this every now and then.'"

"I guess it's like pregnancy—it only takes once."

"True, if it's the right time. I think he decided to become a circuit rider for the DL cause after his diagnosis."

The waiter arrived with the bill and before I could pick it up it was Herbert Marshall signed the check—apparently he was staying at the hotel—and the waiter disappeared.

"The HIV will be released with the coroner's report, won't it?" I mused.

"Probably so, although my guess is they'll delay release until Dr. Howe has been notified."

Boy, I would not want to be the person to have to make *that* call.

Poor Sheila Howe. She'd already lost a fiancé and had her life turned upside down. Now, just when she thought things couldn't get any worse, apparently they were going to.

Herbert Marshall interrupted my chain of thought, though.

"Ms. Powell, there is another L.A. name on that list that you apparently overlooked. It could be part of the answer you're seeking. Would you like a last glance at my folder?"

I had been mentally going down the list, I'd hastily checked, so I nodded.

There it was again, a roster of the black who's who in entertainment, business, sports, and other arenas, all DL:

Several players from the NBA and the NFL.
Dean of an Ivy League law school.
A famous talking head on the Sunday news shows.
A velvet-voiced soul singer.
A graffiti artist whose hectic paintings, especially in the years since his death, commanded millions at auction.
A morning talk show host.
And Hiram Walker.

He was nestled between the NFL tight end and the talk show host, two names that, even on paper, were so famous I'd focused on them to the exclusion of the name I knew. *Hiram Walker*. That explained a lot.

I handed back the folder and looked at Herbert Marshall.

"Six degrees of separation."

"Or less," he agreed. "So you see why I have made you privy to this information: it's important to me that black men stop killing each other and their families this way." He tapped the folder. "This is the message. But it will take months, *years*, to get all this through Legal, especially since there's some question as to who Simp Hastings's beneficiaries really are at this point. His immediate family are all deceased, and he changed his will a lot."

"So the message is lost until a bunch of lawyers okay it—"

"Not necessarily. This is the message, but *you* can be the messenger, Ms. Powell, if you're brave enough. I suspect you are. Please don't disappoint me. You may reveal my name to your editor and publisher if you must—and even that involves risk—but other than that, I need to be kept out of this story."

"Except by anonymous mention."

"Exactly."

He picked up his bag. "I'm back in New York tomorrow night. Here are my numbers." He handed me a personal card with nothing but his name on it, and two sets of numbers inked in below them. "Home and cell. Call if you need to. Thanks for your time."

I watched him walk toward the hotel's bank of brass elevator doors, which opened and swallowed him up. Two seconds and it was as if he'd never been there at all.

Kwaku Halstead had been right: people don't like it when you mess in their business. And when you publicize their business, that's even worse.

Discovering Simp's double book had just widened the possibilities of who'd killed him by . . . well, at least by as many people as were on that list.

Chapter Twenty-three

I left the hotel for a hasty conference with Fine, who, after hearing my information, sighed and called the publisher to ask if we could come up and see him.

"Don't bother. I'm on my way down anyway, I'll stop and see you all," he told us. That's one of the reasons I like him—he's not hung up on titles, statusy stuff: if he's in the nabe, he'll come to you, instead of making you haul yourself up to his place. They should clone him, to make some editors I know act more like him. Very different from his predecessor.

After the three of us talked, they decided we could honor Herbert Marshall's confidentiality and use him in a story if one of the principals independently confirmed the information about them that he had. It would be my job to find them.

"I will be in and out for the next couple of days," I told Fine. "I'll probably have to chase a few folks. But I'll check in."

"Keep your cell on," he instructed, as I left his office. "And Powell . . ."

"Yes?"

"Good work. Be careful out there."

I smiled. "You sound like my . . . like a friend." No sense in putting Paul in all this.

He grunted. "Then maybe you should listen to one of us."

"Maybe I might."

It didn't take me long to get to Hiram Walker's offices. He'd started out in a small place in Leimert Park with a partner. They ran Speed-Walker. But the Speed part of the partnership eventually left for a larger firm, and the business became the Walker Group. Hiram had flourished doing a combination of edgy commercial projects—most of them municipal buildings or other city commissions—and a few high-profile residential clients. The home he had designed for one of the best-known Los Angeles Lakers had been photographed for numerous high-end shelter magazines and had been variously described as "daring," "groundbreaking," and, in one case, "joyously innovative."

Somehow, he and Myron Bournewell had become friendly, and the older man had brought Walker in on a couple of collaborative projects. Since then, Walker's business had gotten even larger, and he'd moved from Leimert Park to a tall building sheathed in copper-tinted mirrored glass. It loomed above the intersection of Wilshire and San Vincente, a little east of Beverly Hills.

Hiram Walker's office suite was on the eighth floor, and looked out over the San Vincente side of the street. A pretty receptionist sat before a blond wood half-circle of a desk and fielded calls. And guarded the firm's principal from unexpected visitors.

"Is Mr. Walker expecting you?" she asked sweetly, after I identified myself.

"He's not, but it's quite important. Please ask him to take a moment," I told her, and gave her my card.

She excused herself and went down the hall to see what he wanted her to do about me. The answer became obvious in about twenty seconds, when she returned, slightly flushed.

"I'm sorry. Mr. Walker has a full day, and he just can't see you today."

Okay, time to play hardball.

"Please suggest to him that it will certainly be much easier for him to see me for a few moments now than to read what I will write about him in the paper tomorrow morning if he doesn't. If you tell him that, and he has no interest in contributing to a story about himself, or participating in fact-checking, I'll leave immediately."

She stared at me, slightly dumbfounded, turned, and went back down the hall again.

But this time the results were, as I expected, different.

"Mr. Walker will see you, for just a moment," she conceded. "Please follow me."

She did the walk a third time and made sure I was following her down the hall.

The white walls were hung at even intervals with stark black-and-white photos of some of the Walker Group's projects.

"Here we are." The receptionist opened the door and stepped through.

"Ms. Powell is here, Mr. Walker," she announced.

"Thank you, Yvette. You may return in five minutes to escort her out."

He was seated, and did not rise to meet me, which was probably supposed to indicate displeasure. Hiram Walker sat behind his large blond wood desk, which had an almost completely clean top, save for a huge brushed-stainless lamp with a sweeping arc of an arm, a small steel clock, and a frosted silicone pad that apparently was used instead of an ink blotter. Next to the visitor's chair opposite the desk was a glass table with a large charcoal pottery vase; it contained tall branches of a flowering fruit tree—quince or plum, maybe—in full bloom.

"Clock's ticking," he reminded me, pointing to the small clock on his desk. "You can spend it quizzing me or critiquing my décor, your choice, but in five minutes, you're gone."

"May I?" I gestured to the chair.

"Whatever. You can do your five minutes sitting or standing, doesn't matter to me."

"But in five minutes I'm out, right?"

He nodded silently.

"Then I will have to be more blunt than I would be if time weren't tight. Again, I am sorry for your loss; I understand your wife, Nora, was a wonderful woman, held in high esteem by a number of people around the city."

He nodded. "I'm sure you didn't need to burst in here to

force me to confirm that for your article." Hostility crackled around him like a force field.

"You're right. But she's part of why I needed to see you."

He waited, unyielding, silent.

I knew my time was almost up. I had to move quickly.

"When Simp Hastings died, he was writing another book."

"He's always writing. He's a *writer*, Ms. Powell. That's what writers do." He rocked gently in his ergonomic leather chair.

One minute forty-five seconds to go.

"Your name was in it." The rocking stopped.

"It was a book about men with whom he had had sexual relations over the past few years. And before you waste what little time I have left denying it, I should just say these words to you: 'Atlanta, three years ago, bachelor party, Ritz Carlton, off the hook.'" It was a guess, but since a lot of prominent black men had been at that party, according to Herbert Marshall's recap of his conversation with his hairstylist, it was eminently probable.

Apparently I was right. Hiram Walker sat stock-still. Then he leaned forward and picked up the phone.

"Yvette, Ms. Powell will be here a while longer. I'll walk her out when she's done."

He quietly replaced the receiver and looked at me; the hostility had been replaced with a weariness that made him look ten years older.

"Who told you?" he asked, running his hand over closely cropped hair.

"A guest at the same party. This person had an on-again,

off-again relationship with Simp for a few years." That was stretching it, but I knew if I contacted Honoré, he would tell the truth; Honoré was not DL, he was unapologetically gay. "Want to tell me what happened?"

He shrugged. "The usual. As you said, it was a bachelor party. The groom was a good friend; we'd all gone to Morehouse together. The bride had been a few classes behind us at Spelman. Big, proud Southern families. Marrying two dynasties together, reunion of the old elite, blah blah blah."

"The groom was marrying her even though he was gay?"

"He wasn't *gay*," Hiram Walker snapped. "The thing with guys was every now and then. It was a preference thing. His *central* preference was women. And he loved the woman he was marrying."

"Then would it be fair to call him bisexual?"

"No, it would *not* be 'fair to call him bisexual,'" Walker mimicked me. "It would be fair to call him occasionally eclectic in his sexual tastes."

"And what about you, Mr. Walker? Are you *also* 'occasionally eclectic in your sexual tastes,' or are you accepting the reality that you're Down Low?"

Walker got up and began to pace.

"This is *ridiculous*. If we were Victorians, we wouldn't even be having this conversation!" he raged.

"True—for a number of reasons. One being the fact that HIV and AIDS did not exist during the Victorian era. It's about more than manners, Mr. Walker. And it's about more than privacy."

"What *is* it with the media and privacy, can you tell me that? Why are you people so committed to prying into every nook and cranny of people's private lives?"

He stopped directly before me and loomed over me. I wasn't worried for my safety, but I have to say his agitation did register on me. I stood to be closer to eye level with him, and he backed up, as I'd hoped he would.

"When it's your private life and it impacts no one else, I'd have to say you're absolutely right. In your case, though, Mr. Walker, your private life and your unwillingness to be honest about it might have tremendous impact on someone else's life."

"How so?" He crossed his arms.

"How long have you been HIV positive, Mr. Walker? And when were you going to tell your wife?"

Tears came to his eyes. He hesitated for a long moment, then spoke.

"She knew. We'd actually fought about it that morning. The morning she died. I broke the news to her the night before Myron's services."

"So she was upset?"

He looked at me with disgust.

"Wouldn't you be, if you were in her position, Ms. Powell?"

There was a timid knock at the door. He answered with none of his customary courtesy.

"*What?*"

The door opened and a very reluctant Yvette popped her head in.

"Mr. Walker, your five o'clock with Ryson Construction is here."

"Reschedule it, Yvette."

"But they've come down from Sacramento and—"

"*Reschedule*, please, Yvette. Tell them . . . whatever. I just can't see them right now."

She nodded, hurt that he'd screamed at her, but still protective.

"I'll tell them you have a family emergency," she whispered.

He looked at me.

"Apparently I do, so that's exactly true. Thanks, Yvette. And sorry."

She nodded and the door clicked softly.

"What else do you want to know?"

"Mrs. Walker suspected she'd been infected, didn't she?"

His shoulders slumped.

"She did. It's why she had the early A.M. appointment at the doctor's. Testing."

I was surprised.

"So she didn't know she was pregnant when she went off to see Leslie Seaver-Smith?"

"As far as I know, she got the last-minute appointment because of the blood test. I think her doctor did the pregnancy test almost as an afterthought. Just in case."

Something was percolating up to the forefront of my consciousness. I flailed at it, hoping to grasp whatever it was, because I knew once I left Hiram Walker's office I would not be allowed back in, ever. I made small talk, stalling for time.

"This has nothing to do with what we were just discussing—it's plain curiosity and feel free to tell me to mind my own business if you want."

He smiled bitterly. "Why start now? It hasn't worked so far . . ."

I smiled back, tentatively.

"Did your parents name you after whiskey on purpose?"

He actually laughed aloud.

"Hiram was my father's name. One of his relatives on his mother's side had the last name Hiram. You know how it is when they hand names down. So my father became Hiram Walker, named by teetotaling Presbyterians who knew nothing about drink and had no idea there is a famous whiskey with the same name. My people are from Yellow Springs, Ohio, Ms. Powell. It was a stop on the Underground Railroad. Preacher country. Nobody knew squat about liquor."

"*Then,* maybe, but what about when you were born?"

"By then, they were used to it, and my father wanted his son named for him. So I became Hiram Richard Walker Junior." He paused for a moment. "And my son, had he been born, would have been Hiram Walker the third."

We listened to the rush-hour traffic below on San Vincente.

The traffic reminded me of another building on another busy street. One in which traffic had been snared and held up and then diverted for hours because a despondent man had sailed over his penthouse balcony. Another piece of the puzzle clicked into its space.

"You and Myron Bournewell were very close."

"He was like an older brother, or a young uncle, take your pick. A great man."

"A great man who was perhaps also DL?"

Hiram Walker looked at me calmly.

"You'll never prove it. There is no biological evidence to support that. And if I read that in your paper tomorrow, I will encourage Lydia to sue it—and you."

"That's why she cremated him at the last minute, isn't it? Not because he was a suicide, and they didn't want him buried as one, but so the DNA would be destroyed, which cremation would have done."

"It was Lydia's decision."

"Is Lydia HIV positive, too?"

He rose and went to the door, and opened it.

"You'll have to ask her yourself. If she'll deign to speak with you."

"She did the last time."

"The last time, Ms. Powell, you were praising her husband. This time, you're trying to bury him."

Let the dead bury their dead. Isn't that what Samuel Johnson had warned me to do?

Chapter Twenty-four

Simp Hastings seemed to be the genesis of it all, the hub from which everything radiated: Simp and Hiram, briefly, led to Nora Walker's infection. Hiram, infected from Simp, had probably passed HIV on to Myron Bournewell. Lenora had been infected—what about Lydia? And was that why she insisted on cremating him?

As I drove down through heavy traffic, down Wilshire toward home, I pondered all the interconnections. And wondered whether Lydia Bournewell would speak with me.

My house was dark and empty when I got in. Paul wouldn't get here till later. I saw the message machine glowing across the room, and, after dumping my bag, I went over to pick it up.

There were two. The first was Paul, saying he'd be home "eightish. Don't wait if you're hungry. If you can wait, I'll take you to dinner someplace close by. You choose. Just as long as nobody anywhere we go has a six-pack or looks like LL Cool J."

Bummer. It would have been great to go back to G Garvin's again.

The second message was a surprise:

"Miss Powell, this is Martha Dexter. We met last week; I'm Sheila Howe's great-aunt. I have something of some urgency I would like to discuss with you. Please call me sometime after seven this evening. Here's the number once more . . ."

Interesting. Did that mean Hiram Walker had called the Howes to warn them I was asking around? I looked at the clock. Too soon to call her back, but I could make a couple of calls in the interim.

The first was down to Norco, to Samuel and Angela Johnson. When he picked up, I filled him in on the fact that I'd found his nephew, and the gist of our conversation. His dogs were still with him. "In fact, he's breeding one of them, so there will be more. I don't want to turn him in to the police, but I don't want to leave his dogs to wander around and terrorize their neighborhood—or someone else's. Especially if they are the dogs that, as I suspect, killed Nora Walker. The police need to know where they are, and that they won't attack anyone else again. Which probably means destroying them. Would you rather talk with him, or should I go the official route?"

Samuel Johnson sighed heavily. "No, I'll do it. Just give me his home and work addresses. I hate that it's gotten to this. I'd like to think that if his mama were still alive, it wouldn't have, but you never know."

"What will you do if he doesn't listen?" I asked.

"Oh, you'd best believe he'll be listening. Not listening is not an option." The rumbly bass held echoes of Samu el-Simba's authoritarian tones. I hoped he was right, and asked him to follow up and let me know what he found out.

I had a bit more time, so I made the call I'd been procrastinating about. I called Lydia Bournewell.

"Mrs. Bournewell, this is Alex Powell, at the *Standard*," I began.

"Yes, Alex. How are you, dear? And thank you for that lovely piece on Myron and his memorial service. It really made him seem very three-dimensional."

"I'm glad you think it sounded like the Myron Bournewell you knew. And I'm sorry to have to call you when I'm sure you're still recovering from all the stress of the past several days, but—"

"It's all right, Alex." She cut me off neatly. "I suspected you might call. I spoke with Hiram not long ago."

"Then you know I wanted to ask you about . . . would you rather I come and see you and have this conversation?"

It had been a full day and I was tired, but it seemed strange talking about Myron Bournewell's sex life over the phone with his widow.

"No, this is fine. I'm actually going out in a few moments. But I don't mind talking with you before then. You are, of course, calling to inform me that my husband was bisexual.

But that presumes this is something I didn't know before your call."

"You *knew*?" I blurted.

"I learned as a young bride, Alex, that Myron had some needs that I could not satisfy as his wife. Was I upset when I discovered he'd neglected to tell me this? Of course. Was I ready to destroy our entire marriage because of it? In the beginning, I wasn't sure."

"How did you make your mind up?"

"I talked with my rabbi, believe it or not. I would not have expected him to be very sympathetic—this was back in the sixties, you know—but he was quite . . . progressive. What he said to me was this: do you love him? Do you have a good life with him? Would your life be better if he weren't in it? And as soon as I heard those questions, I realized my answers were yes, yes, and no."

"Yes, you loved him, yes, he loved you, and no, your life would not be better without him?"

"Exactly. Long-term marriage is a marathon, not a sprint, Alex, and I was in it for the long term."

"Didn't you worry that he might eventually decide to come out completely, Mrs. Bournewell?"

She paused.

"I didn't. I knew Myron loved being married, loved being a father to our children, as much as he loved being an architect. We had a very fulfilling life, for a very long time. And I think we were able to do that within the parameters we drew for ourselves."

"Parameters?"

"When I came back from the rabbi, I told Myron I could stay with him, happily, under three conditions: his dalliances had to be occasional and discreet—our friends, our community must never know about his other life. And I don't think they ever did."

"You said three conditions . . ."

"Yes. The other two were this: no disease. And if he ever fell in love with someone who wasn't me, he had to be honest about that immediately."

I pondered her conditions.

"That was it?"

"That was everything. And it worked just fine. Until recently."

"He was mentoring Hiram Walker and became involved beyond mentoring?"

She sighed. "Yes. I knew they were fond of each other, but there did not seem to be any sexual electricity between them. Not that *I* perceived, anyway. You know how it feels being in a room with two people who should not be attracted to each other—for whatever the reason—but are? I didn't get that with Myron and Hiram. They were just good friends."

"Except apparently they were more than that . . ."

She sighed again. "Apparently so."

How to put this? There probably wasn't a delicate way.

"Mrs. Bournewell, Hiram Walker had just informed your husband he was HIV positive, and had urged your husband to be tested immediately. Did he tell you?"

Silence. Then: "Of course, Alex. He told me nearly everything. And he wanted me to be tested, too."

"Have you been?"

"We both were. I am negative, for now, at least."

"Do your children know?"

"I told them after their father was cremated. They agreed with my decision. They're shaken, of course, but they've been very supportive."

There wasn't very much else to say. I thanked her for her time and cooperation, and a disturbing thought occurred to me.

"Mrs. Bournewell, you sound fine, but so self-possessed, that under the circumstances, I'm worried about you." I heard a doorbell chime in the background.

"That will be Celeste. We're going to dinner in the neighborhood. And thank you, but don't worry about me, Alex. I'm not a candidate for suicide. After what happened to Myron, I would never do the same thing to my children. I plan to be here for a long time. And I believe my friends will be as good friends to me as I have been to them. You come check on me in a month, and see if I'm not right."

I hope she was, for her sake. For all their sakes.

It was seven-thirty, and I called the Howe residence. A frail female voice spoke at the other end.

"Ah, Miss Powell. Martha Dexter here. I have something I'd like to discuss with you, but it's very delicate, and I would not like to do it over the phone." She paused, and waited for me to offer to come up, which she was obviously expecting me to do.

"If you like, I can come see you now for a few moments, but it will take about a half hour to get there," I began.

"I'm old," she said flatly. "I don't know if anybody has told you this, but we old people don't sleep much. I'll be up."

"Then I'll plan to see you somewhere between eight and eight-thirty."

"Very good."

I made a pit stop, then ran a brush through my hair and hit my cheeks with a bit of blush—I was so pale that it looked as if I were coming down with something. Maybe I was.

After I left a quick note for Paul about where I was going to be, I put on the alarm, locked the door, and headed north and east, toward Los Feliz, and whatever Martha Dexter was choosing to share. Driving through the mist—it had been a warm day, but the temperature had dropped fairly suddenly, wreathing the streets in a very British fog—I wondered which tack the old lady was going to take: coercion or intimidation? Whatever it was, I was betting Martha Dexter, doyenne of the Howe family, was not going to permit anyone to sully the family name she was so proud of, even if life and death hung in the balance, as it might for Sheila Howe and others who could have been infected by Simp Hastings.

Chapter Twenty-five

The roads became foggier and foggier as I wound my way up Western Avenue to Los Feliz Boulevard. The old-fashioned street lamps were haloed by milky rings of reflected light. Here and there, on the boulevard, a lone jogger huffed silently by, or a couple walked their dog. But the streets were mostly empty.

I'd used my cell phone as my poor girl's GPS: before I left, I'd just given myself a memo about where I needed to turn. I had set the phone on speaker, so I could hear quite adequately as I passed all the ersatz Tudors, Taras, and Frank Lloyd Wrights. Soon enough, I'd arrived at 4404 Barbary Lane.

I made my way to the glossy front door and rang the bell. It seemed like an exercise more than anything else. The porch lights were on, as were the floodlights on the lawn. But the front windows were dark, and the driveway was empty. I rang several times, but there was no answer. Maybe Martha Dexter had gone to sleep?

I heard the wolfish bark of a good-sized dog. It was answered by other dogs in the neighborhood—the doggy version of CNN. What did they call it in the 101 Dalmations? The Twilight Bark. After a few moments, I turned away and began walking back to my car. Then I heard my name being called.

"Miss Powell? Is that you?"

The doorway was still dark, but something ghostly hovered near the slight space between the doorframe and the door. A jeweled hand beckoned. "Come."

I cautiously walked closer, then saw it was Martha Dexter. She hadn't gone to bed after all, although she looked as if she were on her way. She was dressed in a silk lounging robe and her hair, as usual, was pulled back to the nape of her neck in its customary bun.

"I don't like opening the door at night unless I know who is out there," she apologized.

"I didn't think anyone was here. Are you by yourself this evening?"

"Yes." She nodded. "My niece and her husband went to the movies. They just wanted to do something normal for a moment. Come in."

The Howe home, without its mood lighting and the usual in and out of family and employees, seemed eerie, desolate even. I could hear the spring wind whipping in and out of the magnolias on the front lawn. The branches of the willows at the side of the house flailed back and forth with a brisk snapping sound, like an advertisement for a particularly bad punishment.

The glossy foyer reflected light from rooms in the back of the house; the dark floor glistened like a shallow pool.

"Let's go to the back; it's warm back there."

Martha Dexter turned and I followed.

She was right. The living room glowed with flattering apricot light from the many low-wattage bulbs in lamps scattered throughout the room. On the far wall, a fire blazed merrily in the hearth. The day's *Standard* lay open on a comfortable chair. Martha Dexter went over, folded it neatly, and placed it in a willow basket with some other papers. Then she turned to me.

"Shall we have some tea? It's Dolores's day off, but I'm sure I remember how to dip a tea bag into a pot of hot water. Not that this would be *proper* tea, of course, but it will do in a pinch . . ."

I don't know why being alone with Martha Dexter was so unsettling, but it was. Maybe it was the quiet. But I didn't think so; it had been quiet when I first visited.

I watched the old lady move some things aside on the coffee table to make room for the teapot. She left and quickly returned with a box of cookies and glass teapot, the kind with a glass infuser, so you can see how strong your brew is getting. Two mugs were on the tray, and a pot of honey.

"Phyllis is normally more formal with company, but it's just us two and they're not home. You won't tell, will you?" She winked.

And that's when I figured it out. Martha Dexter was being suspiciously . . . *nice*. She'd been snappish and aloof the first time I'd met her. Very Negro Grande Dame. Could she have been putting on airs for her lofty relatives? Did she want something? Both?

"If I remember correctly, you take honey, but no milk?"

"You have a good memory."

"This is special honey," she said, spooning it into the bottom of my cup before pouring the tea on top. "We have an old family friend up in Santa Rosa who decided to become a beekeeper after her husband died. Now she sells honey to all the fancy places up and down the California coast. She says she never would have guessed that her hobby would secure her retirement. This one is scented with fruit and Santa Rosa lavender, as is the tea." She pointed to the tiny lavender buds blossoming in the infuser.

I brought the mug to my nose. The sunny smell of Provençal fields wafted up. Martha Dexter took a deep draught of hers, too. Then she settled back and looked at me.

"I hear from various people you have been asking around town for the past few days about things that might affect my family. What do you want to know?"

Guess the girlfriend-bonding time was over.

"Well, as you know, I have been trying to figure out whether these deaths actually have a connection we just hadn't picked up on yet."

Her eyes glinted. "And do they? Do you now know who killed our Jamie?"

"Well, I don't know if I do. We have James, who obviously died of exsanguination from a wound to the neck—"

"That would be loss of blood?"

"Yes. And Myron Bournewell, who didn't know Simp—uh, James—at all, and died from a fall from a tall building."

"He committed suicide, from all reports."

"Indicators point to that, yes."

"And how would this be related, please, to James's death?"

"Simp—Jamie, sorry—knew them both. He and Hiram were both Morehouse undergrads. Apparently, they were quite, um, friendly. Which, until yesterday, was something I'd never heard."

"Well, of course not." She sipped more tea and looked at me calmly. "You didn't know them socially."

Ah, the *real* Aunt Martha had returned. The one who subtly or not so reminded the rest of us who counted and who didn't.

"Did you know Nora Walker, as well?"

"Not really. We knew nothing of her family before Hiram. She married up."

And another piece of the puzzle fell into place: who is more preoccupied with his rung on status's ladder than he who has last arrived? I don't remember who said that, but it could account for a lot. And I remembered something Aunt Edith had told me about Martha Dexter over dinner in Westwood.

"No disrespect, but from what I understand, Mrs. Dexter, you'd know a little bit about marrying up, wouldn't you?"

Instead of sputtering in denial, Martha Dexter smiled slightly. "Ah, so you *have* done your homework, Miss Powell. Yes, there's no point in denying it. I did, indeed, come from a very modest background. My parents worked hard for a living. They wanted us to have a better life, of course, as did most Negro parents of a certain type. Back then, middle class was not just money—it was aspiration, values. Things that seem not to be valued today." She took another sip of tea. As did I. It was good, and I hoped it would combat the scratchy-throat feeling I was starting to get. A little light-headedness told me I'd been stupid not to eat something quickly before I came. There had been no lunch, and tea with Herbert Marshall seemed hours ago, although now it was only a bit before nine.

Martha Dexter continued with the family saga:

"At any rate, my husband came from a more elevated background than I, but he had little ambition. He wanted to spend his life doing good works—whether or not he was paid to do them. I was not his family's first choice for a spouse, but the Howes are pragmatists. They realized I'd be good for him—and them. When we married, I promised his mother that I would see that he always kept his eyes on the prize and made sure the family name was upheld. I managed to do that quite successfully." She looked at me squarely. "Until this year."

"You didn't approve of Jamie?"

She shook her head: *no.*

"I told Sheila women marry later and later these days.

She is ambivalent about having children, so it's not as if she felt the biological urgency. Given that, she would have made a wonderful second wife for an important corporate man—someone who is divorced or widowed, preferably someone whose children were grown or at least out of the house. She could have made a brilliant match with someone from our crowd, someone who graced the pages of *Forbes* and the *New York Times* with regularity. Someone like that nice young man who heads American Express—"

"He's quite married," I interjected.

"I said someone *like* him," she clarified impatiently. "Anyway, wives sometimes die, or go off with other, *more* powerful men." Hard to see how a sister could have done better than American Express's CEO, but you never know.

"But Jamie Hastings was Sheila's choice."

Her great-aunt sighed in exasperation. "Apparently so."

I was wishing a window could be cracked. The room had gone from comfortingly warm to almost uncomfortably warm. I loosened a few buttons of my sweater and pushed the sleeves up.

"Are you too warm, Miss Powell? I can see if I can work the thermostat. I'm always cold in this house, so it's probably turned up too high . . ." She made as if to rise.

"No, I'm fine, really. Do please go on. You were saying you didn't understand why Sheila was attracted to Simp, uh, Jamie?"

"I was, wasn't I? Well, just between us, she far outshone him in achievements, didn't she? Came from a much more distinguished family. And was flourishing in a *noncontrover-sial* career."

So unlike Jamie's, was the unspoken finish.

"People are upset by his book and lectures, aren't they?" I asked.

"By that, and other things."

"Such as?"

"Let's start with the fact that he's a fraud. All this talk about who's who and 'our crowd'—his *real* background is a glorified version of his public self. The summer home he goes on and on about? It was *rented.* The coming-out party for his sister about which he writes so glowingly? Done with borrowed money and sponsors—*sponsors!*—just like an ad in *Ebony.* My family may have put its best face forward, but that did not include pretending to be something we were not. Do you know when she came out, his parents had to *bribe* her escort?"

So the rumors were true. Penelope Hastings's much talked-about debut—the swimming pool filled with Champagne, the small sterling frames from Cartier handed out as souvenirs, the A-list photographer who chronicled the white debuts for the *New York Times* society pages—had been paid for with borrowed money, underwritten by her father's ad-sales connections to liquor importers, hotels, and society caterers. That put a different spin on the cover of his book, of the happy nuclear family in formal dress at one of the many cotillion events Penelope Hastings attended. And now she, and her parents, were all dead of cancer. So Simp was fine to reinvent his past.

"What'd they bribe the escort *with*?"

"Job possibilities. Apparently, James the elder knew a lot of people with business connections that an up-and-coming young man might find useful. Just as the young white men get their internships and mentorships, his daughter's escort was going to have access to that, as well."

"But wait—if he *was* her escort, wouldn't he have had access to that anyway? It's not as if just anybody can show up to these things . . . everyone is vetted six ways from Sunday. Or they were, back then."

Martha Dexter gave me an approving glance. After all, I had done my homework.

"True enough. And if a *truly* distinguished family's daughter had been coming out, he hardly would have been asked to be her escort. But what passes for distinguished families today isn't what it was a few generations ago. The haute is much less so in today's haute black bourgeoisie. This boy was good-looking, polite, and, most important, there was no scandal attached to his family's name. So it didn't matter that the father had made his money recently, through a chain of fried-chicken franchises. Or let us say it mattered much *less*."

"Nouveau is better than no riche at all?"

"Something like that."

"And now his family is . . ."

"Dead. All of them. Prematurely. Convenient, isn't it?"

It was getting late. The combination of my lack of sleep over the past few days, the overwarm room, and the increasingly likely fact that I was coming down with something made me want to just pull over the afghan at the end of the chaise and curl up in it.

"Are you all right, Miss Powell? More tea, perhaps?"

"Thank you. It's probably time I go. It's been a long day." I shook my head, which felt very heavy at the end of my neck. "You said you had something to share with me, I believe?"

"Ah, yes, so I did. It's just this, Miss Powell: I don't believe you'll be writing about Jamie's unfortunate death, or his medical problems. They'd reflect very poorly on my family."

"Those were Jamie's choices, Mrs. Dexter, not Dr. Howe's."

"Well, here is the problem, Miss Powell: they are indeed Dr. Howe's problem now. Her precious Jamie, the man she just *had* to have, had other men. And he has made her not only a laughingstock, but a sick young lady."

That cut right through the fog.

"Sheila Howe is HIV positive?"

Her aunt nodded sadly.

"Unfortunately, yes. The coroner was kind enough to call her directly last week and tell her that the disease showed up on Jamie's autopsy report. So they strongly suggested she be tested. The lab rushed the results, as a professional courtesy. They came back this morning—positive. She was beside herself."

Poor Sheila. How awful to have your fiancé be positive— how much worse to be a doctor, and know what might be coming, even as people speculate that you could have protected yourself better? The levels of betrayal she must be feeling.

"You know," Martha Dexter said casually, "every family has its 'perpetual bachelor.' In the old days, we just didn't talk about it, the way people seem to find it necessary to do now. In the best families, the son or uncle or whoever, just would go on his little vacations or business trips from time to time, and it was understood that what occurred there stayed there. The family remained intact. The family name remained pristine."

"But they'd had to pretend to be something they weren't."

"We *all* do that, every day of our lives, in one way or an-other," the old lady snapped. "My niece, for instance, spent an awful lot of time pretending she didn't see what was di-rectly in front of her."

I sat forward, a little crookedly.

"How *is* Sheila?" I asked.

"Very well," Martha Dexter said. "Very well, indeed. Let's go look in on her, before you leave, shall we? She's been nap-ping since just after dinner."

Huh. So everybody wasn't out for the evening. Funny she hadn't mentioned Sheila before.

I rose, made a swipe at my shoulder bag, and successfully attached it to my shoulder. It banged against me as I shakily followed Martha Dexter down the hall to a small, two-person elevator. We took it down to the ground floor, where the bedrooms were located.

"This way," the old lady indicated, moving slowly. "Here we are."

She swung the door open. "As you can see, our Sheila is doing much better."

Sheila Howe lay on the bed, sleeping peacefully, as the willows whipped and snapped against her windows. The covers were pulled up to her neck, and she was perfectly still.

Perfectly still.

"What's happened?" I slurred.

"What's happened is what *had* to happen, Miss Powell. When people ask questions they have no business asking, it can affect all of us adversely. Our Sheila was tortured by the thought that the public would soon know she'd made the wrong choice, and the consequences of that decision. Now she is peaceful."

I lurched over and felt the doctor's forehead. It was very cool to the touch. Feverishly, I ran my fingers down to her neck, where her carotid artery should have been beating.

It wasn't.

"Oh, Mrs. Dexter," I muttered, "what have you *done*?" I sat on the edge of the bed. Sheila Howe's inert body rolled slightly, but that was all.

"It was painless," the old lady said brusquely. "She felt nothing, and neither will you. Neither will I."

What?

"Oh, Miss Powell. It is a kindness that Sheila won't have to deal with the humiliation of what will, inevitably, come out. Her life would not have been worth living after you wrote your story."

"People will still find out," I persisted fuzzily. (That's what my tombstone will read: HAD TO HAVE THE LAST WORD.)

"Of course they will, eventually. But not right away. Which may give my nephew and his wife time to straighten their investments, perhaps leave ahead of the story."

Holy shit. She was completely serious. And obviously, my light-headedness and hot flashes were not a cold coming on, unless we wanted to count the Eternal Chill.

"What was in the tea, Mrs. Dexter?" I asked urgently. *Think,* Alex!

"You might as well get comfortable, my dear. We two have taken a significant jolt of fentanyl—do you know what that is?"

I shook my head no, and it felt like slo-mo.

"It's a painkiller, reserved for very serious cases. Major surgeries. Cancer patients. That sort of thing. It's one hundred times more powerful than morphine."

I tried standing up. It took two attempts. And breathing was getting harder. The fentanyl, or my imagination? Imagination can have powerful physical effects.

"I had back surgery last year; I'd never felt such pain. And they gave me lollipops with fentanyl in them. It was the most ridiculous thing, to see me, a grown woman, with one of those sticks in her mouth." She laughed silently.

"But they *worked.* And even after the pain was gone, I complained of it, so they would give me the lollipops. I was able to secrete away quite a few by the time I left the hospital. Several of them are in the tea you and I—and earlier, Sheila—shared. Look at her, how peaceful she is . . ."

I looked. She did look peaceful. It would be so easy to sit back down and stretch out next to her.

"You're crazy—and I'm leaving."

Martha Dexter settled into the reading chaise in a corner of Sheila Howe's darkened room.

"You won't get very far. Why not arrange yourself so you look good for whoever finds you? Probably my nephew and his wife."

I started to lurch to the elevator. If I could get upstairs and out, the cool air might help revive me.

"Why aren't *you* dead yet?" I wondered aloud.

"I have developed a tolerance, from the surgery," Martha Dexter explained placidly. "But I kept some insurance, just in case." I saw a small white stick wave in the gloom. Jesus. I shook my head to clear it, and slid up the hall.

The elevator gave a sickening lurch and glided upward. I stumbled out, fell on the foyer floor. My purse fell down and I heard stuff roll all over the floor. I didn't care about anything but my keys. I scrambled around like a blind person, touched my fingers on them and wept with relief.

It was getting harder and harder to breathe and I had to move slowly. I inched across the slippery foyer floor, pulled open the door, and was hit with a blast of cool, moist air. It felt good, but it wasn't enough.

The serpentine brick walkway to the street looked as if it went on forever. I don't know how much time passed as I sloppily made my way from tree to tree until I finally got through the gate to the street proper. The streetlight haloes looked like something from a van Gogh. My car was right in front of me. Should I try to inch up a neighbor's walk, or drive down the hill? Or maybe drive to a neighbor's house and just hit the horn?

It took me eight tries—*eight!*—to jam my key into the lock. The heavy door swung open, just as my knees started to buckle. I heaved myself inside. I wasn't sure my feet were even feeling the pedals, but after I stomped on the gas, the little car roared to life.

I fully intended to drive twenty feet to the next-door neighbor's, hit the horn and wait for someone to come and help. But what if they didn't? What if they couldn't hear me?

The car seat was starting to feel awfully comfortable. If I'd had a new car with one of those heated seats, I probably would have given up and lain back, right there.

I wasn't being seduced by heat, just overwhelming fatigue. Which may explain why I hit the gas far harder than I'd anticipated. The car, still in gear, shot forward, glanced off an Escalade parked on the street. The rebound ricocheted me toward the cul-de-sac in which Barbary Lane ends.

Only I couldn't make the car stop there. It went over the guard rail and began a gentle roll down the hill, once, twice. Slow, then faster. I could see the Glendale lights winking through the cracked windows—right side up, wrong side up, then a crunch.

Then silence.

Chapter Twenty-six

I had been dreaming about swallowing sand. I woke up because I was thirsty. When I opened my eyes, I saw dawn coming through a window that was unfamiliar, in a room that was a little too cool. Paul was sitting in a chair right by the bed. Big circles were under his closed eyes, and his cheeks and chin spouted stubble. How many days' worth, I wondered?

Another face appeared to block him out. A pretty Filipina nurse bent down and took my pulse.

"Good and strong." She beamed. "How are you feeling, Miss Alex?"

I tried to move my mouth to make words come out, but all I could do was croak.

She must have gotten the hint, because she reached for the pitcher of ice water, used a slotted spoon to fish out a few chips, put them in a small pleated cup, and lifted them to my mouth.

"Try this," she whispered. "Let them melt slowly, then doctor says I can give you more. Your throat may be a little sore," she warned.

I felt the wet melt in my fuzzy mouth. I tried to swallow. A *little* sore?

The nurse winced in sympathy.

"That's because doctor ordered your breathing tube released when we saw you could breathe on your own, without the bentilator." Spanish. All the *V* sounds were *b*s. She looked over at Paul, who had shifted slightly, to get more comfortable, and smiled.

"Such a good fiancé. He never left your side—except for the bathroom, of course." She giggled softly. "He sleep here, every night, in that chair. We have a room down the hall where he can have a bed, but he refused."

"*Every* night?" I croaked. "How many nights have I *been* here?"

"Two, so far. You're doing good. God's miracle, that you walked away with a cut on your ankle, a bruised sternum, and a dislocated shoulder. It was the drugs," she said, matter-of-factly, as she gave me more ice cubes and fluffed my pillows.

"The drugs?"

The nurse laughed. "You were so relaxed, the seat belt just suspended you while the car rolled over and over. The police say only a heavy old car like that could have protected you." She thumped the bedside table. "Built solid."

Imelda—believe it or not, that was her name—left promising to return with apple juice. "And if you're good, later on, some Yell-O."

I could hardly wait.

I turned to find Paul staring straight at me from his chair.

"Don't do that," I croaked. "You *scared* me."

"I believe that should have been *my* line, Einstein."

He got up, stretched ostentatiously, and walked stiffly over to the bed. "How do you feel?" he asked, brushing his hand across my forehead. I jerked away. "Oops—sorry—that is a little black and blue. How do you feel, though?"

"Lucky."

He sighed. "That's an excellent one-word description of what you are. *Stupid* would probably fit in the same place . . ."

"Oh, come on," I rasped. "Who knew she was going to turn out to be Killer Granny? I thought it was the safest kind of reporting possible—old lady, nice neighborhood, no dog in sight . . ."

"Point taken." He laughed ruefully, picked up my hand and squeezed it. His hand felt warm and large and comforting. I squeezed back. "What do you remember?"

Before I could answer, the door swung open. Jim Marron came in, followed by a doctor who was lecturing him.

"Ten minutes, I'm not kidding. I don't want her tired out."

"Ten minutes, promise." He turned to me. "Welcome back, Powell. Your fiancé here tell you we almost lost you?"

"What is this fiancé stuff, anyway?"

"When we raced to the hospital to see you, it was the

only way they'd let him in with me. So I confirmed this poor sap is, indeed, your betrothed."

I turned to Paul, indignant.

"No jewelry?"

"Hospital bracelet, Einstein. Best I could do on short notice."

That made sense.

"Anyway, clock's ticking: what *do* you remember—anything? Obviously," the detective explained, needlessly, "I'm here in an official capacity."

So I told them the story of tea with Herbert Marshall, and needing to verify some of his info by talking to Hiram Walker. When I got to my phone call to Samuel Johnson, Marron interrupted.

"You were right, Powell. Looks like Malik Fereby's dogs were the ones that attacked Nora Walker. But by mistake. She'd stopped by the community center to pick up some materials Kwaku Halstead had dropped off for her for some project he wanted her to consider. He wasn't actually there—he'd left to go down to San Pedro for a meeting, before hustling back to town for the Bournewell funeral that afternoon."

"So he never saw her?"

"No. But Malik thought they were hooking up at the Center for an actual discussion. So under normal circumstances, it might well have been Halstead walking Nora to the car after their meeting."

"So Nora died completely by accident?" Paul asked.

Marron frowned. "Either Malik isn't the dog whisperer he thinks he is, or the dogs were too stupid to get his signals straight. But you see what the end result was."

We were silent for a moment, contemplating Nora Walker's horrible, needless death. Then something occurred to me.

"Why would Malik want to kill Kwaku Halstead? He doesn't even know him!"

Marron opened his mouth, but before he could answer, the doctor was back.

"Time's up. You need to scoot, Detective. My patient needs her rest."

"Your patient will be in a complete state of agitation unless some of her questions are answered before he leaves," I informed the doctor coolly. "I might get *so* agitated, you'd need restraints. We don't want that, do we?"

Paul and Marron looked at the doctor expectantly.

He came over, slapped a pressure cuff on me, and waited until it expanded and retracted. He shone a little light into my eyes, and took the pulse on the side of my neck.

"If I give them ten more minutes with you, what do *I* get in return?" he asked, peering at me severely over the tops of his glasses.

"Undying gratitude?"

"Nope. Not good enough."

"Name in my next column?"

"Like I care."

"A pliable, obedient patient who will sit back, shut up, and obey orders for the rest of the day?"

"Bingo!" He pointed his finger at Marron. "Ten minutes. Clock's ticking."

"Where was I?" Marron fretted. "Early Alzheimer's."

"Malik's beef with Kwaku," Paul reminded him.

"Oh, yeah. Get this: Malik Fereby wanted to dispose of Kwaku Halstead because he thinks Halstead's dad ruined his uncle's life. Second-generation blood feud. Got it all in confession."

I turned to Paul and explained that Kwaku Halstead was really a Howe, and how.

"But Kwaku doesn't even claim them as family," Paul pointed out.

"He doesn't, but Malik thinks things went downhill for Samu el-Simba after the Royce Hall shootout. He wanted to rebuild Nu Afrika on the bodies of his uncle's old enemies."

"We went to his crib in Hyde Park," Marron said, "and he had notes, graphs, the whole nine, with a list of Nu Afrika enemies. About four other people, all descendants of the Panthers who were offed that day. Of course, they're all bankers and lawyers now . . . it would have been so pointless. But that's how these meatballs are."

"Poor Malik. So mixed up."

"Poor Malik, my ass. Nora Walker died a horrible death because of poor Malik. You need to get your bleeding heart stitched up, Powell."

Then, almost as an afterthought: "Oh, and he also confessed to offing Simp Hastings."

What?

"Yeah, that wasn't personal. It was just a blow to bourgie Negroes everywhere. He happened to read about Simp's reading that night in the paper, and decided to strike a blow against the colored class system. Weird: he left the money, and the watch—he wanted people to know it wasn't your standard ghetto robbery. But guess what we now have?"

"The flash drive with all the info on it that could have gotten Walker killed anyway?"

"As Dr. Kildare back there would say: bingo."

Holy shit.

"Do you remember anything about the accident?" Paul asked.

While Marron took notes, I told them about my shock at seeing Sheila Howe's body, her aunt's insistence that we, too, would be dead soon. Of my panicked, stumbling path to the car. Breaking over the cul-de-sac's guard rail.

"How did you find me?"

"With one of these." Marron touched his hip, where his cell nestled in a holder.

"I didn't call you—"

"Actually, Einstein, you did," Paul said. "You must have banged against something while you were lurching around the Howe house, and hit speed dial. I picked up, but I realized what had happened—you weren't talking to me on the other end, you were talking with Martha Dexter. I got the gist of what was happening, and called Marron. He got somebody up to the Howe house on the double."

"Four squads came up. We found the old lady downstairs, near death. She was DOA by the time we got to Cedars. Dr. Howe had died a couple of hours before that. But that you already knew."

"But how did you find *me*? I wasn't in the house."

"Oh, that. We followed the skid marks, looked over the crumpled railing, and there you were, upside down in that car, which was all beat to shit, by the way."

"It can be fixed," I interrupted.

"Uh-uh," Marron and Paul said, together.

"Uh-*huh*."

"Put it this way," Marron said gently. "We had to use the Jaws of Life to get you out. It looks like an opened orange sardine can."

My car!

It was the only thing I'd heard so far that I couldn't cope with. Almost being killed, everybody else being killed . . . horrible, but somehow the loss of my car was the worst.

The door opened again. Dr. Bossy was back.

"Time's up, gentlemen. Actually," he considered, looking at Paul, "you can stay if you're quiet. You, Detective, can come back this evening, if you leave now and if my patient rests in between. Deal?"

"Deal," Marron told the doctor. "Later," he told me.

The doctor looked at my wet cheeks. "Those had better

be tears of joy about something, missy, or he goes, too," he said, nodding at Paul.

"No! Don't make him go. I won't cry anymore."

Paul excused himself for a moment. "Need to stretch my legs. Back in a minute."

"So, about the emotional upset?" the doctor persisted.

"It's just that . . . Never mind. You're not going to get it."

"Try me." Said not unkindly, but with arms crossed over his chest. Somebody needed to tell Genghis about body language.

"I know I'm lucky to be alive . . . I appreciate everything everybody's done for me . . ."

"You were *this* close. Thank god for epinephrine, yes, but . . ."

"But when my car went over the guard rail, and rolled over—"

"Twice, from what I hear. Fucking miracle you're here at all. Excuse my French."

"Right. But they had to cut me out of it. And it was an old 2002."

"A 2002 isn't very old," the doctor pointed out.

"Not the year—the *model*. A 1976 model 2002. Last year they made them."

His eyes widened.

"A *BMW* 2002? Those are *collector's items!*"

"Duh."

"Oh, I *am* sorry." It was like he turned into a human being, right before my eyes.

"Yeah." I sighed fondly. "That car was my baby."

Genghis flipped over my chart and perused it quickly.

"Speaking of which: you're thirty-seven. If you and the fi-ancé want babies, you'd better get busy. The egg factory isn't open forever, you know."

I sighed. "Did my mother send you?"

He looked over those damn half-moon specs again.

"I'm telling you: doing it the old-fashioned way now is way easier and cheaper than doing it via IVF a couple years from now. Think about it. And now." He slammed closed the chart. "Get some rest."

"After what you just said to me?"

Truth be told, I was sleepy. I don't even remember when Paul got back. I do remember sending him home to sleep that night. That chair was uncomfortable, and it wasn't as if I needed watching over anymore.

They let me out on Easter Sunday. At five A.M., the Right Rev-erend August Holywell appeared in my room, just as the walls were starting to turn pink.

"Up all night—Easter vigil," he explained cheerfully.

"But what are you doing *here*?" I asked. "Isn't this a three-service day?"

"It's most assuredly a two-service day, but I do this every year, although not at the same hospital. Several of us do. When I heard you were here, I asked to come to this hospital. Are you ready, Alexa?"

"For what?"

"Communion, of course."

"Ah. I don't think so, Father H., but thanks."

"And why are you not ready to receive the body and blood of our Savior?"

I squirmed a bit.

"Well, to take communion, you have to be in a state of grace, don't you?"

"Alexa." The prelate put down the little container that held the host, and the portable pitcher of sacramental wine.

"I would say that anyone who has been through what you have been through in the last few days is certainly living testimony to God's grace and beneficence, wouldn't you?"

"I rolled over twice," I informed him.

"And are here to tell the tale and, characteristically I might add, argue with me about it. Well, since of the two of us, I am the one who has the degree in divinity, let *me* be the judge, here on earth, anyway, as to whether or not you are in a state of grace."

I nodded sheepishly.

"I'm ready."

He made the sign of the cross on my forehead, took a wafer and held it out.

"The body of Christ, the bread of Heaven."

He held the cup to my lips.

"The blood of Christ, the cup of our salvation."

A thin trickle of wine dribbled down my jaw. He gently

wiped it away with a soft white napkin that was part of his cleric's traveling kit.

"Christ is risen, Christ is risen," he intoned softly.

"Alleluia, alleluia," I responded dutifully.

"Alelluia, indeed, Alexa," Father H. said. "Go in peace to love and serve the Lord. Alleluia."

By the time I was discharged, families across the city were having their Easter brunch. Sally had insisted on sending a car for me—a ridiculous extravagance. Michael Riley himself came to pick me up. Paul brought going-home clothes.

"Family's back with the wife's people for the holiday." Mike winked. "Grace of God, indeed."

Turned out Sally had invited him to early Easter dinner, and she was going to feed us, too.

Michael asked if we minded if he rolled up the glass divider between us and him. "Need to have a quick conversation with the wife," he explained.

"Sure," I told him. And smiled. I knew he was just being polite.

Paul leaned over and whispered, "No fair trying to read his lips, Einstein."

Busted.

Instead, I watched as families dressed in Easter finery walked up the sunny streets we passed. Little girls in pastel dresses, their fathers in suits. Cars of carefully dressed people on their way to lunch. It had finally turned into real spring weather: the trees were misted in green fuzz, the beginnings of new leaves. The temperature was in the mid-seventies. Perfect.

When we got to Sally's, Michael and Paul walked me through the door.

"Just in time," Sally said cheerfully, although her smile quavered.

I hugged her, even though it hurt my chest. "I'm fine. Stop worrying."

Signe had stayed, Georgie came. Jim Marron pulled up just as Sally was passing Champagne. "Oh"—she paused— "can you have any, I wonder?"

Paul took out his cell and called Genghis.

"Two sips," he relayed. I took one—the bubbles hurt, but it tasted good—and saved the other one for later.

"I called your mother," Aunt Edith informed me. "She was going to come, then I told her maybe to wait until you were home and you could really use the company. We've been talking several times a day. She's worried about you, Alex."

"I'm fine, really. I talked to her this morning, before they sprung me loose."

Edith nodded approvingly. "Good. So when's she coming?"

"Uh . . . we're negotiating that right now."

She gave me the "I don't believe it for a minute" look, but let it slide.

After dinner, we excused ourselves. Time for the nap I promised to take.

The space where my little orange car normally stood looked sadly bare.

Paul reached around and gave me a hug. "Cheer up, Einstein. Maybe we can find another one on eBay or something."

I doubted it, but who knew?

Inside, everything was as it always was. The answering machine was blinking, and I went to play back my messages. Paul stopped my hand.

"First things first. Aren't you missing something?"

"Besides my car, you mean?"

"Yeah, besides your car?"

I looked around. Nothing seemed out of place.

"I don't think so."

Paul sighed as if disappointed.

"Einstein, if it's Easter, shouldn't you have an Easter *basket*?"

"Did you get me an Easter basket? *Did* you?" I yelped.

"Don't know . . . you'll have to look around and see."

I limped methodically through all three of my rooms until I found it, snuggled near a bookcase. It was a square basket, made of twigs, with a big looped handle. Nestled on biodegradable green paper grass were foil-wrapped chocolate eggs, a small box of artisanal chocolates, and a big old-fashioned sugar egg—the kind with a peephole in it with a diorama inside.

I picked it up and looked through it. There was the White Rabbit, holding his pocket watch and looking straight at me.

Scribbled above him were the words "Will you, Einstein? Clock's ticking . . ."

I looked at Paul.

"What's it mean? What clock?"

He sighed and rolled his eyes.

"You are incredibly dense sometimes. Look under the chocolate bunny."

I felt beneath Mr. Bun. There was another square. My hand froze.

"Need help?" Paul plucked the box from the grass, and put it firmly in my hand.

"I was serious last year, Einstein, when I told you I was too old to date around. We should either do this or not."

"That's romantic. What about your job? You know, the one that's three thousand miles away?"

He pulled me to him.

"Funny thing about jobs, Einstein. Sometimes they change. All that traveling I've been doing for the last several days? It's because they've finally realized, back in New York, that important things actually *do* happen out here. So they're beefing up the L.A. bureau. And I was offered a prime cut."

Paul on this coast. Amazing.

"Actually," he amended, "I was offered my choice: editor down here, correspondent up there—in that Other City. I told them I'd get back to them."

"And do you have a preference?" I asked, hopefully.

"My preference is to be near this irritating person who keeps putting herself in harm's way, but I could commute, if this is too close. Or," he said quietly, "I could stay up in the Bay Area if this isn't what you want."

I didn't need to think twice.

"There's been a lot of death around here these past few days," I began.

"One of them yours—almost," he reminded me needlessly.

I pulled away and looked up at him.

"The only death I'm interested in at this point is maybe being nagged to death by you. Regularly."

"Will you do it till death parts us, Einstein?" he whispered, opening the box.

"I will," I whispered back.

Mr. Bun had been sitting on a very generous four-karat stone. It looked an awful lot like the one Aunt Edith usually wears.

"Placeholder," Paul explained as he slid it on. It was a little loose, but not in danger of sliding off.

"Aunt Edith said to let you know this is an IOU. She said to tell you when you get fifty married years under your belt, maybe you'll get one, too."

"Married to you for fifty years? You should be so lucky." I grinned.

Paul laughed. "Oh, I plan to be."

As if on cue, the phone began to ring. The machine picked it up almost at once, and whose voice did we hear but A.S. Fine's.

"Powell, I hear you're back among the living. Call me tomorrow and let's talk about how we're going to do this series. It has Pulitzer written all over it. See ya."

"Need to call him?" Paul asked, biting into one of my chocolates.

He licked a finger. Then I took another finger and licked it.

"Nah. Time enough tomorrow. Let's go show my temporary ring to the others. And have my second sip of Champagne."

He held the door open and helped me out. It had been a long day, and from my place to Sally's felt like a long walk for someone with a badly bruised ankle. It was mildly throbbing, and would feel worse soon. I didn't care; I had help.

"Can I lean on you?" I asked Paul.

He smiled, put his arm around me, and took almost all my weight.

"Einstein, don't you get it? That's what this is all about."

And we walked, slowly, toward Sally's open door.

Epilogue

Kwaku Halstead and the Howe family have had several meetings, and after an uncomfortable start, they seem to actually enjoy one another's company. The Howes are perhaps more interested in a reunion than Kwaku, as he is about the age Sheila was. They offered to help him out financially, but Kwaku is more interested in social justice than personal gain. So the Howe-Halstead Trust, which honors Wilfred, Sheila, and, yes, the late Velvet Halstead, is being formed to help grassroots organizations in South Central L.A. Kwaku will be the trust's executive director, Phyllis Howe its president.

Samuel Johnson, the former Samu-el Simba, and his wife, Angie, continue to live out in Norco where she runs her bakery and he trains horses. They faithfully ride once a month up to Lompoc State Prison to visit Sam's nephew Malik Fereby.

Malik Fereby is doing twenty-five to life for first-degree

manslaughter and lying in wait. He has just received his GED, and is now working on his college degree—via correspondence, of course—and majoring in American history and political science.

Lydia Bournewell continues to sit on the board of several Los Angeles charities, and has formed a new one, the Myron Bournewell Memorial Fund, which gives grants to organizations seeking to destigmatize HIV and AIDS. She enjoys a robust social life, and as she predicted, her friends did not desert her. She remains HIV-negative.

Herbert Marshall published *DL: Undercover Brothers and the Down Low Life* and, as promised, the incendiary book became an immediate national bestseller. Marshall has been given his own imprint, BrownMan Press, by his publisher.

After a brief leave, Hiram Walker remains the head of his architectural firm, but spends considerable time lecturing around the country about the need for the black community to accept gay black men. People are still shaking his hand (or their heads, depending) at the heated argument he and a famous black evangelical minister got into on *Nightline*. "You will go to HELL!" the good reverend thundered, his jowls shaking for emphasis. "And I will have company," Hiram replied. "My own personal spiritual advisor, won't I?" There had been rumors about the minister in question for years, but until then, no one had ever called him on the hypocrisy behind his rampant homophobia. It's the only time anyone can recall Ted Koppel being flustered enough to cut to commercial early.

Signe went back to New York and wrote a very interesting profile of Herbert Marshall and his role in the whole to-do for the *New York Times Magazine*.

Georgie has been happily thumbing through bridal magazines and planning my wedding—even though I've told her a million times I have no idea when that might happen. Whatever. It keeps her and Sally out of my business.

Aunt Edith has dined out for months on the "Why Simp Hastings *really* Got Killed" story. She's like Dominick Dunne after O.J.—people can't get enough. The ring she loaned Paul so he could propose is safely back on her finger. "You'll get it back, eventually," she promised. "It's in my will."

Sally still spends time fretting over me, but happily, less time than she used to. She and Hamilton Smith have become an item, so once a month she's down there, once a month he's out here. The rest of the time they send salacious e-mails to each other. ("If Homeland Security ever commandeers those, there's going to be lots of agents going home to see their wives at lunch," Ham once told me, winking. Lordy.)

True to its word, the *Times* moved Paul out here for his new position as West Coast editor. He's been staying with me since he moved, but it's clear we need something bigger, soon. So we've started to look for a house. Not in Sally's neighborhood, of course. Can't afford it. But we'll find something. Meanwhile, when Aunt Edith's four carats left with her to go back to New York, my own true engagement ring appeared: a two-karat square-cut solitare.

And me? I wrote a series, "Black and Blueblood," that

traces the destruction Simp Hastings wrought on several lives, and looked at why so many black men are DL. I'm happy because it's done. A.S. Fine is ecstatic because he did indeed nominate it for a Pulitzer and it's on the short list. "Of course, if you get it, you'll be impossible to live with," he snorted when he told me the news. "Yup, and if I don't, *you'll* be impossible to live with," I pointed out. The newsroom is taking bets as to which would be worse.

Finally, after its roll down the Los Feliz hill, my poor little orange 2002 was, indeed, almost a total loss. But in true organ donor fashion, parts of it were harvested so other 2002s could live on. Which leaves me in need of a car. So far, I've rented (on the insurance company's dime) a Volvo convertible (Paul's choice), a Mercedes (Georgie, duh), a Ford Escort (Marron thought I should "see how the other half lives . . ."), a Lexus sedan (Sally's suggestion), and a Saab hatchback (Signe). None of them felt right.

My next car is out there somewhere, and I suppose I'm going to have to find it before my six weeks of covered car rental draws to a close.

Stay tuned. And if, as Dionne sings, you see me walking down the street? Pull over. Help a sister out.

Want More?

Turn the page to enter
Avon's Little Black Book —

the dish, the scoop and the
cherry on top from
KAREN GRIGSBY BATES

Karen Grigsby Bates:
The Interview

By Alex Powell

AP: *You don't look comfortable.*

KGB: I'm not. Usually I'm the person *asking* questions, while the *other* person squirms.

AP: *Well, is it possible that after we finish this interview you'll have renewed appreciation for what your interviewees are going through?*

KGB: What's possible, kid, is that I'll get tired of this whole undertaking and stand up and leave.

AP: *Well, it won't be the first time that's happened, but let's see how far I get, shall we?*

KGB: Fire away. First question?

AP: *A lot of people will assume that you and I are the same person, Are we?*

KGB: No. We have some things in common: a short temper

and a smart mouth. We're both journalists. And we both, at one point, had a little old 2002. But that's about it.

AP: *How are we different, then?*

KGB: I cook often, you don't. I have a good relationship with my mother, while yours is . . . difficult. We'll see that in future books. There are probably other differences . . .

AP: *I'm lots younger than you.*

KGB: And way less diplomatic, missy.

AP: *Where did Paul Butler come from—and thank you, by the way.*

KGB: You're welcome. Try to deserve him. Paul is a composite, as are virtually all the characters in my books. He's a mixture of men I love and/or admire, including my husband, the husbands of a couple of dear friends, and a couple of men I've been friends with for decades.

AP: *He's like a man-smorgasbord?*

KGB: Well, if you insist on that badly thought-out food analogy, I prefer to think of him as a lovely gumbo of black masculinity. Stop rolling your eyes!

AP: *Sorry. And are Signe and Aunt Edith also composites?*

KGB: Signe is; she's a blend of two sister-friends who are diehard Southern belles. Aunt Edith was jacked completely and totally from a real live relative, who gave me dispensation to use her however I like. I could not make this woman up!

AP: *Both your books explore newsroom politics to some extent. Why?*

KGB: You know why—you work in one. But for the record: how newsrooms are composed and who runs them has a lot to do with what appears in the papers, on television, and on the radio each day. The fewer people of color there are in newsrooms as reporters, editors, and producers, the less likely you are to get a multidimensional reflection of the real world. So I explore newsroom diversity—and lack thereof—and the ethnic tensions that sometimes arise in newsrooms because it's a very real part of life for most journalists of color, and certainly it is for black journalists.

AP: Are you telling me that the same thing has happened in newsrooms you've worked in?

KGB: I would say you're a smart cookie—draw your own conclusions.

AP: Where do the ideas for your initial story lines come from?

KGB: Usually they're something I've seen or heard and can't get out of my mind. For *Plain Brown Wrapper,* it was watching a venerable editor dodge three dates at once at a black journalists' conference. For *Chosen People,* it was a panel about black upper-class life, which was the catalyst for some heated—even explosive—Q and A from audience members when the panel took questions. It just gave me another opportunity to illuminate some of the dialogue that goes on in some parts of the black community.

AP: Right. So, what's next for Alex—uh, me?

KGB: I think you're going to travel with Paul up above Santa Barbara to a gathering of antique sports car aficionados. The highest bidder at the annual auction gets the car—but is also found in it, dead.

AP: Are you always going to be killing off people in your books?

KGB: It's more socially acceptable than real-life homicide. That's a *hint*.

AP: I'm going to take it, too! Thanks for your time. That wasn't so bad, was it?

KGB: More fun than a colonoscopy; less fun than four hours in line at the DMV.

Alex's Stuff

*(with apologies to all the magazines that
make these kinds of lists):*

What she drives: "old, old, *old* BMW 2002 orange coupe. They
will have to cut me out of it." (Hey Alex—guess what?)

Gas: "whatever's on sale."

Newspaper: "The *Los Angeles Standard*, duh. But I also read the
New York Times and the *Washington Post*."

Guilty pleasure: *People, Allure*, and *Lucky*.

Magazines you'll most often see her with: *The Nation, The New
Yorker, Town and Country*.

Toothbrush: Oral B electric

Toothpaste: Crest Vanilla Mint. "Good enough that I skip breakfast some days!"

Watch: "An old Cartier American Tank I got at a pawn shop. It
was on layaway for months."

Scent: Annick Goutal's Eau d'Hadrien in the summer, Calèche
in the winter. And in the evenings.

Favorite shoe: Stuart Weitzman black suede loafer, for work. Delman ballet flats for evening. Keds for the weekend.

Purse: Whatever catches my eye at Target.

Tote: "I alternate: a denim messenger bag from Old Navy; a caramel leather tote that Paul brought back from a quick trip to Rome."

Wouldn't be caught without: "A Bic rollergel pen, my ATM card, my sunglasses, and something good to read."

Wouldn't be caught with: "matching shoes and purse. Not at my age, anyway."

Favorite designers: "Vintage Saint-Laurent (my ambition is to find a real Le Smoking in a swap shop), vintage Chanel (post-WWII, pre-Lagerfeld), vintage Norrell. (I know: don't hold my breath, right?)"

Favorite places to stay: the W in Seattle; Campton Place in San Francisco; the Relais Christine in Paris; the Bauer-Grünwald in Venice, Shutters in Los Angeles, the Plaza Athénée in New York. Uncle Webb's house at the Vineyard.

An Alex Powell
Cookbook

(Really.)

Believe it or not, Alex is a fine cook—she just doesn't like doing it unless it's absolutely necessary. She has an affinity for cooking, but she keeps fighting it: "If you cook well and people know it, then they expect you to do it regularly. Uh-uh, not me."

Until she and Paul Butler became a regular item, Alex's favorite recipe for entertaining could be boiled down to five words: Let Someone Else Do It. But Paul is highly social, and a good cook to boot. And frankly, Alex is competitive enough that she doesn't want him to be known as the better cook of the two of them. So they often cook together, and when nobody is looking, she cooks for him. ("Do not tell anyone I do this," she warned him once. "Or you and the Colonel can become *very* good friends.")

She and Signe also like to cook together; when they do,

they often divvy up the tasks into two categories—glam work and scut work. "That way, nobody feels abused."

Georgie Marks doesn't even *pretend* to cook. "I know how to visit people who do, and I know how to make reservations," she says pleasantly. "Pass the martinis!"

The following recipes have been gathered from Alex and her friends. As you can see, they're not hella specific (as Signe likes to say) about measurements. Or, Paul would point out, *some* of them aren't. "Some of us actually use measuring cups and spoons."

The gang hopes you enjoy these.

Avon's Little Black Book

Alex Powell's American Paella

In *Chosen People*, when friends, relatives, and Alex's significant other all descend upon Los Angeles in the same evening, Alex has to break down and entertain them. She drags out her huge paella pan, and fills it with a California version of this classic dish. Like gumbo, you can improvise. And like gumbo, the leftovers are better the second day.

good quality olive oil	*1 cup frozen peas, defrosted,*
4 boneless, skinless chicken	*rinsed w warm water,*
breasts	*drained*
4 boneless, skinless chicken	*¼ cup roasted red peppers in*
thighs	*oil, drained and slivered*
½–1 lb medium shrimp, peeled	*1 dozen pimento-stuffed green*
and deveined	*olives (optional)*
½ lb turkey smoked sausage or	*2 tsps saffron*
turkey andouille, sliced	*4 cups low-salt chicken broth*
2 cups short grain white rice	*1 tsp kosher salt (or regular)*
1 medium onion, coarsely	*black pepper to taste*
chopped	
6 cloves garlic (or to taste),	
coarsely chopped	

Heat the olive oil in a wide, shallow pan—don't let it smoke. Sauté the chicken parts until partly cooked, remove to a plate and cover. Sauté the sausage, remove and keep warm. Add the garlic and onion, and sauté till golden (you might need a bit more oil . . .) Add all but 2 tablespoons of the chicken broth, and the pepper. Dissolve the saffron threads in the warmed chicken broth, then stir in. Cover and let rice mixture cook down for about 20 minutes, adding broth or water as necessary. (Or, as Georgie likes to suggest, when she oversees the process, "wine. I never saw anything cooked that wasn't made better with wine.")

Meanwhile, cut the chicken into large, bite-sized pieces. About 10 minutes before the rice is completely done, push chicken pieces, shrimp, and sausage into the hot rice mixture, cover, and continue cooking until rice is tender and chicken and shrimp are cooked through. Scatter the peas over all, place olives and red pepper strips in a decorative pattern. Serve with warm French bread and a big green salad.

And (we didn't forget, Georgie!) wine.

Serves 10–12

A Big Green Salad with Stuff in It

Sometimes when Alex returns from a hard day's work aggravating her editors (or the police chief, or the head of the Los Angeles City Council, or the mayor . . .), she's too tired even to order takeout. That's when she throws together this salad. And the variations depend on what's lying around.

3 cups of mixed salad greens, the kind you can buy in a bag at the grocery store

A cooked, boneless, skinless chicken breast (preferably grilled)

2 tbs candied pecans, coarsely chopped

¼ cup chopped fruit—apples, or grapes, or sometimes Alex uses dried cherries

A few tablespoons of chèvre (a creamy, mild-flavored goat cheese*) to taste

Rinse the salad greens and drain.

Chop the chicken into 1-inch cubes

Toss the greens with the nuts and fruit and your favorite vinaigrette dressing. Add chicken and chèvre and toss once more.

Put on a nice plate and pour yourself a glass of wine.

*(Look for chèvre in the imported-cheese section of your grocery store.)

Josefina's Halibut with Tomatoes, Olives, and Capers

Sally's maid/companion, Josefina, doesn't just excel at dessert—she makes a mean halibut dish. Sally has her serve it at an early spring cocktail party in *Chosen People*. Even people who don't like fish like this dish. In the winter, Josefina likes to serve it with potatoes au gratin. You could also use couscous, orzo, or rice pilaf, and a big green salad with assorted baby lettuces and artichoke hearts.

1½ lbs skinned, boneless
  halibut, cut in four pieces
4 tbs butter
4 Roma tomatoes, seeded and
  coarsely chopped
2 heaping tsp capers in brine,
  drained

¼ cup pimento-stuffed green
  olives, coarsely chopped
2 cloves garlic, finely chopped
½ cup dry white wine
freshly ground black pepper

Heat 2 tbs of the butter in a skillet large enough to hold the four halibut fillets. Sear the halibut, and remove before it's cooked through. Take care that you don't burn the butter. Add the tomatoes, garlic, capers, and olives, and about half the wine, cooking it down until the liquid is about half what it was. Add the remaining butter, stirring till melted, and a splash of wine.

Return the fish to the pan, spoon the tomato-olive-caper mixture over the fillets, and add a bit more wine if necessary. Add a few grinds of pepper. Cover and cook until the fish is tender—about another 5 minutes.

Remove the halibut, put a piece on each plate, and spoon the vegetable mixture over each piece of fish. Dust with black pepper.

Serves 4

Paul Butler's Grilled Salmon for Sally

Alex's boyfriend, Paul Butler, is a man who knows his way around the kitchen. When he visits Alex in Los Angeles, they eat out a lot. But her landlady, Sally, has a gorgeous "outdoor kitchen" next to the pool, and she says it doesn't get nearly enough use. So when Paul is in town, he'll often visit a local fish market and come home with fish to throw on the grill. "And"—he nods towards Alex—"a rib eye for the barbarian."

Here's his recipe for Sally's favorite grilled salmon:

4 boneless salmon fillets*	*2 cloves of garlic, crushed*
½ cup teriyaki sauce	*fresh black pepper*
½ cup dry white wine	*kosher salt, finely ground*

Combine the marinade. Place the salmon in a heavy zip-top plastic bag or a glass storage dish. Pour the marinade over, and leave for about 4 hours. Try to flip the fillets at least once. Drain and grill over medium-hot coals until the fish is tender in the middle, about 5 minutes per inch thickness. Serve with couscous or rice pilaf and grilled asparagus (see below).

Serves 4

*Fresh ahi or tuna work well, too, if you're not a salmon fan. And if you're a red meat eater, substitute 2 half-pound rib eyes for the fish, and use red wine instead of white in the marinade.

Grilled Asparagus

1 lb asparagus, trimmed
2 tbs olive oil

kosher flake salt
ground pepper

Pat the asparagus dry. Place in a shallow pan, drizzle with the olive oil, then grind pepper and salt over it. Toss on the grill (perpendicular to the grill's grids, or you'll lose half your dinner!) Cook till just slightly wilted—about 5 minutes.

Josefina's Tres Leches Cake
(Alex's shortcut version)

Alex's landlady, Sally Fergueson, has lived with her house-keeper, Josefina, for longer than Alex has been alive. Josefina sometimes makes this cake for company. She knows it's one of Alex's favorites. Alex has mastered a quickie version of this delicacy from Josefina's Mexican homeland. It's based on yellow cake made from a mix. (Don't tell Josefina—she'd be horrified!)

1 box of yellow butter cake mix, baked as directed

1 cup sweetened condensed milk

1 cup (unsweetened) coconut milk

1 cup heavy whipping cream

¼ cup sugar, or to taste

2 tsp pure vanilla extract*

Preheat oven to 350 degrees.

Grease a 9" × 11" cake pan.

Chill the beater to your electric mixer, and the cream.

Using your favorite butter cake recipe from a box, mix and pour into the greased pan. Bake at 350 degrees until the cen-

*You can use almond extract or rum instead of vanilla, if you'd rather.

ter of the cake springs back when touched, or a toothpick or skewer emerges clean. Set aside.

While the cake is baking:

Mix the condensed milk and the coconut milk together and let sit while the cake bakes.

While the cake is cooling, poke it full of holes with a toothpick or a skewer. The more holes, the more the cake will absorb the milk mixture.

While the cake is still warm, carefully pour the coconut condensed-milk mixture over the cake, pausing to let the cake absorb the liquid. It's okay if a little of it pools at the bottom of the pan.

Cover the cake tightly, and place in the refrigerator for at least 8 hours, preferably overnight.

Just before serving, whip the chilled cream with the chilled beaters, and when it forms soft peaks, add sugar to taste, and vanilla extract. Serve each square of tres leches with a generous dollop of whipped cream.

Fruit Poached in Wine

This is a dessert for people who normally pass up dessert. It's made with fresh fruit—that's healthy, right?—that has been poached in wine (more fruit!) and a little sugar, and served with a bit of crème fraîche. You can find crème fraîche on the shelf in many grocery stores, or make your own (see below). The tang of the crème fraîche offsets the richness of the fruit. Serve it in a pretty glass, and pass a plate of fancy cookies if you think your guests will rebel at "only" fruit. (Paul says this is "a very sexy dessert.")

SUMMER VERSION:

four ripe peach halves   *4 basil leaves, shredded*
white wine syrup (see below)   *crème fraîche*
a squeeze of fresh lime juice

Serves 2

WINTER VERSION:

six dried Kalamata or   *1 cinnamon stick*
    Dakota figs   *2 cloves stuck in a fresh orange*
or four pear halves, peeled   *peel*
    and cored   *crème fraîche*
Red Wine Syrup (see below)

Serves 2

Wine syrup: Winter or summer, the process is the same: take ½ cup of sugar and ¾ cup of wine (red or white, depending on your taste and the time of year). Boil until sugar dissolves. Place remaining ingredients in pan and simmer for about 10 minutes. Add fruit and simmer for about ½ hour. Allow fruit to cool. Remove from pan, place in glass bowls. Strain syrup through a sieve and pour about ¼ cup over fruit. Top with crème fraîche. Can serve at room temperature in the winter, or chilled in the summer.

Crème fraîche: Literally, "fresh cream"—tangier than whipped cream, and nicely offsets other sweets. In one cup of whipping cream, mix 2 tbs buttermilk. Place in a glass jar, cover tightly, and leave at room temperature for 8 to 12 hours, or until cream thickens considerably. Then store in refrigerator.

KAREN GRIGSBY BATES

KAREN GRIGSBY BATES is a correspondent for NPR News. For several years, she wrote for *Time* magazine and was a contributing columnist to the *Los Angeles Times*'s Op-Ed page. Her work has also been featured in the *New York Times, Essence, Vogue,* and the *Washington Post. Chosen People* is the second novel in the Alex Powell series. Bates lives in Los Angeles with her husband and son, where she is currently at work on *Finding Finney,* a novel about black college life in the 1970s.